Death Notice

by

Alicia Dean

A Monroe Donovan Novel

Death Notice

Cover Art by *Lisa Dawn MacDonald*

The Wild Rose Press, Inc.
PO Box 708
Adams Basin, NY 14410-0708
Visit us at www.thewildrosepress.com

Publishing History
First Edition, 2022
Trade Paperback ISBN 978-1-5092-3984-9
Digital ISBN 978-1-5092-3985-6

Published in the United States of America

I stripped off my clothes and turned the shower on full blast. I stepped under the hot spray, enjoying the almost painful sting of the water. I shampooed my hair and scrubbed with ginger-citrus body wash, staying until the hot water was almost gone.

Toweling off, I stood in front of the mirror, naked, and partially blow-dried my hair. As I reached for my robe, I heard a thump, then a scraping sound, and froze.

My legs went weak and a tremble worked its way from my toes through my chest.

What was that?

Even living alone, I wasn't prone to being skittish or imagining noises. I seldom became frightened. Wasn't the least paranoid.

That had been something, though. Some noise inside my house. I pulled the robe over my still-damp body and belted it.

I didn't have a weapon in the bathroom, or in either bedroom. There was a gun in the living room and knives in the kitchen, but in this part of the house, nothing. My phone was in the front room, too. Although, what would I do if I had it? Call 9-1-1 and tell them I thought I heard a noise?

I rummaged through the cabinets beneath the bathroom sink and came up with a spray bottle of Tilex. Tough on mildew, had to be tough on exposed eyeballs.

Slowly, I eased the bathroom door open and crept to the front of the house. The living room was empty.

I made my way carefully to the kitchen and pushed the door open.

My hands tightened on the spray bottle and I gasped, drawing the attention of the man seated at my dining table.

Dedication

To my sisters, Christi and Janis, and to my beautiful
nieces, Madison, Amanda and Jenny.
Thank you for your love and support.

Acknowledgments

They say it takes a village and that was pretty much true with this book. I'd like to take this opportunity to thank all the 'village people,' who contributed, although I know I am leaving someone out. I can assure you, if I am, it is simply an oversight and I truly appreciate the help I've received from everyone.

I'd like to thank Meredith, for believing in me. I'd also like to thank my mentor, Mel Odom; my friends and support group… Rhonda, Judith, Faith, Claire, Janet, Natasha; all those who've read the book, or part of it, and offered numerous helpful suggestions… Martha, Julie, Johanna, Mary, and Lori. Also, my friends and critique group… Christy, Betty, Sheila, Kelly; the members of my OKRWA group, Erin, Danell, Silver, Colleen, Diana, and my beta reader, Calisa, for catching many errors I didn't. The members of my HERA group, Judy, Derek, Janice, Goldie. Jeff Paris, for reading for me and inadvertently providing me with the terrorist remark, and especially Major Vincent Cannon, whose expertise helped me to get the police stuff at least partially accurate. Any and all mistakes are my own.

Chapter 1

Before I found out that a murderer was using my obituary column to forecast his kills, my biggest concern was the promotion my boss/ex-lover, Adam, had promised me.

I'd been writing obituaries for the *Northland Chronicle* for two years, but that was about to change. Today, Adam was promoting me to the crime desk, something I'd wanted since leaving my job at the *Kansas City Star*.

I'd given up a coveted career as crime reporter because I was in love, and because Adam swore that when the crime desk came open at the *Chronicle*, it was mine. Two years, and one very bad break-up later, the position had opened up. Last month, when one of the crime writers turned in his notice, Adam promised me that he wouldn't let our break-up stand in the way. Today was when we made it official. I could barely contain my excitement as I drove to work, leaving earlier than I normally did, since I hadn't been able to sleep anyway.

Although it was October, summer had lingered longer than it should have and autumn was just now establishing its rightful place. I took a moment to appreciate the scenery—the beauty of the blue sky and the trees—some still fat and green, others with leaves that had turned scarlet, gold, or burnished orange.

When I arrived at the newspaper and climbed out of

the car, cold wind snatched at my coat and whipped my hair around my cheeks, making me hasten my trip from the lot to the office park where the newspaper was located.

I halted long enough to toss a few pennies into the fountain that dominated the square outside the *Chronicle*. Water spewed from multiple spouts, bathing the marble statue that depicted Pandora in the motion of opening her infamous box. Kansas City was known as the City of Fountains and was rumored to have more fountains than Rome. In a few months, the water in most of them would be frozen, but they'd still be lovely to look at.

In the break room, I made a pot of what my co-workers called my truck-driver sludge. I had my own pot because the others preferred something resembling tinted water more than coffee.

Adam arrived as I was pouring my second cup. He headed to his office without speaking to me, but he opened the door moments later and stuck his head out.

"Monroe, I need to see you."

His voice was hard. Harder than a man about to promote a valued employee.

I stepped inside and shut the door.

He sat on the edge of his desk, holding a newspaper. Before I could sit, he thrust the paper toward me.

I took it and saw that it was folded back to the obituary page, with one of them circled in red.

"Read that for me, please," Adam said.

"Why?" I grinned. "Are there words with more than two syllables?"

He gave me a look. He was not amused. I read.

Richard James Hebringer, 33, of Kansas City,

Missouri, passed away unexpectedly on October 24th. Richard is survived by his parents, Hank and Patricia Hebringer, sibling Cassandra Hebringer, and extended family members. He will be interred at Macon Cemetery on October 24th.

"Shit!" I sank slowly into the chair across from his desk.

"Yep. *Shit* is right."

Today was October 23rd, which meant the guy died tomorrow. What really sucked was that I was the one who'd overlooked the error.

"How'd you happen to catch it?" I asked. "You were reading obits?"

"No, my grandmother saw it. She reads them every morning. Likes to use the old joke about making sure her name's not in there."

I smiled faintly. "Sorry. I can't believe I let this through."

"Yeah. We're just lucky no angry relatives have called...so far," he added ominously. "Can't imagine they'd be too happy with us."

He said 'us,' but his accusatory look said 'you'—as in me.

"I assume the guy actually died on the twenty-first or twenty-second. I'll check, but I'm sure the email had the twenty-fourth listed. Whoever sent the obit to me had the wrong date." My excuse was lame, even to my own ears, but I ran it by him anyway.

"Maybe so. But it's your job to check these things before they're published."

"I know. Want me to print a correction?"

"Let's hold off. If no one notices, that will just bring attention to it."

I nodded. Although in the grand scheme of life, this was a very small infraction, I, of all people, knew how serious it really was. Having been raised with a mortician father, I knew better than anyone of the solemnity and seriousness of death. The smallest thing that seems mocking or disrespectful can send already grieving family members into deep despair.

I tossed the newspaper on Adam's desk and changed the subject. "When do I start my new job?"

Adam's gaze slid away from me, landing where his hands were clasped between his thighs. "About that..." He sighed heavily.

"About that, what?"

He looked at me now, his eyes pained. "Roe, I'm sorry, but there's been a change of plans."

My body tensed, but I tried to remain calm. "What do you mean, a change of plans?"

"You're not going to be writing crime."

I opened my mouth to speak, but he lifted a hand and rushed on, "At least not right now. I'm not saying it won't happen. I'm just saying it's not going to happen as soon as we planned."

I was humiliated to feel tears at the back of my eyes. Determined not to let them fall, I cleared my throat. "This is because of Tabitha, isn't it?"

He shrugged. "She feels a little threatened by the fact that my ex-girlfriend still works for me."

"Even though you chose *her*? While we were still together, I might add."

Adam stood and shoved his hands in his pockets. Turning his back on me, he walked to the window, staring outside. "Tab knows you and I would be working more closely together. She feels my giving you a promotion makes it look like I'm still in love with you."

"Hmmm." I snorted a humorless laugh. "You'd think the fact that you fucked her on my birthday would negate that theory."

He turned to face me. "Come on, Roe. You know I'm sorry about all that. I thought you'd forgiven me. That we'd gotten past that."

"Jesus, Adam. I did, too. I *am* past that, but apparently, Tabitha's not. And it's pretty damned unprofessional of you to let your girlfriend dictate how you deal with your employees."

"I know. It's just…well, her father does own the newspaper, and right now is a bad time to make her feel threatened. Especially since—"

He stopped, and I saw something like dread in his expression.

"Since what?"

He blew out a breath and took his hands out of his pockets. Crossing his arms over his chest, he looked down at the floor as he spoke. "We're engaged."

A bolt of pain shot through my chest. It surprised me that I could still be hurt by Adam. But, his news did hurt—and shock me. I'd always thought of Tabitha as just a fling, never dreaming she'd be the kind of woman he'd marry. Adam had just gone through a divorce when he and I started dating and, at that time, he was more than just gun-shy. He was as opposed to getting married again as an atheist was to prayer. That worked for me, since I wasn't interested in marriage, either. Especially to Adam. I would never, ever marry a man who was prettier than me. With his golden hair, smooth, tanned skin, and intensely green eyes, Adam definitely fell into that category.

I'd always wondered what he'd seen in me, and now realized I was a no-pressure rebound girl after a bad marriage. Not the kind you kept around for long, but the kind that would do in a pinch until a woman more suitable came along. Still. I never figured Adam would get married again. Well, I knew he wanted to settle down someday. He'd mentioned wanting children. I just figured it was a long ways off. Like the Millennium had seemed in the early 90's.

I sucked in a deep breath and bunched a handful of hair on top of my head, a habit I had when I was stressed or sad or angry. My hair was mussed a great deal of the time.

"Congratulations," I said, but it sounded more like, 'I want to rip your heart from your chest and feed it to you bit by cheating bit.'

"Thanks. I hope now you understand why I have to keep Tabitha happy. Once she's more secure in our relationship, maybe after we're married, you and I will talk about that promotion."

"Aw, gee, thanks, Adam." My voice oozed sarcasm. "You're awesome!"

"Come on, Roe. Please just be patient with me. Hang in there."

Then it hit me. Maybe what he and his future wife were hoping was that I *wouldn't* hang in there. "Is she trying to run me off? Get me to quit? Are you?"

"No. I mean, *I'm* not." He leaned slightly toward me as if to punctuate his sincerity. "Trust me. I want you here, Roe. I don't want you to leave."

"Why not? It's not like you couldn't easily replace me."

He sighed. "I still care about you. I like working

with you, and I know you deserve that promotion. I wish you'd hang in there with me, just a while longer, until I'm able to make it happen."

I thought about that. I'd hung in with him for two years and where had it gotten me? Nowhere. I didn't trust Adam, and he'd just shown me why. Again. My job at the *Star* was no longer available, but that didn't mean I couldn't get some position there, or somewhere else. Anything was better than staying around here, letting Adam kick me around some more.

"This is bullshit, Adam, and you know it."

He cocked a thumb toward the newspaper, still folded open to the obit. "You did screw up on that obit."

I didn't respond. He and I both knew that minor mistake wasn't enough to keep me from getting that promotion. He was just being a dick.

"Hey, don't sweat it," he said, coming back around to sit on the edge of his desk. Leaning forward, he clasped my hand in his. "Just be patient, please?"

I stared down to where his fingers massaged the back of my hand. His touch warmed me, but at the same time, made me ache. Most of the time, I really thought I was over him. Then, at other times, the old feelings came flooding back, catching me unaware. This was one of those times.

Then I remembered the way he'd treated me—was still treating me—and the warm feeling went away with the speed of a NASA launch.

I jerked my hand away and stood, wanting to use all the curse words I knew—and growing up with three brothers, my arsenal was extensive—but I held back, deciding to practice a little decorum.

"Screw you, Adam." I wanted to say 'fuck you,' so

I still considered I'd handled it with class. "I quit."

"What?" He stood and lifted his hands out to his sides in a pleading gesture. "You can't do that. Please. Give me some time."

I stared into his beseeching eyes, his heart-stoppingly handsome face and felt… nothing. I inwardly sighed with relief and slowly shook my head. "I've given you more than I should have, Adam. So much more. Consider this my notice."

"Monroe, wait—"

I ignored his plea and stalked out of his office, forcefully slamming the door behind me. "Unbelievable," I muttered under my breath as I headed toward my cubicle and tried to still the quaking in my chest.

"What is? Your wardrobe? What's the occasion?" My friend and co-worker, Asia Martin, stood near my cubicle, hands on hips, apprising my outfit.

"Occasion?"

"You." She waved a hand out like one of those game show models presenting a prize. "All dressed up like that."

I looked down at my black slacks and soft white sweater, which for me, was dressing up. It wasn't exactly high fashion, but it was about as girlie and dressed up as I ever got. The first six years of my life, I hadn't realized I *was* a girl.

Asia, however, was most definitely in touch with her feminine side. Although slightly overweight, she was gorgeous, and her wardrobe was that of a wealthy socialite rather than a newspaper employee. Today, she wore a bronze linen suit with a silky chocolate shell underneath the jacket. I was sure it was by some designer, but I didn't know Gucci from Prada, so I had no idea which. The color suited her, setting off her caramel skin and the blonde in her stylishly braided hair.

I plopped down in my chair so that my view of Adam was blocked. The staff work areas were separated by chest-high partitions and Adam's office overlooked our cubicles where he lorded over us in his glass-encased kingdom. "I just felt like dressing up a bit," I said.

"For him?" She sneered and jerked her head toward Adam's office.

"No, not for him. Just because I was in the mood."

"Well now you seem to be in a pissy mood. So, what changed since this morning when you dug through your sweatshirts and Levis until you came upon this?" She plucked at the shoulder of the sweater.

"I'm not getting the promotion."

"I knew it," Asia hissed. "That son of a bitch. Who's getting it?"

"I don't know."

"*He* probably doesn't even know. As long as he can appease the bitch, he's happy. You need to… to… Ah, hell. I don't know what you need to do." She clenched and unclenched her fingers. I assumed she was imagining Adam's neck between them. "You need to quit. That's it. No, wait. Then I'd be stuck here without you. Shit."

"I did quit."

"*What?*" Her expression was horrified.

"I'm not going to stay here and let that asshole treat me that way any longer. I'm done. I gave my notice."

"Nooooo," she wailed. "I can't stand this place without you."

I looked up at her, feeling a twinge of guilt at

abandoning her. "I'm sorry. Surely you understand."

A long dramatic sigh left her. "I do. You've worked your ass off and he… he… Dammit, I can't think of anything bad enough to say about him."

"I know." I attempted a smile. "Hey, at least we have thirty days until I leave. Maybe we can make his life a living hell."

"He's hooked up with Super Bitch. I think she did our work for us." She reached out and squeezed my hand. "I'd better get to work. You okay?"

"I'm fine."

Asia walked away, and I checked the clock on the wall. Not even lunch yet. The day stretched out long and unhappy before me. As soon as it finally crawled to an end, I was going to head home and plant myself in front of the TV with a cup of rich hot chocolate, pillows of whipped cream floating on top. Maybe I'd watch the World Series. None of my favorite teams had made it, so I didn't care who won. Not caring about something for a little while sounded like heaven.

"Well, well, look who's here," I heard Asia say, her voice an appreciative murmur. She'd stopped halfway between her cubicle and mine and was staring out the glass walls to the reception area.

I stood and followed her gaze. Two men were at the reception desk. One was tall and muscular, with a shaved head and goatee. His eyes darted around the lobby and through the glass into the newsroom, his expression intimidating. Had it not been for the suit jacket, I might have mistaken him for a UFC fighter.

The other man was a tad shorter with dark, tousled hair. Beneath the gray suit jacket, his shirt was in need of pressing, his charcoal tie askew. The clothing gave the impression of having been haphazardly tossed on, rather than actually donned. His shoulders were slightly hunched, as if bracing for a blow. His eyes also roamed, but unlike the other man's, they seemed to drift, hesitant to settle on any one object.

As we watched, Mary, the receptionist, returned to her desk and spoke to the two men.

"You know them?" I asked Asia, reluctant to take my eyes off the dark and disheveled one.

"Mmmhmm," she nearly purred. "They're detectives. The messy, dreamy one is Detective Lane Brody."

My lips twitched, the closest I could come to a smile after my chat with Adam. "Did you just say *dreamy*?"

"No other word for it, girlfriend. Just look at him. I met him at the bar." Asia's husband, Darion, owned a sports bar called The Blitz. Darion was a big, tall hunk of a man who had briefly played football for the Green Bay Packers before suffering a career-ending injury. Not only was he sexy, he'd known Brett Favre. Talk about a catch. "Him and Darion hit it off. They've kind of become buddies." Her lips stretched into a leer. "Wouldn't mind him being *my* buddy, if you know what I mean."

"Yeah, I think I cracked your code," I said dryly. "Speaking of Darion, I was beginning to think you'd forgotten you already have a man."

"Lane Brody could make a woman forget her own name," Asia said. "He's every heterosexual woman's wet dream and every lesbian's temptation to convert."

I laughed, studying him again. Yes, he was good-looking, but not drop-dead gorgeous. The appeal wasn't so much his looks as it was the overall package. There was something about him… something sexy and vulnerable all at once.

He turned our way, staring at us through the glass. His gaze landed on me, and I caught my breath, then tried to swallow back the flutter working its way through my chest and throat. He gave me a half smile. Even from this distance, I could see his eyes crinkle at the corners.

Asia sighed. "Look at him. Don't you just want to… I don't know… *fix* him?"

She said 'fix' like it was a step of the Kama Sutra.

Mary glanced back toward us, then picked up her phone. Mine rang and I answered.

"There are two detectives here to see you," Mary said.

"They want to speak to me?"

I looked at Asia, whose eyes rounded in excitement. She pointed at the detectives, then at me, lifting her brows questioningly.

I nodded and said to Mary, "Send them back."

I watched them come through the glass door, wondering what the hell they could want with me. I'd never been in trouble with the law, couldn't imagine what they were doing here.

"You are *so* lucky," Asia said quietly. "I don't care if they're here to arrest you for murder, you're lucky."

"Right," I replied, just as quietly, "an arrest would be the perfect ending to this glorious day."

"At least handcuffs would be involved."

I rolled my eyes, but before I could respond, the detectives were standing in front of us.

"Hello, Lane. Good to see you," Asia said, reaching out a hand.

The sexy one took her hand in a brief shake and gave

her that smile-not smile. "You, too." His voice was smooth with an underlying rasp. Up close, I could see the color of his eyes, an unusual combination of aquamarine with tiny sapphire bursts in the center.

Asia glanced from the men to me, then back to the men. "I'll get out of your way," she said, giving Detective Brody's frame a quick, lascivious up and down before she disappeared behind her cubicle. Hopefully, I was the only one who'd noticed.

"Miss Donovan," the taller one said, "I'm Detective Webber and this is my partner, Detective Brody. We'd like to ask you some questions. Is there somewhere we can talk privately?"

I glanced around and saw Adam standing at his office door. His eyebrows were drawn together in a scowl, making me wonder if this had something to do with him. Could he be in trouble? The thought made my spirits lift, and I smiled at the cops. "Sure. Right this way."

I led them to the conference room, as aware of Adam's eyes following us as I was of Detective Brody just a few feet behind me.

I shut the door and took a seat at the conference table. Detective Brody remained standing, while Detective Webber sat across from me, flashing a thousand watt smile that I figured was meant to either charm or disarm me. "Miss Donovan," he said. "Can you tell us where we might find Josephine Detweiler?"

An alarm bell rang in my head. Josie was in trouble again. Josie had been my best friend since childhood. She was a drug user who had a no-good, asshole boyfriend she couldn't seem to stay away from. Josie would breeze into town from time to time when she needed to get clean or have a safe place to crash. My house was always that place, but she hadn't been around in a while.

I swallowed, praying it was a minor offense. "No, I mean, not right now. I haven't seen her in a couple of weeks. Is she okay?"

"We just need to ask her some questions about her boyfriend, Matt Lovell. Have you seen him lately?"

I tried to keep the dislike out of my voice as I answered. "I haven't seen Matt in months." *And that's not nearly long enough,* I silently added. "What's this about? Is Josie in trouble or is Matt?"

"We're conducting a homicide investigation and need to ask Mr. Lovell some questions. We were hoping Miss Detweiler could tell us where we can locate him." That smile again. He leaned forward and lowered his voice, as if for intimate conversation. "We understand she stays with you when she's in town?"

They were looking for Matt about a murder? What had he done now? My heart started beating too fast. Whatever it was, he'd better not hurt Josie. Or, at least, not any more than he already had.

My gaze wandered to Detective Brody. His arms were crossed, and I noticed his glance flitting around the room, but something told me his attention hadn't strayed. I guessed that his relaxed, casual attitude was a smoke-screen for a keen mind that missed little.

"Yes, she does. But she hasn't been around in a while."

"Do you know how we can get in touch with her?"

I shook my head. "I have no idea. She doesn't have a phone, and I don't know where she stays when she's not with me."

His charming smile was replaced by a disbelieving frown. "You're her best friend and you don't know how to reach her?"

Skepticism 101. He must have been at the top of his class.

"No. I don't. I wish I did, but she comes and goes without warning. I never know when I'll see her or when she'll take off again."

"What about Mr. Lovell? Do you know how to reach him? Or any of his friends we can contact?"

"I doubt if Matt has many friends, and if he did, I wouldn't know them. Or want to know them. I'm sorry. I really don't know how I can help you."

Detective Webber fell silent, staring at the notepad he held, his brows drawn into a frown. I didn't know if he was reading something, or just thinking about how much he doubted my story. I inwardly shook my head. Cops.

"It's very important that we find Mr. Lovell."

"So," I said slowly, "what you're trying to tell me is that you'd like to speak to Matt?"

Not missing the sarcasm, Detective Webber gave me a look, but I saw a small smile playing around the corners of Detective Brody's mouth. He hadn't spoken since they'd come in the room, but for some reason, I was more acutely aware of his presence than that of his talkative partner's. Although I'd only heard it briefly, I liked his voice and wanted to hear it again.

"Is there something you want me to tell her if I see her?" I directed the question to Brody.

His eyes captured mine for a moment, and his whisky voice said, "Could you please have her call us?"

This time, I detected the hint of a southern drawl. He

handed me his card, and I wanted to touch my fingers to his as I took it, but figured it would be too obvious. Besides, a gold band circled his ring finger, glinting reproachfully at me.

Immediately, I mentally kicked myself in the ass. Freshly out of an extremely bad relationship, and here I was having schoolgirl fantasies about a married man. I swung my gaze to Webber.

"I'm sorry I couldn't be more help. I'll have Josie call you as soon as I speak to her."

"Please do."

I followed them out of the conference room and went back to my cubicle, ignoring Asia's hungrily inquisitive gaze. Dropping Detective Brody's card on my desk, I leaned back in my chair, gnawing my lower lip as worry gnawed my gut. My best friend was in trouble, or at least her abusive boyfriend was, and that had to compute to trouble for Josie, too.

Chapter 2

Life, Rich Hebringer decided, was a lot like drowning in a swimming pool filled with shit. It stunk, it was hard to swim through, and most of the time, just when you thought you might break the surface, you were sucked right back down to the bottom of the festering, reeking pool.

As he reflected on the theory, he grabbed the trash bag from the can behind the registration desk and headed to the back door of the bed and breakfast where he was oh-so-fortunate enough to be employed as the night desk clerk.

The frilly, pink, rose-patterned curtain on the window of the door lifted and brushed his face as he tugged on the knob.

Goddamit.

He hated all this frou-frou bullshit. Hated the giddy, love-struck couples who stayed here. Tonight, only three of the six rooms upstairs were occupied. One couple had gushed to Rich that they were on their honeymoon. Another couple, a few years older than the honeymooners, were obviously having an affair. They'd had that flushed look, that naughty sparkle in their eyes, and had covertly glanced around the entire time Rich was checking them in. The other couple was two dudes. The gay thing kind of gave him the willies, but what the hell. To each his own, right?

He despised everyone who stayed here—flamers, heteros, whatever the fuck. He despised the way most of them, immediately after checking in, fled to their rooms, so anxious to start banging each other, they couldn't hang around long enough to say, "So, how are things for you, Rich? You happy? You like being stuck here like some kind of piss-ant dick munch who didn't complete high school, let alone acquire a college degree? Oh, really? You *have* a college degree? And you're working *here*?"

Rich shook his head and stepped out onto the path at the back of the B and B. The 'path' was actually a sidewalk, but when it wound through delicately landscaped lawns, and was lined with lilies—all sorts of lilies in pinks, oranges, purples, every color of the fucking rainbow, and every type in God's creation—you couldn't really call it a 'sidewalk.' Even though it was October, the owner, Lily Highland, made sure her precious lilies were in abundance by replacing them with fake lilies when the blooming season was over.

Kind of ironic the place was infested with a flower that was a sign of purity, when it was a hotbed for illicit affairs. Funny, really. Not funny as in ha ha, stand-up comic funny, but there were so few things in life Rich found amusing these days, he'd take whatever he could get.

He juggled the bag of trash in one hand as he dug for a cigarette with the other. He paused midway down the path and touched the lighter to the tip of the cigarette. Inhaling deeply, he drew the smoke into his lungs and let it curl out of his mouth into the night sky.

It was against the rules to smoke on the grounds—even on the fucking *grounds*—of Highland Lily Bed and

Breakfast. How fucking controlling and pretentious was that? It was fucking *nature*, man. Animals ate, shit, and copulated on these precious grounds, but a guy couldn't have a smoke to release a little tension? Well, fuck her and her rules. He'd had a rough day, a sucky night, and he needed some goddamned nicotine. After all, he was in a pool of *shit*, man. What harm was a little smoke going to do?

He headed to the dumpster, mentally expanding his shit-pool hypothesis. He had never considered himself much of a philosopher, but he thought this new analogy had a lot of merit.

In this pool were a herd of vicious, deadly, ravenous crocodiles. One wrong move, one stroke of really bad luck, and one of those beasts would yank you down into the mire and devour you. You'd be gone, nothing but a fading memory to the other poor souls struggling in the same muck. Thing was, you wouldn't really mind when this happened. Might actually welcome the blessed jaws of death. At least then, you would be free from the endless dream-sucking feces.

This new—and somewhat negative, though insightful theory—was a result of Rich's failed job interview. He'd been working the front desk of this lame-ass bed and breakfast in this go-nowhere shit town for two years. Today, he'd had a job interview with an accounting firm, thinking he could finally put his degree in business management to use. But, they'd told him at the end of the interview that he wasn't *right* for the job. What the fuck was that supposed to mean? How much more *right* could he be? Intelligent, good-looking, personable—oh yeah, and a fucking *degree* in business management.

He tossed the bag into the dumpster, glancing around the shit-pool. All was peaceful. The guests were humping their asses off in the rooms upstairs, and not a creature stirred. The moon shone down through the branches of trees that were just beginning to lose their leaves. Off to the left was the prissy-ass garden with its wrought iron benches and trickling fountains and year-round blooming plants.

Funny how it didn't *look* like a shit-pool. That's what made it even more dangerous. Here you were thinking life was all happy and wonderful and things were finally going to work out like you hoped. Then, something in the shit-pool reaches up to suck you down once more.

As he took a last drag off the cigarette, he sensed a movement to his left. He turned and, coming toward him from the garden, was a man dressed all in black. In his hand, he held a gun. Rich wasn't familiar with firearms, didn't know what the fuck kind of gun it was, but he knew all he needed to. The gun was big, it was deadly, and it was pointed straight at his chest.

Oh fuck, he thought, nearly gagging on the lungful of smoke trapped in his throat. The butt trembled in his fingers and he dropped it, leaving it smoldering on Lily Highland's beloved grass. He probably would have wet himself if everything in him hadn't locked up the instant he saw the pistol.

At that moment, staring into the gleaming barrel of the gun, he had an epiphany.

Turns out the crocodiles *are* worse than the shit.

****

I was picturing a soothing bath, fluffy robe, hot chocolate, and baseball when I pulled into my driveway and climbed out of my car. All I needed was an evening to decompress, alone, without interference from the outside world.

"Marilyn! Marilyn!"

It was Linus, my eighty-two-year-old neighbor. He called me Marilyn instead of Monroe because he got a kick out of it.

I sighed, debating whether to ignore him as I saw my fantasy of warm chocolate and solitude slipping away.

Humanity won out over indulgence. I smiled brightly and waved at the old man, heading toward him.

Linus Tompkins was one of three neighbors in my cul-de-sac. Each of the four houses sat twenty feet apart. Far enough that we didn't feel like we were rubbing against one another but close enough to prevent total privacy.

Linus had been my neighbor for nearly five years and in that time, we'd formed an odd friendship. I would run errands for him—doctor's appointments, grocery store trips, etc, and in turn, he entertained me with stories of the outlaw, Jesse James. Linus was a relative, a descendant, although I wasn't sure of the exact relation. Once in a while, Linus would give me a piece of James' gang memorabilia.

I joined him on the faded cedar porch swing, catching a whiff of Old Spice and Mentholatum. Tufts of gray hair were all that remained on his freckled head. He wore tan pants with blue suspenders, a plaid shirt, and a ratty blue cardigan sweater.

"How was your day?" he asked.

"It was good."

"You don't do that well."

"Do what?"

"Fib." He chuckled and patted my knee with his wrinkled hand. "You're troubled about something. Anything I can do?"

"No, thanks. Everything's fine."

His faded blue eyes stared at me shrewdly, but he didn't say anything. For a while, we sat and gently rocked in silence. Across the street, Don Chathum was pulling his roller trash can to the curb. He raised his hand in greeting, and we both waved back. A cool wind gusted over the porch, and I pulled my coat more tightly over my sweater.

"Life's not so simple anymore," Linus finally said.

"Not so much," I agreed.

"Back in my day, things were far from perfect, but you can be certain they were a sight better than now."

"I'm sure they were." I settled back, preparing to be on the receiving end of one of Linus's lengthy ruminations.

"Shows like *I Love Lucy* and *Gunsmoke* are a thing of the past. Now you gotta have a bunch of naked people and filthy language to get a hit TV show." He looked out over the yard, but I guessed he was actually looking back fifty years. "I know you just think I'm an old fool and things weren't as perfect as they were portrayed on TV, but they were, in general, much better than now." He shook his head. "You know what kids are doing these days? Kids. Teenagers—fourteen, fifteen years old? They're taking naked pictures with their cell phones. Pulling crazy stunts, even killing themselves live on the Internet. You seen this stuff?"

"Yeah. It's crazy."

Apparently satisfied with my allegiance to his cause, he went on, "The public sees way too much of what goes on these days. The media puts everything into visuals. Just like the wars, and all this police brutality caught on tape. Don't get me wrong, I'm not saying it's right when that happens. The police shouldn't be doing it, but does the public really need to see it when they do? Can't it just be given to the proper authorities and handled there? There's enough of a breakdown in respect for the law as it is. Don't need to give people more reason." He sighed, a drawn out, rattling sound. "Yep. Things sure have changed. I long for the days when everybody wasn't hooked up to some kind of electronic doohickie. It'd be nice if someone went to show you a picture of their kid and pulled out a billfold instead of a blasted cell phone."

I smiled indulgently, gritting my teeth on the inside. Normally, I didn't mind listening to him for hours. But tonight, I was cold and feeling antisocial. I wanted to wallow in self-pity all by my lonesome.

I stared out over the neighborhood, my eyes straying to the graveyard next to my house. Shadows were starting to blanket the evening, casting the tombstones in a shroud of darkness.

"I sense you're not really with me this evening, Miss Marilyn."

My gaze turned back to Linus. "I'm sorry. I didn't mean to be rude. Just a little tired."

"You better get rested up. You've got a long evenin' ahead of you."

"Why's that?"

He nodded toward my house. "You have a visitor, and she seems in a bad way."

Josie. I didn't ask why he was just now mentioning it. I figured it had just now occurred to him. Linus's memory wasn't always in top form. Plus, he wasn't

Josie's biggest fan.

I blew out a breath and stood. "Thanks, Linus. I'd better go check on her."

"Can I ask you something, missy?"

"Sure," I said wearily.

He peered up at me with his wise old-man eyes. "Who checks on you?"

A lump rose in my throat, but I forced it away and smiled down at him. "You check on me, Linus. That's who."

He smiled back, sadly, and nodded. I stepped off the porch, shot him a parting wave, and headed home.

Rather than joy at my friend's arrival, my heart was filled with dread. Selfishly, I was disappointed at missing out on the 'wallow-in-misery' evening I had planned. On the other hand, I was relieved that Josie had lived to see another day. Each time she vanished, usually without warning, I would wonder if I'd ever see her again. Between the drugs and the asshole boyfriend, I just didn't know.

I took off my coat and hung it on the rack inside the foyer. Even if Linus hadn't told me of Josie's arrival, I'd have known immediately. The smell of cigarette smoke assailed me and I nearly tripped over a ratty pair of Timberland boots. Those same boots had left a puddle in my entryway. I took a towel from the kitchen and dropped it on the hardwood floor to absorb the water.

I heard the television and moved into the living room. Josie lay on the sofa, my burgundy micro fiber throw resting half on, half off her sleeping form. A bottle of Blue Moon beer sat on the coffee table next to her splayed hand. One of my Tupperware cereal bowls, full of cigarette butts, rested next to the beer. It wasn't that I didn't have ashtrays, it was just that Josie couldn't be bothered to dig one out and had used the first thing she'd found. I was just grateful she'd used something other than the floor.

"Josie?" I shook her shoulder, some of my irritation ebbing when I felt how tiny and fragile her bones were beneath my fingers. She didn't stir. I could let her sleep, but I needed her awake so I could check her out. See how far gone she was. Was she high or in the coming down stages? She knew she couldn't stay here and do drugs, but if she needed me or was ready to get off of them, my home was open to her.

"Josie," I said more loudly. She didn't open her eyes, but her thin fingers shot out and gripped the front of my sweater.

"I won't leave you," she murmured, her voice sounding raw and panicked. "I promise, Katie, I won't leave you. I won't leave you…"

I flinched as a long-ago memory washed over me. Katie. Poor, sweet, Katie.

Poor, sweet, murdered, Katie.

It had happened when we were twelve. Josie, Katie, and I were best friends. Josie and Katie were at a sleep-over at my house, in a tent in my back yard. Sometime during the night, Katie disappeared. Hours later, her body was found. They never caught the guy who killed her, and the tragedy of that night had stayed with us all these years. Especially with Josie.

I took hold of both Josie's wrists and shook her some more. "Josie, it's me, Roe. Come on, hon, wake up."

Her eyes snapped open, and she rose to a sitting position, her gaze taking in everything in the room before settling on me. Recognition dawned, although she still looked confused. "Roe?"

I searched her pupils to see how dilated they were. Not bad. Maybe she was coming off it.

"Yeah, it's me."

"Katie?"

So, she wasn't quite with me yet.

"No, honey, it's me, Roe. Katie's gone."

Confusion gave way to sorrow, and tears streamed down her cheeks. "I shouldn't have left her."

I pried her fingers from my sweater and put my arms around her, settling next to her on the couch. "You didn't leave her, sweetie. It's not your fault. You were just a kid. We all were."

She cried softly for a few moments, then stopped, pulling away from me.

"Are you okay?" I asked.

She nodded in a quick, jerky movement. "I will be. I just need to…" She ran a trembling hand through her limp, unwashed hair. "Just need to get my head straight, you know?"

Yes, I knew. I'd been through it enough times, I should. I just wondered how many times would be enough. If Josie would ever quit the drugs for good.

I looked at her, seeing a cut on her lip that was trying to heal. A bruise shadowed her right cheekbone. Anger washed over me, but the anger was toward her almost as much as it was toward Matt.

Why did she keep going back to him? What was it about her that made her think she deserved to get the shit beat out of her?

Thinking of Matt reminded me of the detectives. I needed to tell Josie they wanted to talk to her, but she was in no shape to deal with that right now. Maybe in the morning would be better.

What she needed now was a hot meal and a shower. Her stained AC/DC T-shirt and tattered jeans looked like she'd been wearing them for days. I could smell stale sweat, along with the odors of booze and garbage, like the stench that rose from the gutters of Bourbon Street.

Standing, I took her by the hands and pulled her to her feet. "Go take a shower. I'll fix you something to eat."

She nodded like an obedient child and headed unsteadily down the hallway.

****

By the time Josie finished showering, I had a pot of potato soup with chunks of ham simmering on the stove. I made it from canned potatoes, because raw ones would take too long to cook, and Josie needed something in her stomach quickly. Not the healthiest of meals, but it was substantial.

Josie came into the kitchen wearing a pair of my navy blue sweats. The clothes hung loosely on her frame. I wasn't particularly large, but Josie was skeletal. Even before the drugs, she'd been tiny, but now she looked as though a puff of wind would blow her away. Her pixie-ish, waif-like appearance brought out protective instincts in most people. Except for Matt. For him, it seemed to bring out the desire to inflict pain.

Her wispy, pale blonde hair was clean now, but she still looked street-worn. Dark shadows rimmed her eyes, and her pallid cheeks were sunken in. The signs of her beating stood out like blips on a radar screen.

What had happened to make her choose this life? She'd had a good childhood, great parents, a loving sister. Her mother had died a few years ago, and now it was just her dad and sister.

"Have you called your dad?" I asked as I poured glasses of tea for us.

She shook her head.

"I'm sure he's worried about you. You should call him."

"Right. So he can lecture me about Matt?" She took a seat at my black lacquer dining table and sipped the tea.

"He just wants what's best for you."

"He has no idea what's best for me. Can we drop it?"

I sighed. "Yeah. Sorry."

As far as I knew, she never contacted her family anymore. When she came into town, she stayed with me. Although he loved his daughter, there was a great deal of tension between her father and her. He wouldn't accept that she was a drug addict. He thought she just liked to party too much. Neither of her parents had dealt well with her grief after Katie died, figuring if they ignored it, it would go away. Instead, Josie went away, into the drugs.

I slid a plate of sliced tomatoes in front of her, and she curled her nose.

"Eat a few of these, you need the nutrients." I sounded like my mother. I cringed. "The soup will be ready in a minute."

"Fine." She sighed and picked up the fork.

She'd finished two of the tomatoes by the time the soup was ready. I dished up a bowl for each of us, taking a seat across from her. We ate in silence and, after finishing more than half the bowl, Josie leaned back and linked her hands over her non-existent stomach.

"I'm about to pop," she groaned.

It was more than I'd expected her to eat, and I nodded approvingly. She waited until I finished eating before lighting a cigarette. Standing, I rummaged through the cupboards until I found an ashtray, then slid it in front of her.

"So, how are things going with you?" she asked, sounding more like my long-time best friend and confidante.

An unexpected rush of tears came to my throat, and I had a sudden, overwhelming desire to unburden myself, to tell her about Adam's engagement and his lying to me about the promotion.

I opened my mouth to tell her and looked into her bruised, haunted eyes. Her skin was so pale, so thin, I could almost see her skeleton beneath the surface.

"Fine," I said. "Everything's fine."

She frowned, maybe noting something in my tone. "You sure?"

"Yeah," I forced a smile. Everything was not fine, but it could wait. She was a little too fragile right now to take on my problems, too. "I'm sure. Everything's great."

After I washed the dishes, we watched some television—sitcoms, not baseball as I was the only one of the two of us who liked it—for a few hours, before Josie's yawning made me realize that, even after her nap, she needed sleep.

I made up the guest bed for her. Once she was under the covers, I sat on the edge of the bed.

"You remember Snowball?" Josie asked.

I did. Snowball was a Pekingese Josie owned when we were kids. Toward the end of our sixth grade year, the dog became ill. The vet said someone had to stay with her, awake, all night, or she could die.

"I didn't want to stay with her," Josie went on. "Jerry Vanderpool had asked me to the dance." She looked up at me, her bloodshot eyes defensive. "I'd had a crush on him forever. It was the end-of-the-year dance. We were going off to different junior highs. Our last time to be..." she let the words trail off and shrugged.

"It's okay," I said soothingly. "Katie wanted to sit with Snowball. She loved animals."

"Yeah, but Snowball was my dog. My responsibility." Josie scooted up until she was sitting, leaning her back against the headboard. She fumbled around in the nightstand drawer and extracted a pack of cigarettes. As she lit one, I went back into the kitchen for the ash tray and returned, placing it on the nightstand beside her.

We sat in silence, both lost in the memories. Josie rested her head back on the headboard and blew a stream of smoke toward the ceiling. Drops of moisture glinted in the corners of her eyes, but the tears didn't fall.

"You remember when we went over there the next morning?"

"Yeah." I smiled at the memory. Katie, although exhausted, had an elated glow about her. *Snowball's fine*, she'd said, her voice brimming with excitement. *I took care of her all night and she's fine now, look.*

The tiny dog had bounded up to Josie, yelping and wagging her tail.

I know what I want to do, Katie had exclaimed. *I want to be a veterinarian when I grow up. I want to save animals.*

She'd talked about nothing else from that day until

mid-summer. She'd stopped talking about it then because that was when she'd been murdered.

Josie put out her cigarette and slid down, laying her head on the pillow. Her eyes closed, and a small sigh escaped her lips.

"Should have been me," Josie mumbled. "Katie would have done good. I'm just a nothing. A waste of air."

"That's not true," I whispered, tucking the covers around her.

But she'd already gone to sleep, one hand resting beneath a wan cheek.

I hadn't mentioned that the cops wanted to talk to her. I knew I should, that I'd have to eventually, but not now. For now, she just needed to feel safe.

Chapter 3

The song sounded familiar… Pina Coladas… caught in the rain…

Rich slowly opened his eyes, trying to figure out where the music was coming from and why he…

Oh, shit!

He remembered. The man. The gun. The blow to his head.

His limbs were heavy, his head thick and muddled. It was more than being knocked out. He'd been drugged. Now he felt the motion of the vehicle and realized he was tied up in the back seat. There was enough light for him to see the back of the man's head. The man in the driver's seat. His abductor.

How long had he been out? What the fuck did the guy want?

Rich was sure he didn't know him, so why?

He sucked in a breath through clenched lips. The motion of the car and the headache from the blow were making him queasy. He swallowed against the bile. *You can't throw up… you can't throw up…*

Not only did he hate throwing up, it would get the psycho's attention. He would know Rich was awake and then…

Rich didn't want to think about what would happen then. He needed to be positive, figure a way out of this. He was afraid like he'd never been in his life. Whatever the guy wanted, it couldn't be good for Rich. If he'd wanted Rich's opinion on social issues, or wanted directions, or maybe wanted to take Rich to dinner, there would have been no need for the gun or the abduction.

Nope, whatever nut-fuck had in mind, it wasn't good. Rich was screwed. In comparison, the shit pool that was life was starting to look pretty good. It was most definitely preferable to whatever this asshole had in mind. The guy hadn't worn a mask or a disguise of any kind. He'd let Rich see his face. Rich had watched enough television shows and movies to know that only meant one thing.

Rich's face was pressed into the cloth of the car seat, and the ropes were digging painfully into his wrists. He hadn't moved since he'd regained consciousness, but his head was pounding, and he was getting a cramp in his shoulder. Before long, he'd have to shift his position. He lifted his head and stirred, just a little bit, but it was enough.

"You awake?" the man said into the rearview mirror. His voice was smooth, calm, not at all what you'd expect from a blunt-object wielding, gun toting, kidnapping maniac.

Rich didn't respond.

"I know you're awake. You can stop pretending. Do you know why you're here?"

Because you knocked my ass out and dragged me here, motherfucker.

Rich said nothing.

Outside the car windows, Rich saw only trees and the faint beginning of dawn breaking. How long had he been out? Where were they heading?

"You're here because you're one of them."

33

No sense pretending, the guy knew he was awake. "One of whom?" Rich asked, his voice hoarse and quivering.

"You're all a part of it. She's the one, the truly guilty one, but you and the others had a hand in it."

"A hand in what, man? I didn't do shit."

The man chuckled but didn't say anything.

The song ended, then started up again. The same song. Rich hated this song, but he damned sure wasn't going to complain about the music. He had much bigger issues to worry about.

The car slowed to a stop, and the man cut off the engine. He climbed out and opened Rich's door. He was average height, nice-looking—if a dude could think another dude was nice-looking. Pleasant features, clean-shaven. Pretty normal, actually. So true what they say. Killers don't always look like killers.

Wait, Rich, he might not be a killer.

Yeah, right. He brought you out here for a fucking picnic.

The guy reached in and grabbed Rich's shirt front, yanking him from the car. Rich stumbled but remained on his feet. The world tilted, and the trees spun above his head. Rich closed his eyes, trying to push back the nausea. He did not want to throw up. Hated it. Never understood how bulimics could do it. He'd rather weigh six-hundred pounds.

"Come on." A gun went into Rich's ribs. "Move."

Rich moved.

The gunman led him twenty feet into the woods and told him to stop.

"Get on your knees."

"What? Why are you doing this, man? Whatever

happened, I'm sure I can explain. I didn't mean it, man, I promise." Rich was shaking, and tears poured down his face. He was so fucking *scared*. His stomach tingled, the feeling going all the way down his legs and up into his chest.

"On your *knees*, now!"

The look on the maniac's face didn't invite argument. Rich obeyed.

"You really don't know what you did, do you?" The man shook his head and chuckled in a 'can you believe it' sort of way. "That's the worst part of all. That you think it's just *okay*. No big deal, right?"

"What's just okay? Man, please, tell me what you're talking about and I can explain. I promise."

The man went on like Rich hadn't spoken. "Since you're not as culpable as the others, I'm going to show you mercy."

Rich nearly wet himself with relief. "Oh, thank you. Thank you so much. I'm sorry for whatever I did. I won't say anything to anyone, I promise. You won't regret that you let me live."

The man's eyes narrowed, and he gave a quick shake of his head.

"I didn't say anything about letting you live." He pointed the gun at Rich's head and cocked the hammer. "Since you're not as culpable, I'm going to kill you quick."

****

The sound of bulldozers and drills accompanied me as I walked toward the door of the newspaper. I hadn't slept much the night before, and the noise of the construction going on next door gnawed at the fringes of a headache I was working on.

The professor was in his usual spot by the Pandora fountain. Today, he had a couple of friends with him. He stood as I approached. The others did not. One was leaning back against the fountain, his eyes closed, the other sat next to where the professor had been, wearing headphones and rocking back and forth. The headphones were hooked to a small, portable CD player but I wondered if it was actually playing. Could the homeless afford to keep batteries in their electronics?

"Good morning, Miss Donovan." The professor smiled, showing surprisingly well-cared for teeth. He was tall with slightly stooped shoulders and gray hair that, although receding from his forehead, was long in the back. His voice was cultured, making him sound like Batman's butler, Alfred.

"Good morning, Professor. How you doing?"

"If I were any better, I'd be delirious with the pure joy of it, my dear."

I smiled. The professor was one of the most optimistic people I'd ever met. Considering he lived on the streets, it was pretty impressive. The rest of us could take a lesson on attitude from him.

"Who are your friends?" I dug out a few bills as I spoke and dropped them discreetly into the bucket that sat at the professor's feet.

"Headphone and Carl. Headphone doesn't talk much, but he's good company." Neither man looked up. "Headphone only appeared recently. Not sure where he came from or how he came to be in his current circumstances."

I'd chatted with the professor off and on during the year or so since he started hanging around the newspaper. I'd gleaned that he was once *actually* a professor. He fell on hard times because of alcoholism. Lost his job, his wife, wound up on the streets. He'd stopped drinking but hadn't put his life back together.

"Perhaps, like me," the professor continued, "he prefers the simple life."

I glanced at the tattered clothing all three men wore. Their coats were barely sufficient to keep out a strong breeze, let alone the biting wind. "I can't imagine choosing to live out on the streets."

"You'd be surprised, my dear. In many ways, street life is preferable to the rat race of the world. Do you realize how many people live a life of constant stress? They hate their jobs, their very lives. This is stress-free. There is no pressure. No luxury, either, but luxury doesn't really make you happy. This is the perfect existence for those who are miserable, day in, day out, not doing what they truly want to do. Those who dislike having others expect something from them. This is freedom."

"So you're saying people who are homeless prefer it that way?"

"Not all, not by any means. There are those who would like to get back on their feet but either do not have the means or can't kick their addictions. But some, like me, are content to live this way. I like being *off* my feet." He smiled. "Especially when it allows me to make the acquaintance of charming and lovely people such as yourself." He made a small bow. "You are a rare individual. You see us as people and don't ignore our existence. For that, I'm grateful."

I smiled. "And I'm grateful to you, Professor, for keeping me grounded."

I said goodbye and headed to the door, cursing my

timing when I reached it at the same time as Adam and Tabitha. She brought him to work every morning and met him for lunch every day. Apparently, eight hours apart was just too much.

"Hello, Monroe," Tabitha said. She had this nasally, cartoon voice that always set my teeth on edge. She was a big-boobed, small, athletic blonde, who came from a wealthy family. Superficially, the entire package was quite a catch, I had to admit, but I didn't know how Adam could stand to listen to that voice for the rest of his life.

"Tabitha. How are you?"

"Great, thanks." She held possessively to Adam's arm. "Just heading to spinning class."

Spinning class. Figured. The closest I'd ever come to spinning was watching the turntable through the microwave door while my food cooked.

I looked past her to Adam, who squirmed uncomfortably. "Well, I'll let you two lovebirds say goodbye," I said. "I've got to get inside. Those obituaries won't write themselves." I gave Adam my best smartass look and strode past the couple into the building.

****

Lane sat with his hands linked between his knees, leaning forward in his chair as he watched Catherine brush her hair. She wore a blue silk robe, the same color as her eyes.

She sat in front of the window, the lights shining in making a hint of lavender shimmer in her auburn hair. She was beautiful. Even after all this time, all they'd been through, she was still an amazing-looking woman.

"I saw the Emersons today," he told her, wanting to make small talk, anything to fill the silence.

She didn't respond, but then, she seldom did.

Lane tried again. "They said to tell you hello. They still live in the old neighborhood. He just retired and they bought a travel trailer. Going to hit the road for a few months."

Finally, she lifted her head. Wide, unfocused eyes stared at him. "Joseph?"

The name sliced through him like a knife to the gut. Still had that effect. Even after two years.

"No, it's Lane."

Her brows drew together. "Where's Joseph?"

"I don't know," he replied wearily. *In hell, I hope.*

She gave him that blank yet desperate stare, the one that said she almost knew who he was, but not quite. He had to look away. His gaze roamed over the room. In addition to the bed, there was a metal desk with a few drawers that held Catherine's belongings. No mirrors. Too dangerous.

Even if he didn't already know where they were, the smell would give it away. The hint of ammonia that couldn't quite mask the odors of sweat and madness.

The Riverbend Psychiatric Hospital was nicer than the one she'd been in before. He'd had her moved here when his transfer with the force came through. He'd had to get away from St. Louis. Too many memories. All bad. He'd hoped a change of scenery would help. So far, it hadn't.

A sound at the door caught his attention, and he turned to find his mother-in-law, Miriam, standing behind him.

She was nearing sixty but looked no older than forty-five. Her blond hair barely showed the gray and her face, thanks to what he suspected were a few tucks here and there, was nearly wrinkle-free. She was tall and willowy, just like her daughter. Her gaze went from Lane to Catherine.

"How is she today?" she asked, tight-lipped.

Lane shrugged. "The same."

"Did she ask about him?"

He didn't reply. That was all the answer she needed. She moved further into the room and stopped next to her daughter's chair, tossing an oversized red handbag onto the bed.

"Why do you put yourself through this?" She spoke to him but still stared at Catherine.

"I could ask the same question of you."

"She's my daughter," Miriam bit out, like it was a curse rather than a blessing.

"She's my wife," he responded, much the same way.

Miriam's lips tightened further. She took the brush from Catherine's hand, the gentleness of her movements at war with the tension in the set of her shoulders. She began brushing her daughter's hair. Catherine sat like a statue, unaware of Lane's or her mother's presence.

"I wish I'd gotten help for her sooner," Miriam said.

"You did all you could. She'd been in therapy for years."

Miriam shook her head in a short, impatient motion. "I could have done more. Could have started when she was a child. Even then, I saw signs that her emotions weren't quite stable. I should have warned you before you married her."

"I knew she had issues. None of us could have predicted what would happen."

She made a motion that was somewhere between a nod and a shrug, as if in acquiescence, and said, "You should sign those divorce papers."

"I will, eventually. It's just difficult. I made a vow."

She let out a scoffing chuckle. "Too bad your wife didn't feel the same."

A pang stabbed his chest. He didn't need a reminder of how Catherine treated their vows. Suddenly, it was too warm in the room. Too stifling... too much.

He was searching for a plausible reason to escape when fate handed him one in the form of a call from his partner.

"Break's over," Tony said. "Got a call that a body was found out on Macon road." He gave Lane directions.

"I'll meet you there." Lane ended the call and turned to his mother-in-law. "I need to head out."

Miriam nodded but didn't speak. Lane left her humming softly to her daughter, tears glistening in her eyes as she lovingly slid the brush through Catherine's hair.

****

Twenty feet was as close to the crime scene as Lane could get in his car. He parked and walked the rest of the way through the trees, letting the light bars on the squad cars guide him. The air around him smelled of rain and damp earth. He tensed at the anticipation of the odor that would soon join those.

A patrol cop met him at the perimeter of the barrier tape.

"You're lead, right, Detective Brody?"

"I am," Lane said, snapping on a pair of latex gloves.

"We got an anonymous call and when we arrived, found the victim."

Lane walked with the guy to the tape where a handful of patrol cops guarded the perimeter. Tony was waiting for him.

"What do we have?" Lane asked.

"Caucasian male, mid-thirties," Tony answered as they ducked underneath the tape.

Lesli, a crime scene tech, squatted next to a body lying on its side, hands tied behind the back. Lane stopped next to Lesli and she looked up, her lips set in a grim line.

"Apparent trauma to the left temple. Looks like a gunshot wound." She gestured a gloved hand to a round hole with a stream of dried blood beneath.

Lane squatted next to her and ran his gaze over the body. The man's eyes stared blankly in front of him, a cloudy film over them. His lower body was twisted at an unnatural angle, meaning the gunshot had come suddenly and unexpectedly. Lane glanced at the ground around the body. Based on the two sets of footprints, and the fact that there were no drag marks, the murder had likely happened here.

Lane looked at the fingers. No visible evidence of defense wounds, but he was tied up, so how much defending could he have done? Lividity had settled in the lower areas, and the corpse was stiff, which meant he'd been dead less than thirty-six hours.

Lane stood and glanced around. "Got a take on the entry and exit points?"

Tony pointed the direction Lane had come. "That's the only way in or out to the road."

"What about casings, weapon?" The chance that the weapon was left behind was almost nil, but sometimes they got lucky.

"One casing from a Smith and Wesson .38," Tony said.

"No weapon left at the scene?"

Tony snorted. "Did you think there would be?"

Lane shrugged. "A little optimism never hurts, right?"

"Coroner's here," one of the patrols said.

Byron Keaton, the county coroner, was tall and lanky, with a thick head of curly hair. He nodded to Lane and Lesli as they stood to let him in next to the body.

Lesli reported what they knew so far, while Lane stood patiently, waiting for Keaton to complete his initial exam.

"Lividity fixed. Rigid. Only visible signs of trauma an apparent gunshot wound to the left temple."

Lane took notes as Keaton spoke, although he doubted he'd find anything they didn't know already. Not until he did the autopsy.

A commotion behind Lane made him turn. Two coroner's assistants approached, carrying a gurney with a body bag lying on top.

"Hell of a long walk," the one in front complained. He was young, with longish hair and a put-out expression.

"Be glad you're walking it instead of being carried," Keaton barked.

The guy flushed but didn't respond.

"You can take him," the coroner said, standing and pulling off his gloves.

There was no more grumbling as the two of them worked the body into the bag and placed it on the gurney, then, one on each end, carried it back the way they'd come.

Once the coroner had gone, and the CSI techs finished photographing and videotaping the scene, Lane walked the perimeter, searching for any more spent casings, more footprints, anything to tell him what had happened. He found a white dusty footprint and knelt to study it.

"Did you guys lift a print of this?" he called to one of the techs.

"Not yet, but we'll get it, Detective."

Lane turned back to the print. Chalk? Some kind of talcum powder? He touched a finger to it and brought it to his nose. No scent. Not talcum powder. He placed a versa-cone next to the footprint, marking it as evidence.

Being extra careful not to disturb the crime scene, Lane moved slowly through the area. The sound of leaves crunching beneath his feet was unnaturally loud in the silence left behind by the dead.

"Did you know that an average mature oak tree sheds around 700,000 leaves during the fall?" he said to Tony.

"Nah," Tony said, "but thanks for the 4-1-1. Now that I've got that question answered, I'll be able to sleep at night."

"Cool." Lane grinned as his partner meandered in the opposite direction.

After a few fruitless minutes of not finding any clues, Lane heard a shout from Tony.

"Hey, come look at this."

Tony stood near a gigantic oak tree, pointing at the trunk. The words, 'Partners in Crime' were written in dark red.

Dread settled in the center of Lane's chest… a dread that told him it wasn't just a random shooting. Not a robbery or a fight that got out of hand. Something about it had the mark of a person with a mission. He felt it in his bones.

"This ain't his first rodeo," Lane said quietly. "Or at least, not his last."

"Nope. I'd say this guy has some kind of plan in mind. You think that's blood?"

Lane shook his head. "The victim didn't lose enough blood for this. Plus, the color's not dark enough." He called one of the techs over to take a sample.

A rustling above them made him look up. A squirrel perched on one of the branches peered down at them suspiciously. "If only you could talk," Lane muttered.

They were losing what little light they'd had. There was no moon out, or if there was, the thickness of the trees blocked its glow.

"Want us to set up flood lights?" a tech who'd been sweeping the leaves and bushes with a metal detector asked.

"No," Lane said. "I'll do another walk-through, but I think we've got all we're getting for tonight."

He watched as the techs packed up their equipment. Looking around the scene, he found himself wishing the dead man had simply pissed someone off and this would be the end of it.

His gut told him he was shit out of luck.

Chapter 4

On Saturday morning, I stopped for coffee on my way to the bi-monthly family dinner. I'd had coffee at home but realized at my current speed, I was on pace to arrive early at my parents.' Another cup of coffee was a preferable option.

I was next in line and tried to curb my eagerness as the pungent aroma of coffee teased my taste buds. My gaze fell on the lemon bars in the glass case. Someone had captured sunshine in the bright, yellow rectangles of perfection while angels sprinkled their heavenly dust over the top. Or maybe that was just powdered sugar.

I considered having one. If I did, I wouldn't be hungry at mealtime. My mother would interpret this as a sign of an eating disorder.

If I *didn't* have one, I'd be ravenous at lunch and eat too much. My mother would scold me about watching my weight.

You'll never find a man if you get too heavy, Monroe. You're already past thirty-five and the weight won't come off like it did in your twenties. Men don't like chubby girls.

"Can I help you?" the perky barista asked, thankfully snatching me away from the specter of my mother's admonishments.

After a few brief mental arguments, I decided against the pastry and ordered my usual. "Large

Columbian blend with an extra shot of espresso."

The girl called out my order over her shoulder as one pink-tipped nail poked at the register.

A voice behind me said, "I hope they serve a chisel with that."

I turned to find Detective Lane Brody standing at my shoulder.

"Detective," I said, sounding a little too breathy and pleased for my liking.

"Miss Donovan. How are you?" His clothing was more informal today, jeans and a dark green button-up shirt. The tail hung out, making him look casually mussed. I wondered if that was the look he was going for, or if he just couldn't be bothered with fashion.

"Fine, thanks." I paid for my coffee and moved aside so he could order. Suddenly, an unpleasant thought overtook my pleasant ones. "Are you following me, Detective?"

His mouth quirked slightly at one corner. "In a professional or non-professional sense?"

"Professional."

"No." He gave his order to the girl, leaving me to sort out the meaning of his cryptic response. Did that mean he was following me in a *non*-professional sense?

No, of course not. He probably wasn't following me at all, but my pulse was jittery and my insides fluttered, getting me all confused.

The young guy behind the counter called out that my order was ready. I took the coffee from him, sipping cautiously from the opening in the lid.

"Well, nice to see you," I told Brody, turning to head to one of the tall, shiny-topped tables.

Brody followed.

"Mind if I join you?"

His tone was friendly, but I wasn't fooled. His interest was business. I wondered if he had more questions or was just trying to get a read on me, see if I'd lied about Josie. I hadn't. But I was probably going to. I couldn't let the cops at her now. She was too fragile.

Even knowing his interest wasn't personal, I was self-conscious about my appearance. I wore a sweatshirt and Royals' cap, no make-up. My mother hated it when I "dressed like a vagabond," so I did so more often than not when I knew I'd see her. Now that I'd run into Brody, my plan to annoy my mother had back-fired.

"Not at all," I said, pointing at the chair across from me.

Brody sat his coffee and a lemon bar down on the table. It looked even better up close.

We sat across from one another at the table and I raised my eyebrows at Brody. "Did you really just happen to be here at the same time I am?"

"I swear. It really is coincidence that I ran into you," he said, taking the lid off his cup. "I was heading—" He stopped and looked down at the table, took a breath, and brought his eyes back up to mine. "Heading somewhere I'm not in a hurry to be."

"This is more of coincidence than you think. So was I."

"Well, I guess it's fortunate we ran into each other." He took a bite of his lemon bar and while he chewed, I tried to think of something to say. I didn't want to bring up Josie, so I searched my mind desperately for something that would keep him from doing so. Nothing came to mind. Probably because I was trying too hard.

My gaze wandered around the coffee shop, although

there wasn't much to see. Few of the tables were occupied. Most patrons took their injection of caffeine on the run.

In the corner, two young girls sat slumped in a booth, rumpled clothing and smeared make-up indicating they'd pulled an all-nighter. Three young guys at a table next to them alternated between checking out the girls and engaging in conversation too loud and too animated for a lazy Saturday morning.

At a table a few over from ours sat a middle-aged couple, she with her muffin, he with his newspaper, held in front of his face like a barrier.

I turned my attention back to Brody and watched with envy as he took another bite of the lemon bar. He swallowed, then pointed at my coffee. "That's some pretty strong java."

"Yeah. You'd think I'd have trouble sleeping the way I drink the strong, dark stuff. But it doesn't seem to affect it."

"Actually, the lighter coffee beans contain more caffeine than the darker roasts. The darker beans are roasted longer, and the longer a coffee is roasted, the more caffeine burns off in the process."

"Fascinating," I said mockingly. "How did you know that?"

"I know tons of useless information." He cocked a head toward the three men, whose conversation seemed to have become more heated and had most definitely increased in volume. "For example, they're arguing about whether or not *Texas Chainsaw Massacre* is a true story."

"The original or the remake?"

"It doesn't matter, they're both about the same—"

He stopped when he saw my grin. "Ah, you're just being a smartass."

"Sorry. Continue."

"Well, it's not a true story. It was inspired by Ed Gein, who did his deeds in Wisconsin, not Texas. He was only known to have killed two people, although not with a chain saw. Part of the idea for the movie stems from the fact that he used body parts for dishes and furniture and wore the skins of his victims." He sipped from his cup and shrugged. "Like I said, I'm a veritable plethora of useless information."

Suddenly, after that gruesome tidbit, I was glad I hadn't gotten a lemon bar. "Wow. I'm impressed. As a cop, wouldn't it be better to know tons of *useful* information?"

He grinned. "You're probably right. I know a little of that. Speaking of which, any word from your friend since we spoke?"

Damn. Me and my big mouth. I knew Josie needed to speak with the police, but she wouldn't be much good to them until she was straightened out. And they damn sure wouldn't be much good to her.

"I'm afraid I haven't had a chance to talk to her about it." It was only a 'sort of' lie, and I almost didn't feel guilty about it. I took too big a gulp of the hot coffee, burning my tongue. My eyes watered.

"Are you okay?"

"Yeah, fine," I told him, in spite of my scorched mouth. "Listen, I really need to know. Is Josie in trouble?"

"Not as far as we know. We really are just trying to find her boyfriend. So far, that's all we want with Miss Detweiler."

So far. I didn't like that he'd felt the need to add that disclaimer. I let out a sigh, wondering if I should have left Josie home alone. The only other solutions were missing my family get-together, for which I would be forever lambasted, or bringing her with me. God knows, the poor girl had been through enough without that.

"Your boss seemed to be watching us pretty closely yesterday," Detective Brody said. "Like our visit was some kind of problem."

"*Adam* is the problem."

"Yeah?"

"We used to date." I shrugged, not telling him about Adam cheating or the lost promotion.

"Must be awkward at work."

"A little. But we manage."

I fiddled with the cardboard heat protector on my cup, not sure what to say next. Winging it, I said, "You're not from around here, are you?"

"How could you tell?"

"I hear a bit of an accent."

He spread his hands. "You got me. I moved here from St. Louis."

"No," I said, smiling. "I mean, originally. Where are you from?"

"I was born and raised in Montgomery, Alabama. Moved to St. Louis when I was eighteen."

"Ah. That explains it. You don't have a strong accent, but you didn't quite get rid of that southern drawl."

"No, ma'am. Try as I might," he said, purposely making his accent more pronounced. "The guys at the station call me Huck because of my accent. Funny thing is, Huckleberry Finn is from right here in Missouri."

I laughed. "Of course, you'd know that, with that wealth of trivia stored in your cranium."

"Yeah. But I thought everyone knew that. Especially people *from* Missouri. Did you know that The Adventures of Tom Sawyer was the first novel ever to be written on a typewriter?"

I lifted my eyebrows. "More of the trivia?"

He grinned, his face going a few shades darker than pink. "Sorry. I get carried away sometimes. So, tell me about you. You from around here?"

"Born and bred, right here in the Kansas City area. Blue Springs, actually." Which reminded me. That was where I should be now. We'd both nearly finished our coffee and I was on the verge of being late to my mother's. That wouldn't bode well for the afternoon. "It was nice seeing you," I said, standing. "Much as I dread it, I'd better head out."

"Yeah, me, too." He stood also and we picked up our cups, walking to the door.

"Hey, don't worry," Brody said. My expression must have revealed my anxiety. "I'm sure your friend will be fine. If you talk to her, be sure to tell her we want to see her." He opened the door to let me pass. "And tell her she might want to stay away from Matt Lovell."

Tell me something I don't know.

"I will," I promised.

We said our goodbyes and I hurried to my car, watching out of the corner of my eye as Lane climbed into a blue Crown Vic. I didn't know if that tight, nearly painful tremble in my chest was due to concern over what Josie might be involved in, or because Detective Lane Brody was just so damned sexy… almost frighteningly so.

****

My parents still lived in the house where I'd grown up. The back yards on their side of the street led into a wooded area where my brothers hunted when they were younger. Not only did my brothers no longer hunt there, we all avoided even the mention of those woods nowadays. Deep within them is the place where Katie was killed.

Most of the houses were brick, which was the first sign the neighborhood had been around for a while. A majority of the new homes in the Kansas City area had vinyl siding, making them look like duplicates of one another, other than the subtle changes in color.

Halloween decorations from witches to scarecrows to elaborate grave yard scenes were prominent in nearly all of the yards. My parents' house was one of the exceptions. They hadn't bothered to decorate for any holiday other than Christmas since their children moved away.

My brothers were already there. Of course, they would never dream of being late. My oldest brother was Coburn, then came Mitchum. My brother just older than me, the one I was closest to, was Gable.

My mother had named them after Marilyn Monroe's co-stars, Charles Coburn, Robert Mitchum, and Clark Gable. My mother was obsessed with Marilyn Monroe. A testament to her lofty expectations for me was that she named me after a gorgeous sex symbol she idolized. If she'd known how I'd turn out, she could have saved herself the disappointment and named me Jane, after Plain.

Fortunately for her, my three handsome, successful, nearly perfect brothers prevented her foray into motherhood from being a total bust. Coburn was tall with sandy-blonde hair that fell over his forehead with just the right amount of devil-may-care stubbornness. His wife, Naomi, was a petite red-head, who was pregnant with their first child.

Mitchum was a stockbroker, and although the least good-looking of the Donovan trio, he was still extremely popular with the ladies. His twinkling hazel eyes, lopsided grin, and charmingly reckless personality had them swarming like ants on a crumb.

Gable's hair was the color of a raven's wing and with his white-toothed smile, naturally bronze skin, and jet-black eyes, he was the best-looking of my brothers, but it was a waste, at least, where women were concerned. Gable was a priest. My family had always been Easter/Christmas, hit and miss Catholics. Gable had been more miss than hit. That's why it had surprised everyone when he'd announced, at fifteen years old, that he wanted to be a priest.

Gable had been rowdy, headstrong, bordering on wild until the summer of Katie's death. The way it happened had had an effect on my entire family, each of us in different ways. It seemed to have a sobering effect on Gable. He'd grown up overnight. He'd entered the seminary as soon as he graduated from high school and hadn't looked back since. It made my parents extremely proud, although it hadn't increased their devotion to Catholicism.

I took off my coat and said hello to my sister-in-law and each of my brothers, suffering a top-of-the-head knuckle rub from Gable.

My dad rose from his recliner, standing long enough to give me a hug, then planted himself back in front of the television. Funny how when I was growing up, he'd seemed so big. Now, with his thinning gray hair, his old man spectacles, and stooped shoulders, he seemed like a shrunken version of the man I'd once thought was larger than life. He wore the same hangdog expression he'd worn for years. I wondered when he'd started to be so miserable, or if he'd always been that way and I just hadn't noticed as a child. I thought of what the professor had said. Would my dad be one of those people who'd be happier on the streets? He couldn't be any more miserable, that's for sure.

"Monroe Rachel Donovan. You're late." My mother came into the living room from the kitchen, wiping her hands on a white strawberry-patterned apron. Her hair was impeccably coiffed, her make-up slathered on, her navy slacks and white blouse crisp and spotless, even though she'd probably been cooking for hours. She was just now starting to get plump with age, although with her diets and made-to-flatter clothing, she was fighting it every step of the way.

"I'm sorry, Mom."

"Stuff your sorrys in a sack, young lady. I don't know what's wrong with you." She gave me a peck on the cheek, all the while haranguing me. "Your brothers managed to make it here on time and they have important jobs, families." Unspoken were the words, *And what do you have?*

"I know. I didn't get much sleep last night and I woke up later than—"

"Out partying 'til all hours? You look terrible. Come in the kitchen and help me finish up with lunch."

I followed her into the overly warm kitchen where the smell of lasagna was strong and should have been tantalizing, but I felt no more pleasure than a death row inmate anticipating a last meal.

"You have to start showing some responsibility. It's obvious you're not going to have a husband to look out for you."

"Why is it obvious?" I asked, even though I doubted it as much as she did.

She turned and gave me 'the look.'

"You're thirty-six years old, dear. I don't see men lining up. What about that Adam, are you two back together?"

"No. And we won't be. He's engaged to another woman."

"See?" she said, shaking her head like I'd done something wrong. "You'll never give me grandchildren. I've resigned myself to that."

I wanted to say, "If you've resigned yourself to it, why don't you quit bitching at me about it?" But that would only increase the bitching. Here I'd been cheated on and dumped by my boyfriend, and Mom's only thoughts were how it affected her.

We finished cooking the meal in relative silence. Mom called my brothers and father to the table and we all sat.

After each of us had satisfactorily praised my mother's cooking, she launched into her homage to my eldest brother—and her favorite—Coburn. Coburn's already exalted status had been elevated a few months ago when he and Naomi had announced their impending parenthood. He would be the first to fulfill Mom's dream of being a grandmother. I tuned her out, not even minding the ode to Coburn. At least it would keep her off my back for the remainder of my visit.

****

Lane sat at his desk, rubbing the spot between his eyes with his forefinger, his thoughts wandering from his caseload to his wife. Always, his wife. He'd gone to see her when he left the coffee shop, but had cut the visit short. It was even more depressing than usual, with her not speaking, not moving, just lying in bed, staring at the ceiling while tears leaked from her eyes.

The usual questions hammered away at him. Should he divorce her? Would she ever be fit to stand trial? Did he really even want that? To dredge up everything again? Did he really want her to pay for what she'd done, or did he just want things back the way they were?

Right. Want the impossible. That's healthy.

Unbidden, another thought crept in with the usual fare. Monroe Donovan. Something about her had captured his attention, although he wasn't sure what it was. She was pretty, that was a given. But he saw countless pretty women every day of his life. What was it about her that tugged at him?

There was something warm and inviting about her, a vitality… some kind of light that drew him. He was sure her life wasn't exactly smooth sailing, but she had an upbeat, 'ain't life a bitch, but ain't it kinda funny' amusement hovering in her brown eyes. He recalled the way her generous mouth intermittently twitched at the corners. When she offered a full smile, a dimple creased just her right cheek, as if she only found life half-funny. Just thinking about her could almost invoke her scent… light and crisp, fresh, like spring grass and summer rain.

A file slapped loudly on his desk, startling him, bringing him back from a place he shouldn't have been.

Lieutenant Michelle Karakas dropped into the seat

next to his desk, plunking her feet on the arm of his chair. He looked at her feet, then at her, but didn't tell her to move them. She grinned at him but didn't offer to.

Karakas was tall and squarely built, with short blonde hair, manly features, and a pug nose that didn't match the rest of her face.

Tony joined them, perching a hip on one corner of Lane's desk.

"Okay," Karakas said, opening the file. "Our unfortunate soul was one Richard James Hebringer, thirty-three years old, night desk clerk at the Highland Lily Bed and Breakfast. Don't know if she changed her name, or if corny luck made it turn out that way, but the owner is a widow, Lily Highland." She cocked a brow. "Cute, huh?"

"Adorable." Lane said.

"Mr. Hebringer moved here from Chicago two and a half years ago. No family here but he lived with his girlfriend, exotic dancer, Susan Quintero, aka, you guessed it, Susie Q. Mr. Hebringer was last seen by guests at the B and B at around ten p.m. on Thursday night, when a Mr. Pruitt asked if there was a condom machine on the premises. There wasn't. The guest came down once more after eleven to ask where the nearest convenience store was, but Hebringer wasn't at the desk. Hebringer's shift was eight p.m. to six a.m. He probably disappeared sometime around eleven. If he'd still been there, he should have been at the desk. Pruitt waited for several minutes, but Hebringer never appeared. Detective Woodson learned all this after speaking with the B and B owner on the phone, and also with the horny Mr. Pruitt." She looked up from the folder. "What kind of lab reports you get in so far?"

Lane picked up the paperwork he'd received on the labs. "So far, only a few. Blood found at the scene belongs to the victim. It appears the footprint was some kind of construction dust. Mr. Hebringer's DNA was not in the bank. Thus far, no DNA matches on anything recovered from the scene. The words on the tree were written with paint. They're testing it now to see what kind. Still waiting on ballistics."

"We need to divvy up the interviews. You girls wanna mud wrestle over who gets the stripper?"

"The PC term is clothing challenged," Tony said. He looked at Lane. "I'll fight you for her, man, mud and all." He feigned putting someone in a headlock.

Lane held up his hands in surrender. "I figured you'd be all over that like stink on a garbage truck. You take the stripper. I'll take the bed and breakfast."

"The mother's on her way in from Chicago," Karakas said. "You can both have a crack at her. Miss Q apparently has friends on the force, because she called us wanting to know if we'd found her boyfriend's killer yet, less than an hour after the body was found, before we even had a positive ID. I told her someone would be out to see her."

"Either she didn't want to wait," Tony said, looking over the lieutenant's shoulder, "or someone called dial-a-dancer."

Lane followed Tony's gaze and deduced, as Tony had, that Susie Q had decided to pay them a visit. She wasn't tall, but the six-inch heels she wore gave that illusion. Her legs were bare and nicely shaped, as were her overly large breasts. Her hair was dark, streaked with blonde highlights. She wore a tight, blue stretchy skirt and a blue and white striped blouse that had to work hard to keep her flesh encased.

She headed straight toward them, led by Detective Lucinda Rochester. Lucinda's gaze found Lane's and she rolled her eyes, probably not liking the threat the woman represented. Lucinda had somewhat of a reputation. She was curvy and attractive, with sultry eyes and long, thick, chestnut-colored hair. Since Lane's arrival in Kansas City, Lucinda had been on a mission to bed him, not caring about his marital status. Thus far, Lane had just barely avoided her clutches. Not an easy task. Especially when he didn't particularly *want* to avoid them.

Lucinda brought the woman to Lane's desk. "This is Susan Quintero. She'd like to speak to the detectives on the Hebringer case." Lucinda left, giving Quintero a less-than-friendly once-over as she did.

"Are you Lieutenant Karakas?" Quintero asked the lieutenant, who'd dropped her feet and stood by the time the woman reached Lane's desk. "I'm Susan Quintero. I'm here about Rich's murder."

Karakas shook her hand. "Please, Miss Quintero, have a seat. We're very sorry for your loss. Our detectives were just about to come and see you. You saved them a trip. Have a seat and I'll let my detectives talk to you. Let me know if you have any problems," Karakas said, although Lane knew she didn't really want to hear about any problems the woman might have.

The lieutenant went back to her office, and Susan Quintero sat in the vacated chair, crossing her legs. Despite the low temperatures, her skirt was so short she was in danger of giving a free show right there in the squad room. Conversely, she also wore a heavy, rabbit fur coat.

"Miss Quintero." Tony stuck out his hand. "I'm

Detective Webber."

She shook his hand, then dabbed at tears that filled her eyes. "Do you know what happened to my Rich?"

"No, ma'am. Not yet, but we're trying to find out."

The body had been found less than twenty-four hours ago, and she wanted to know who'd killed him. Of course, it wasn't unreasonable. On television, they solved murders in an hour.

Tony opened his notepad and leaned a little toward Susie Quintero. No doubt it offered him a better view of her bosom.

"I'd like to ask you some questions about Mr. Hebringer and the last few days of his life. If you're feeling up to it."

She nodded. "I'll do anything I can to help you find the bastard."

"Thank you. Your cooperation will help us tremendously. Do you know of anyone who might have had a grudge against Mr. Hebringer? Who might have wanted to harm him for any reason?"

"No. Rich didn't have many friends. He hadn't lived here very long. But, no one hated him. I'm sure of that."

"Did you two live together?"

"We stayed together most nights, but we each had our own place. Rich needed his space. You know, men."

Tony smiled. "Yes, ma'am. I do. When was the last time you saw him?"

She wrinkled her brow, as if thinking was something she didn't do often. "It was Wednesday night. Well, no, wait. Thursday morning. But I barely saw him. I was asleep when he left. I opened my eyes once when he was getting dressed, but nodded back off."

"Did you speak to him after that?"

She uncrossed and re-crossed her legs, slowly, like it was a part of her stage routine. "I talked to him on the phone at around ten-thirty or eleven that night. We had plans for the weekend, so I wanted to talk to him about them." A rush of tears welled, then spilled down her cheeks. Tony grabbed a tissue from the box on Lane's desk and pressed it into her hand. "I thought I'd see him on the weekend. But I didn't. I'll never see him again." Her breath hitched and a sob tore from her throat, her shoulders quaking with her grief.

Not wanting the interview to get off track, Lane allowed her a few moments to regain control, then jumped in. "Did he seem upset when you spoke to him? Anything to indicate something might be wrong? That he was frightened or under duress of any kind?"

Quintero shook her head.

"You say he didn't have many friends, but was there someone he was particularly close to? Someone he might confide in about any problems he might have had?"

"What kind of problems?" she asked with an edge to her voice.

"Any kind. Gambling, drinking, drugs, women."

"Rich didn't do any of those things. I mean, he drank a little, and we... *he*," she hastily amended, "smoked dope occasionally, but nothing that was a big deal. Nothing that would get him murdered." Her voice rose on the last word and the sobbing started again.

Again, Lane waited for her to gain control. After a brief time, she took a deep breath and dabbed at her eyes with the second tissue Tony provided.

"Do you know what he did on Thursday after he left? What he did between then and eight that morning when he went to work?"

She shrugged. "I slept 'til nearly three in the afternoon. I work all night," she added defensively, as if they'd called her lazy. "I didn't hear from him all that day. Have no idea what he did." Suddenly, her face brightened. "Wait. He had a job interview. I know that."

"With?"

"That I don't know. Some accounting firm."

Lane made a note. Probably would lead nowhere, but it wouldn't hurt to have all the facts.

"Did he have any hobbies? Any activities outside of work?"

"Why do you want to know that?"

"We're trying to track all of his movements. All of his associations. You never know what kind of link will lead us to solve a crime."

"He liked to watch TV. Liked sports. Watching them, that is. And fucking. Pretty much it." Her head bowed as she blotted tears.

Tony waggled his eyebrows over Quintero's bent head, and Lane guessed he was indicating his willingness to take over for Hebringer in the 'fucking' arena. The man had no compunction when it came to his dick.

"I think that's about it, Miss Quintero," Tony said, rising from the edge of the desk. He took the woman's hand and helped her to her feet. "We'll be in touch if we learn anything or if we have more questions."

"You promise? You'll let me know when you catch him?"

Tony nodded solemnly. "You have my word." He slipped a card into the hand he still held. "Call me, any time, day or night if you need anything at all."

It was a variation of the offer normally made to family members and witnesses, a little more intimate, more personal. Susie may or may not have gotten it, but Lane definitely did.

Tony walked her out while Lane took the contents of the folder Karakas had left, along with the files from the lab, and filed them in the murder book.

He resumed his between-the-eye rubbing, trying to think about Richard Hebringer instead of Catherine… and the man she'd loved, then murdered.

Chapter 5

My home was decorated in what I like to call 'cozy cluttered.' I know nothing about interior design and wasn't interested in learning, so my furnishings were a hodgepodge of mismatched items I'd bought just because I liked them. My favorite piece—and the oldest—was a cowboy desk dating back to the 1890's. It was solid oak with a drop-front writing surface and intricately carved spindle legs. I'd bought it from a guy in Miami, Oklahoma who refinished antiques.

That was where Josie normally left her notes. Since I didn't see Josie right away, and I lived with perpetual worry over her, my eyes automatically went to the desk.

No note leaned in its usual spot against the beveled mirror, but it could be one of those times she hadn't left one.

"Roe?" It was Josie's voice, coming from down the hall.

I let out a relieved sigh that she was still there, not realizing until then how worried I was that she wouldn't be.

I walked into the living room, arriving there at the same time as Josie. She looked better. Some color had returned to her cheeks and the bruises were starting to fade. She wore jeans and a mint green blouse she'd left here on one of her previous stays. She could make do with wearing my sweats around the house, but no way would anything in my wardrobe actually fit her.

"Hey, how are you?" I asked as I pulled off the ball cap and slid my hair out of its ponytail holder, massaging my scalp.

"I'm okay. Better, actually. Feeling almost human again." She crossed her arms and shook her head. "You make me sick. Your hair looks great even after you've tortured it with bondage all day."

Her comment was in keeping with our mutual admiration/envy of one another's appearance, left over from childhood. Josie wished for my busty, dark-haired, dark-eyed look, while I would have happily traded it for her petite, blonde, ethereal prettiness.

"Right." I rolled my eyes. "Hey, how about if I change clothes and we drive around looking at Halloween decorations, then I take you out to dinner?"

"Sounds great. I'm going stir crazy."

"I'll be ready in a jif," I said, heading down the hallway. Although I'd subjected my mother to my grubby look—and unintentionally subjected Lane Brody—I wouldn't do it to Josie, or the other restaurant patrons.

I changed clothes and was ready to go in ten minutes.

Josie and I drove through the streets at dusk, just the right time to ogle Halloween decorations. There was a house a few miles from mine that always had an impressive display.

I slowed as we approached, pointing out the life-sized vampire, the Michael Myers dummy holding a bloody knife, the witch stirring a cauldron, all the delightful creatures of the season.

"Nice," Josie said. "Wouldn't scare little kids a bit."

I laughed. "I know, but you have to admit, it's pretty cool."

"For a wacko like you, yeah, maybe. But you're twisted."

It was good to hear her light-hearted banter, and to talk about nothing, like we had in the old days. I needed to bring up the detective's visit, but it could wait. I wanted her to eat dinner first, and if I told her, it might spoil what little appetite she had.

Of course, I was sure once she finished eating, I'd think of another reason to put off telling her. I wanted her to have a tasty dessert first, a pleasant evening, a good-night's rest, a hearty breakfast, blah, blah, blah. Truth was, I didn't want to tell her at all.

The hostess who greeted us at Chili's was young and pretty with those thick, unruly eyebrows that looked good on people like her and Brooke Shields. If I tried to wear mine like that, I'd look more like Oscar the Grouch.

There was a twenty-minute wait, and when we told the girl that was fine, she exclaimed, "Awesome!" with wide-eyed enthusiasm normally indigenous to cheerleaders and lottery winners.

We walked outside, and I huddled in my coat, watching the traffic zip by on Barry Road while Josie smoked.

"How was your visit?" she asked.

"Oh, the usual. I was treated to a list of my shortcomings, along with a list of my brothers' virtues. On the upside, their list was longer than mine."

She smiled, but her expression turned pensive, and I wondered if she was thinking about her family. I knew she had to miss them. In spite of her problems with drugs, it was a mistake to completely drop out of their lives. They loved her and I was sure they still wanted to maintain a relationship.

Josie and I were silent as she finished smoking, each lost in our thoughts. When she stubbed out her cigarette, we went inside to finish our wait.

The smell of Fajitas made my stomach growl. I almost let out a cheer when—in just under the twenty-minute prediction—we were led to a table.

We shared southwestern egg rolls and an order of chicken fajitas. I wouldn't have hated splitting a dessert, but was afraid *I* might split if I did. Dinner over, there was nothing to do now except lay it on her.

"So, what's up with Matt?" I asked as an opener. "You're still with him, right? You two have a place together?"

She shrugged. "Here and there. We stay with friends mostly. We got into a fight." Her eyes darted to mine, and I couldn't help but glance at the lingering signs of their 'fight.'

"I took off while he was out and haven't talked to him since. That's when I showed up at your place."

"Do you know how to get in touch with him?"

Her eyes narrowed. "Why?"

I sighed and dug in my purse for Detective Brody's card. I slid it across the table. "The cops need to talk to him. They asked me if I knew where he was. When I said I didn't, they wanted to know if you were in town. They want you to call them."

"Why?" she asked again, looking down at the card like it was a poisonous snake, not picking it up.

"They have some questions about a murder."

Her head snapped up and her eyes widened. "Murder? No way. Matt's got nothing to do with any

68

murder."

"I don't think he's necessarily a suspect. But he's wanted for questioning."

I could see the hesitation in her face, and she still didn't reach for the card. I put my hand over hers. "Josie, we're talking murder here." I lowered my voice. "Probably a drug deal gone bad or something. If Matt knows anything that will help the police, you need to help them find him."

"I don't know where he is," she said, quietly, vaguely.

"Just talk to them. Please. I told them you'd call."

She nodded and picked up the card, slipping it into her jeans pocket, but I didn't think she'd call. I'd give her a few days, and if she didn't, I'd call them myself.

****

Lane's first impression of Highland Lily Bed and Breakfast was that it looked like something out of one of those sappy romance movies he used to watch, just to indulge Catherine.

A sidewalk flanked by what had to be artificial flowers led to a wrap-around porch that held a pink, wrought iron bench and white porch swing. The home itself was a white, two-story, with pink shutters and a pink turret at each corner.

No bell, so he lifted the old-fashioned door knocker and tapped it lightly.

Although the bed and breakfast was essentially a hotel, it was also the owner's home and a sign next to the door requested that guests knock for assistance. He wondered if the killer had knocked.

The door was opened by a woman who looked as though she'd been crafted specifically for this house. She was in her mid-sixties, with hair so silver it looked artificial. She wore round, rimless glasses and a blue dress with tiny, pink embroidered flowers. Her features practically twinkled with homespun friendliness.

"You must be Mr. Brody," she said in a soft, low voice.

"Detective Brody, ma'am. Yes."

"Please, please, come in." A frown momentarily erased the sparkle from her face. "I never dreamed we'd have need of a homicide detective at Highland Lily."

Lane wondered if it felt odd to transpose her name in order to refer to her house. Like he'd feel if he lived on Brody Lane.

He walked through a foyer into a sitting room filled with antiques. An old-fashioned rocking horse stood in one corner and a black piano in the other.

"Won't you sit, Mr. Brody? Would you like a nice cup of tea?"

He didn't correct her on the title this time. She gestured toward a fragile looking sofa and he gingerly sat, worried the spindly legs might give under his weight.

"No, thank you."

She settled on a similarly fragile wing-backed chair caddy-corned to him. "Just ask whatever you'd like. Don't worry about offending my sensibilities." She looked around as if afraid someone might overhear, even though they were the only ones in the room. In an exaggerated whisper, she said, "I watch 'CSI' all the time," like she was confessing to a porn fetish.

"I understand Mr. Hebringer was working here Thursday night."

She nodded gravely. "Yes, he was. He worked every night except Sunday and Monday. Those nights I covered myself. We aren't very busy on those nights and that gives—gave—Mr. Hebringer somewhat of a weekend."

"Were there any other employees here on Thursday night?"

"No. Mr. Hebringer was my only employee. Every day, I fix breakfast and lunch, then retire to my room. Guests fend for themselves for dinner, and Mr. Hebringer would be the only one around in the evenings."

"How many guests stayed here on Thursday night?"

"We have six rooms and only three were occupied that night."

"I'll need the names and addresses of those guests."

The cloud passed over her sunny countenance again. "Oh, my. My guests value their privacy."

"As do we all, Ms Highland, but this is a homicide investigation. Catching the guilty party takes precedence over your guests' desire for privacy."

She twisted her hands in her lap. "I just don't know."

"I can come back with a warrant. One way or another, I'll see your guest list."

"Very well," she said with a dainty sigh. She stood. "Excuse me. I'll get the register for that night."

She was back quickly, considering her objection to the task. She handed him a lace-covered notebook turned to Thursday, October twenty-fourth. There were three entries—two couples and a lone man's name.

"Did Mr. Bray stay here alone?" Lane asked. That had to be unusual for a bed and breakfast.

Her lips tightened. "I didn't ask Mr. Bray about his business, including who his guest would be, or if he would be having a guest at all, for that matter."

"You weren't interested in whether he had a guest?"

"Not in the least. None of my business with whom he chooses to spend the night."

"So, if he'd brought an orangutan in an evening gown, you wouldn't have a problem?"

Her chin lifted and her nose scrunched as if sniffing something repugnant. Her voice was tight with disapproval when she spoke. "Of course I'd have a problem. Animals aren't allowed."

Great. Lane jotted down the names and addresses of the guests and handed the notebook back to her. "Do you know of Mr. Hebringer having any problems with guests?"

"Problems?"

"Conflicts, disagreements, fights."

"Oh, my, no. That just didn't go on. Not here."

"How about away from your establishment?"

"No. I mean, I don't know of any problems Mr. Hebringer had with guests at all. Not with anyone, actually. He was a good employee, and I didn't get involved in his personal life."

"How long did he work for you?"

She put a finger to her lip, thinking. "Going on two years now."

Lane nodded. "Can you show me where Mr. Hebringer worked? Where he checked guests in? And take me through some of the duties he might have performed that night?"

Lily Highland led him to a small room off the living area. In it was a counter that was obviously the registration desk, a table with a coffee pot sitting on it, and another fragile-looking sofa.

"This is where he spent a great deal of the evenings,

although he had free run of the downstairs. He would sit on a stool and watch his little portable television when he wasn't taking care of guests."

"What did he do throughout his shift, as far as chores, responsibilities, things of that nature?"

She lifted her shoulders in a shrug. "Mostly making sure the guests were happy and taking care of their needs. He straightened up in here, took the trash out, kept the coffee made, that sort of thing."

Lane went behind the counter. There was a tall stool and a few shelves built beneath the counter that held pens, paper, a twin to the notebook Lily Highland had shown him, magazines, and DVD's.

A tall, round trash can sat next to the stool.

"I'd like to see where he took the trash."

She gave a quick nod, but he could tell that her hospitality was waning. Dropping the notebook on the counter with a little more force than a delicate flower such as herself should use, she swept toward a door that led outside and opened it. Lane followed.

They walked down a winding path to an outbuilding. A dumpster stood beside the shed.

Ms Highland pointed to the dumpster. "He put the trash in there. That's it. You've had the complete tour."

"Thank you," Lane said. "I think that's all I need for now. I just want to look around some. I'll see myself back to the front. I appreciate your time and I'll let you know if I have more questions."

"Yes," she said, as in 'I'm sure you will.' "Goodbye, then."

She turned and hurried back inside, no doubt anxious to lose herself in her idyllic world that didn't include murdered employees and visits from homicide detectives.

He checked carefully around the dumpster, not finding anything unusual.

Hebringer had most likely been taken from here. The guests reported he wasn't around when they came downstairs to check out. But, was he actually taken from here or did he get called away? Did he know the killer and leave his job to meet him?

A wall of trees lined the back of the property. The house was set back from the road and the nearest neighbor was a quarter mile away. An entire army could have converged on the property and snatched Hebringer without anyone noticing.

****

I typed in the seemingly endless list of names, keeping one eye on the dates of demise and the other on the desk next to Asia's.

Who had Adam given the promotion to? He hadn't told me, so I was curious, and a little suspicious. It was close to quitting time, and, so far, no one had appeared to take over the desk. I wouldn't be surprised to see Tabitha sashay in and rest her toned, cheating butt in the chair. She did, after all, have connections. Of course, it wouldn't make sense for her to take a job writing for a newspaper, I was pretty sure she'd need help writing a grocery list. I wouldn't put anything past Adam, though.

"MPM night, you going?"

Asia's question interrupted my spiteful thoughts. I took my hands from the keyboard and looked up at her.

MPM night was Melting Pot Mojito night. The Melting Pot was a fondue restaurant in the Plaza near downtown Kansas City. They made the absolute best Mojitos in the world and every Monday night, Asia, myself, and some of the other girls in the office met there after work for happy hour.

"Sorry, I can't."

"Can't? There's no 'can't' on Mojito night. What's wrong with you?"

I picked up an ink pen as I spoke, clicking the top over and over. "Josie's at the house."

Asia rolled her eyes. "You're not her mother, you know."

"No," I replied shortly, "If I were her mother, I'd be dead."

Asia had the grace to look ashamed for about five seconds before shaking her head. "You can't fix her, Roe."

I was working on a suitable reply when movement at the crime desk caught my attention. Phillip Conan dropped a briefcase and a photo of his wife and kids onto the surface and gave me a chagrined wave. I waved back, proud of my magnanimity.

So, Phillip had gotten the job. I liked him. If I couldn't have the position, I was glad it had been him. I glanced toward Adam's office. He stood on the other side of the glass, watching me. Waiting for me to fall apart? Well, to hell with him. *No show for you today, asshole.*

"You're sure you won't go?" Asia was still at it.

"I'm sure. Next time, 'kay?"

"Fine," Asia sighed dramatically, "I'll tell you all about it tomorrow and you'll be jealous."

"I'm already jealous."

Asia looked toward Adam's office. He was still standing at the window.

"What the hell's he doing?"

"He wants to see if I'll lose it since he passed me over for the promotion."

"I think he wants in your pants."

I was starting to get on my own nerves with the pen clicking, so I stopped, tossing it onto the desk. I shook my head. "He gave that up when he hooked up with Tabitha."

"Maybe the tabby cat doesn't take care of his needs. He's wanting some of what he let go."

"Maybe his ego is such that he wants every woman he sees."

"He's hot, I'll give him that," Asia said. Then she shuddered. "But he's such a freakin' pig I can't imagine actually screwing him. No offense," she added quickly.

Asia was right. I was amazed I hadn't seen Adam for what he really was while we were together. "None taken," I replied. "I plead temporary insanity for the two years we dated."

Asia nodded. "I'll accept that." She grinned and tugged on my sleeve. "Come on, walk me out."

I followed Asia out into the cold evening air. The professor and Headphone were huddled against the building. They each wore coats, but they were the same ones they wore year round, thin and tattered. Headphone had a beanie cap pulled over his earphones. Temperatures had been dropping steadily and now hovered just above freezing.

"Hey," I said to the professor. "Shouldn't you guys be at the shelter? Seems a little chilly to be outside."

Headphone rocked to his music and ignored me. The professor smiled and said, "Cold is a state of mind. If one never experiences the bite of bitter cold, one can ever enjoy the comfort of blessed warmth."

Asia snorted and muttered, "If one never visits the world of the sane, one will never know how fucking whacked out one is."

Although said quietly, it was loud enough to carry to the professor. I sent a quick, apologetic look his way and he smiled, lifting his eyebrows as if to say, what can you do?

I dropped a twenty into his bucket instead of my usual five. A payoff for my friend's rudeness. It wasn't enough.

Asia and I parted ways in the parking lot, she to the delights of MPM and me to the unknown. My stomach knotted with dread. I never knew what I'd find when I arrived home during Josie's visits.

Would I find her still straight, feeling relatively normal, or would I find her in the throes of DT's? Or, in the false and fleeting ecstasy of the high heroin gave her? Or, worse case scenario, would I find a note telling me she'd taken off again?

Ever the optimist, I bet on the first scenario and swung through the drive-in at Kentucky Fried Chicken for a bucket of extra crispy.

I got home and opened the door, my gaze immediately going to the cowboy desk. Again, no note. But the house seemed unusually quiet, and although I smelled stale smoke in the air, there was no sign of fresh smoke. Even though the dread in my chest told me she was gone, I searched every room of the house.

No sign of Josie or her meager belongings.

Actually, *this* was the worst case scenario. Although she'd seemed much better last night, when Josie bolted without even leaving a note, it meant she was really in a bad way.

****

Good friend that I was, I decided since Josie was no longer in my care, I'd join Asia and the others after all.

I circled the parking garage on Pennsylvania until I found a spot, then walked down the steep, winding drive out to the street. The Melting Pot was a few quick turns, up one block, then two blocks left. The walk in the cleansing air felt refreshing and in no time, I was entering through the doors of the restaurant.

Asia was sitting with Mary, Elaine, and Beth from the newspaper. My friend's face brightened when she saw me come in, and she waved me over.

As I made my way to the women, a waitress stopped by their table, and I saw Asia speak to her and point to me.

Bless the girl and her future offspring, she'd ordered me a Mojito.

There were hugs all around when I reached the table and took a seat. My cocktail arrived not long after I did.

The Mojito was lovely—clear and effervescent with a bright, green, bobbing lime and green sprigs of mint that clung to the sides of the glass like tiny barnacles. Perhaps its appearance appealed to me as much as its taste. I took a grateful sip. Nope, I was mistaken. It was definitely the taste.

We shared cheese fondue with apples, vegetables, and bread for dipping. I made a determined effort to join in on the chatter of my co-workers, but my thoughts kept straying to Josie.

Questions stabbed at me relentlessly. Where was she? Was she on the drugs again? Was she hurt? In jail? Cold, hungry, on the streets while I indulged in decadent fondue and Mojitos? Was she with Matt getting the crap beat out of her?

What really bothered me was that I hadn't called the detectives and told them she was in town. If I had, maybe they would have brought her in for questioning, held her as a material witness, arrested her as an accomplice, something, anything that would have kept her from whatever fate might have befallen her now. Whatever was happening to her at this moment was my fault.

Rum and cheese-soaked bread rose to my throat in a wave of nausea. I wished I hadn't eaten, and that I hadn't had that third Mojito. Well, mostly I wished I hadn't eaten.

Panicked concern for Josie brought me to my feet. "Did you drive?" I asked Asia, raising my voice over the noise of the crowd.

She shook her head. "I rode with Beth."

"Are you okay to drive?" I asked Beth. I was not going to have the endangerment of yet another friend on my conscience.

Beth held up a non-alcoholic O'Douls and gave me a thumb's up.

"Where are you going?" Asia asked when I rummaged through my purse for cash to pay my share.

"I have something to take care of."

"You shouldn't be driving, girl."

"I'm calling Gable," I told her, which was true, but I was going outside to do it. I wasn't going to call a priest from inside a noisy bar.

Asia's eyes narrowed suspiciously. "You on a rescue mission?"

I didn't answer.

"You gotta let her make her own mistakes or nothing will ever change. You're enabling."

I knew all that but couldn't help it. Couldn't throw Josie to the wolves.

I nodded and kissed Asia's cheek, waved goodbye to the rest of them, and stepped outside.

I looked at my phone to check the time. Nearly ten. Hopefully, Gable was still awake. He answered on the second ring.

"You weren't getting ready to go to bed, were you?" I asked.

"Are you kidding? Priests never sleep. It's part of our penance."

"I thought your penance was that you could never have sex."

"Uh oh…" he said slowly, drawing out the words. I laughed. "What's up, sis?"

I paced back and forth in front of the Melting Pot as I spoke, trying to stay warm. I pretty much had the sidewalk to myself, other than an occasional couple who strolled by. The Plaza wasn't busy—this being a Monday night—but it also probably had something to do with the new Power and Light District taking away a lot of business from the Plaza.

I took a breath. "I've been drinking, and—"

"Of course you have. It's Monday."

"Anyway," I said firmly, "I'm worried about Josie—"

"Of course you are. You're breathing."

"Geez. Aren't priests supposed to *listen*?"

"You're right. Sorry. Go on, my child."

I ignored the sarcasm. "Josie's been staying at my house the past few days, but when I got home this evening, she was gone. No note. Nothing. I haven't been able to get her off my mind. I'm really worried."

"You want me to pray with you?" he asked, being deliberately obtuse.

"Are you sure your calling wasn't actually a stand-up comic?" I snapped. "I want to go look for her but I can't drive because I had two Mojitos."

"Three. At least."

"What?"

"Two is the number all drunks use. No one would believe you only had one, and three would be too many, so you always say two."

I'd found him mildly amusing at the beginning of the conversation, but now he was just pissing me off. "Never mind," I said through gritted teeth. "I'll call someone else or take a freakin' cab and run up a five-hundred dollar fare looking for Josie."

"Cool your jets, sis, I'm almost there."

"You are? Almost where?"

"At the Melting Pot. I've been on my way since you first called."

"How did you…?"

"Monday night. Melting Pot Mojitos. You think I don't know what my baby sister's up to? I just had to give you a hard time. If you want my help, you have to live with it. See you in ten. Be outside."

He hung up before I could say, 'bite me.'

****

Gable's '92 Grand Prix belched and lurched along the darkened streets. The car was clean, but smelled funny, like fast food and pine air freshener. The stuffing beneath my leg protruded from a rip in the seat cover. But I was grateful for the ride, no matter how primitive.

I peered out my window, searching the desolate faces for Josie. I knew it was pointless. If Josie were on the streets, she most likely wasn't out in the open, hanging with the other street people gathered around the trash, or strolling with the street-worn hookers. She would be holed up in some corner, lying in an alleyway on the cold, filthy ground, lost in the drugs. I wouldn't be able to spot her from the car.

"Pull over and let me out," I said suddenly.

"What? Are you out of your mind?"

"I can't find Josie from in here."

"You want to walk these streets? Alone?"

"I don't want to walk them at all, but I want to find Josie. I can't ask you to go with me, so yes, alone."

He stared at me longer than he should have, considering he was behind the wheel of a moving car.

"I…" He shook his head and pulled his gaze back to the windshield. "I… just… can't… I'm speechless."

"Then I guess I've accomplished something tonight."

"You're about to accomplish giving me a stroke. If you think I'm letting you go out there," he jabbed a finger toward my window, "alone, you're completely insane."

I didn't respond, just sent my irritated vibes his way.

It worked. He heaved a loud sigh, jerked the car into the parking lot of a convenience store, and slammed the gearshift into park.

He lifted his right hip and removed his billfold. "Take your wallet out of your purse, and leave any important documents—driver's license, credit cards, whatever—in the car, along with anything in your purse you don't want to lose. Just keep a little cash in your wallet." As he spoke, he removed cards from his own billfold.

"Why not just leave the purse and wallet in the car?"

He tilted his head back, closed his eyes, and shook his head like I was the most ignorant creature on the planet. "For one, if someone sees your purse in the car, they might break a window to get it. We could put it in the trunk, but thieves usually get in there, too. You can slide your loose items under the seat, and maybe if no one sees them, they won't bother with the car. Plus, if we're mugged, they'll expect us to have *something* on us. If we don't, they'll hurt us. You have any more questions?"

I didn't. We climbed out of the car. His movements were agitated, his head shaking dramatically, his walk an exaggerated stomp.

"Come on," he bit out, grabbing my arm and pulling me alongside him. "If you have a death wish, no sense putting it off."

Once we were in the midst of the street world, I realized Gable had been right. I was insane.

A group of guys—two Hispanics, one black, one white—with tattoos, piercings, baggy jackets, and low-hanging crotches, gave us hard stares as we walked by. Some of the people looked menacing, others just pitiful. Most of them gave us distrusting looks, a few were downright hostile.

I searched the sea of faces for Josie, or even Matt, but didn't see anyone who looked the least bit familiar.

Gable didn't lose his nervous agitation as we trolled the streets. If anything, it increased.

One of the alleyways I insisted on checking out was where his dire prediction came true.

Chapter 6

A few lone figures lay at intervals along the sides of the alley. Debris crunched beneath my feet as I followed behind Gable, searching the sleeping forms for Josie. In truth, I was beginning to hope I wouldn't find her. I couldn't stand the thought of delicate, vulnerable Josie exposed out here in this filthy, dangerous alley.

As I knelt next to one of the blankets toward the end of the alley—the last person I saw that we needed to check out—Gable's hand landed on my shoulder.

"Hey, I'm not sure you should—"

Before he could complete the sentence, an arm shot out from beneath the blankets—thin, but incredibly strong. Claw-like fingers latched onto my neck. A grimy face appeared above the ragged blanket. He had a ratty yellow-gray beard and wore a tattered watch cap. A musty, sour odor rose to my nostrils, mixing with my fear, and I swallowed back a gag that seized my throat.

"What the hell do you think you're doing, bitch?" a man's voice rasped.

"Ah... I was just..." I choked, grappling at the fingers. I couldn't loosen his grip.

"Hey, asshole." I'd never heard such fury in my brother's voice. "Let her go."

I don't know if the vagrant would have obeyed or not, because Gable didn't leave him any choice. He came up beside me and bent down, chopping an elbow into the guy's forearm. The man grunted and released his hold, the grimy fingers of his other hand clamping onto his injured arm.

Gable took me by the hand and hauled me to my feet.

"Hey, man," the gruff voice slurred, "bitch was in my space."

Gable opened his wallet and tossed two ten's onto the ground next to the man, then tugged me toward the mouth of the alley. He was silent as he yanked me along the street so quickly I could barely keep up with him.

We received some strange looks and a few raised eyebrows. A transgender hooker shouted, "Oooh, baby. When you're done with her, come back for me."

Gable ignored her-him, continuing to drag me stumbling along until we finally reached the car.

Once we were inside, he whirled to face me. "Are you happy?" Without giving me a chance to answer, he slammed his palm on the steering wheel. "Do you have any idea what would have happened to you if I hadn't been there? Any idea at all? And, you do realize, he was right? You had no business approaching him like that. I should have let him at you."

"I know. You're right." The sudden realization of what could have happened washed over me and I began to tremble, suddenly stone cold sober. "You could have been hurt, too."

"Ya think?" Even in the darkness, I could see a muscle twitch in his jaw.

"I'm sorry," I said, close to tears. "I'm really, really sorry."

He closed his eyes, sighed, shook his head. "You were trying to do the right thing. Trying to help your friend. But there comes a time when you need to realize that some people have to help themselves."

"You sound like Asia."

"So, it appears at least someone in your posse has some sense." He softened the words with a smile and reached out and took my hand. "Even as a priest, I have to be able to tell when someone is ready for my help. You need to do the same."

I nodded.

He started the car and pulled out onto Independence. "Now, let's get you home. I'll pick you up in the morning and take you to get your car."

"Can you take me to get it tonight?" When he gave me a look normally reserved for the profoundly insane, I quickly said, "I'm totally sober now. I swear. I want to drive out to the lake house and see if she's there."

Josie and I co-owned a cabin on Lake Viking. Her parents had owned half a dozen cabins they rented out, but, after their mother passed away, her father had wanted the girls to have one of their own and had given each of them a choice of the six. Josie added my name to the deed without charging me anything. My contribution was to pay the utilities and take care of the upkeep.

Gable stared at me for a long time. A *very* long time.

"Did you hear one word that I just said to you? Do you realize I'm a priest and hundreds of people come to see me, on purpose, one to five times a week, just to hear what I have to say? And you..." Another head shake. "With you, I might as well be talking to a lamppost. You can't help her, sis, you just can't."

"I at least need to know she's okay."

"She's not okay. She's a self-destructive junkie, and the more you help her, the longer she'll stay that way."

I leaned my head back against the seat. "I just need to know she's safe for the night. I won't be able to sleep until I do."

"And if you don't find her at the cabin?"

I shrugged. "I still won't be able to sleep, but I'll know I've done all I can for the moment."

"Okay, then. You have me so wound up now, I can't sleep anyway. So, I'll take you to get your car *after* our road trip."

"You're going with me?"

"No. You're going with me."

I wouldn't exactly call a one hour drive a 'road trip,' but I was glad to have him along. I was grateful for the company and happy he no longer seemed to be mad at me.

I reached out and punched the power button on the radio. "Black Water" by the Doobie Brothers burst from the speaker.

"Road trip, it is," I said.

****

Outside on Lane's deck, the light was attracting bugs, even though they were scarcer than they would be in warmer weather. Lane needed the air, though. Felt better than his lonely, stuffy house.

At least it wasn't the home he'd shared with Catherine. He'd rented this one when he transferred to Kansas City. Catherine had gone directly into the hospital. Her stuff was in storage, so there was nothing around to remind him of her, other than the ghost of their marriage.

He sipped a beer as he studied the list of Highland Lily Bed and Breakfast guests. The list was for the past six months. Lane had decided they should go back further than Thursday night and had gotten the records from a reluctant Lily Highland.

One of the past guests could have had a beef with Hebringer. The names were being fed into the computer, searching for a match on anyone with a record, but Lane wanted to look it over himself, see if anything jumped out at him.

He and Webber had been running down leads all day and so far, no hits. Tomorrow, Webber would speak to one of the couples, and Lane would take the single male guest. The other couple—of which the male was condom guy—lived in Michigan. They'd talked to them on the phone, but neither had been able to offer any pertinent information.

Lab reports on the white powder at the crime scene revealed that it was dust. Most likely from a construction site. There was construction going on next door to the newspaper office. Lane would pay a visit to Monroe Donovan tomorrow. Not that he had any reason to believe she, or anyone else at the paper for that matter, was involved in the murder. He needed to ask her about Josephine Detweiler, anyway. He was still looking for Lovell and the girlfriend might lead them to him. He was wanted for questioning in a drug shooting. Lovell knew both the victim and the suspect, so they wanted to talk to him, badly. So far they hadn't been able to locate Detweiler or Lovell.

Lane drained the rest of the beer and went inside to get another. He'd left the television on, and the discordant sounds of a car chase or something equally intense traveled to him in the kitchen. Some kind of noise-maker was always going in the house, whether it be the TV, the radio, the police scanner... something. He couldn't stand the silence. Or maybe he just couldn't stand being alone with his thoughts.

Popping the top off the Heineken, he went back outside and dropped into the plastic chair. He tilted the bottle to his lips and glanced over the railing. His deck looked out over his back yard and into the back of the next neighborhood over. A large Doberman in the yard directly behind his had been gripped in a paroxysm of frenetic barking ever since Lane had come out on the deck. The dog must have worn himself out, or damaged his vocal cords, because now he stood at the fence, challenging Lane to a staring contest. Conceding to the dog, Lane went back to the list. A name caught his eye and his breathing slowed for a brief moment.

Adam Utley, the editor for the *Chronicle*.

The construction near his newspaper, now this. Two possible ties to the murder. They were weak, very weak. There was construction all over the city. Highland Lily Bed and Breakfast was a popular get-a-way for lovers, so no big surprise Utley had been there. Yeah, weak. But it bore watching.

Utley had stayed there four months ago. Probably with Monroe Donovan. Envy bloomed in Lane's chest and spread its tentacles down through his gut, catching him by surprise.

What would it feel like to be closed up in one of those rooms with Monroe? To fall together into a thick, soft mattress and...

And what?

Was he actually fantasizing about making love to Monroe Donovan? True, he hadn't had sex in a long time. Not since the last time he'd slept with Catherine. He'd been tempted, sure. But he was married.

He didn't *feel* married. Hadn't felt married for a while. Technically, though, he was. He still wore the ring. That had to say something. So, he hadn't given into temptation, although there were times he'd certainly wanted to. Monroe Donovan wasn't the first woman he'd been attracted to, but she was the one he seemed to think about the most. He found the thought unsettling. He'd only laid eyes on her twice. It was crazy.

Briefly, he wondered if Monroe were mixed up in anything shady, since she and Detweiler were such close friends. His instincts said no, but they had been dulled by the shit that had happened in the past few years. He didn't trust them. But, hell, he didn't trust much of anything these days.

****

The moon shone white between the branches of the nearly skeletal trees that shrouded the cabin. The wind tried to yank the door out of my hand as I climbed out of the car.

The cabin backed up to the lake, the screened-in rear deck no more than ten feet from the water. We stepped onto the front porch and I knew right away she wasn't here. The cabin was dark, deserted. I looked down at the mat. WELCOME stared up at me, and my heart sank.

Josie and I had a system. Normally, we let the other know when we were using the cabin and whether or not we wanted privacy. As an extra precaution, because sometimes we couldn't reach one another, and cell signals rarely worked out here, we used the welcome mat as a signal. If the mat was face down, with the WELCOME hidden, the cabin was occupied. The word facing up confirmed she wasn't here, although it was possible she'd just been so out of it, she hadn't thought to flip it over. Or, she was here and didn't need privacy, but I didn't think so.

We went inside, using the key Josie and I kept above the door frame.

The cabin was small and rustic with a tiny kitchen. Josie's bedroom was downstairs and mine was in the loft upstairs. I looked around and confirmed what I already knew. Dark. Dusty. Deserted. Josie wasn't here.

Still, we flipped on lights, calling out for her. I went into Josie's room, while Gable checked mine up in the loft.

The bed was unmade. Towels and clothing were strewn all over the floor. Nothing unusual.

I heard Gable shout but couldn't make out the words. Racing out of the bedroom, I yelled up to him, "Did you find her?"

He appeared above, leaning over the cedar railing. "No, but I found something I wish I hadn't." In one hand, he held a packet of condoms. In the other, a set of fur-lined handcuffs. My cheeks flamed, not from embarrassment, but from fury.

"Didn't know you were into this stuff, sis. Didn't *want* to know."

"They're not mine," I gritted, heading up the stairs.

I marched into my bedroom. At first glance, everything seemed in place. I let my gaze run over the patchwork quilt my grandmother had given me, spread over my queen-sized bed with the black iron headboard. The photo of me and my brothers at our camping trip to Yosemite still rested in its silver frame on my nightstand. The black and gray woven rug was in its place on the hardwood floor.

But, something was different. Felt different.

Even without having seen the condoms and cuffs, I would have known someone had been here. Using my room. And I knew who it was.

The son of a bitch.

Adam and I had spent several weekends here and he knew about the key. He'd brought Tabitha here.

"Hey, are you okay?" Gable asked, and I realized I was crying. I thought they were mostly tears of rage. How dare he bring her to my cabin? Who the hell did he think he was? It was the final humiliation in a relationship that was doomed from the start. After all, it's difficult to successfully mate with a serpent.

I scrubbed a hand over my face. "Please take me home," I said quietly, suddenly so weary I would have fallen onto the bed in exhaustion if I didn't know what had taken place there. "My sheets." My voice was hoarse. I was oddly devastated, my hurt over Adam's betrayal suddenly looming larger than my concern over Josie. I felt terrible about it, but I couldn't seem to control it.

I didn't know how to keep Adam from using the cabin again. I couldn't just take the key or change the locks. Not until I'd spoken with Josie. I had to make sure she'd be able to get in.

Gable put his arm around my shoulder and led me down the stairs and out into the cool night air.

"I'll be right back," he told me after helping me into his car.

He disappeared inside. After a few moments, the lights in the cabin went out, one by one. Gable stepped out onto the porch, holding a large, black trash bag. I watched him drop it into the dumpster.

"What was that?" I asked as he slid into the driver's

seat.

"The sheets from your bed. I sprayed the mattress with Lysol and hairspray."

"Hairspray?"

"I couldn't find any Febreeze. I figured as strong as hairspray smells, it would cover any scent."

I smiled. He was a priest, but he was such a guy.

"Ma gave me a brand new bedding set a few weeks ago that I've never even opened," he said. "I'll come out this weekend and put it on the bed."

A new swarm of tears—and love for my brother—surfaced. "If you give me something Mom gave to you, that'll really chap her ass."

"An added perk I hadn't even considered."

He grinned and I immediately felt better.

"Love you, bro."

"Back at ya, sis."

Gable drove me home. We decided he'd take me to get my car in the morning, but I'd call into work. Not only was I sleep-deprived, Adam had pissed me off and he deserved it. Besides, it would give me an opportunity to job hunt.

I called the newspaper's voicemail from my phone and left a message saying I was sick and wouldn't be in.

Gable took me home, helped me inside, then waited while I brushed my teeth and slipped into my pajamas. He tucked me into bed, kissing me on the forehead.

"Night, Roe," he said at the doorway, then flipped the light switch.

I think I was asleep before the room got dark.

****

The next morning, bleary-eyed and still annoyed, I climbed out of bed. After jabbing the button on the coffee pot, I stumbled into the shower. I once more put on pajamas—flannel ones with a sweat shirt—not seeing the need to dress.

I poured a cup of coffee and stood at my kitchen window staring in the direction of the cemetery, although I couldn't see anything because of the fog. I shivered. It was warm enough in the house, but outside looked cold and bleak.

My head was pounding, partly from the Mojitos, partly from the stress over Josie, and partly from anger at Adam. I don't know why, after all he'd done, that this seemed such a betrayal. I guess because the cabin was *mine*. A part of my world I'd let him into. Not something he should have shared with another woman. I mean, who does that? He broke into my cabin and screwed another woman there. Jesus.

I had just poured my second cup of coffee when the doorbell pealed. I started, sloshing coffee onto my hand. Showed what an all-nighter on the streets can do for a person. I dabbed at the hot liquid with a towel, feeling only minor pain from the burn.

I wasn't expecting company, didn't want company, but went to the door anyway.

Detective Brody was on the other side of my peep hole. I looked down at my ratty clothes and ran a hand through my tousled hair. Damn. Caught again looking less than glamorous. Of course, it wouldn't really be easy to catch me looking glamorous.

I debated briefly about not answering, then opened the door. He wore washed-out jeans and a grey jacket, almost fading into the mist hovering in the yard behind him.

"Seems we're destined to meet over coffee," he said,

gesturing to the cup in my hand.

"Seems that way." I stepped back. "Come in. Would you like a cup?"

"No, thank you," he said as he came inside.

I shut the door and followed him into my living room. He stopped in front of my Jesse James display. There was a duplicate of a Colt .45 Jesse James had used and a couple of coins that were thought to be his, although it couldn't be authenticated. There was also a tin cup he supposedly drank from and a tie tac that came from Linus's great-grandfather, who was Jesse James' cousin, or step-cousin, or something like that, I wasn't exactly sure of the connection.

"This stuff looks pretty old," Lane said, pushing back the edges of his jacket to rest his hands on his waist.

"The pistol is a replica. Most of the other items are authentic." I pointed to a *Kansas City Times* newspaper with an article covering Jesse James' death. "Like that. It's over a hundred years old."

He turned to me, his eyebrows raised, an expression either of amusement or wariness on his face. I couldn't tell which. "You collect Jesse James memorabilia?"

"I didn't intend to, but yeah, I guess I do."

"You are aware he was a criminal? A killer?"

I shrugged. "That's one version. Some people consider him the Robin Hood of the West."

"Regardless of his benevolent nature, Robin Hood was also a criminal."

"Well, now you're just talking like a cop."

He smiled and crossed his arms. "I am a cop." Then he said, in an exaggerated western twang, "I'd sure hate to find myself on opposite sides of the law from such a pretty miss as yourself."

Although I knew he was joking, and I felt decidedly 'un-pretty' at the moment, Asia's remark about handcuffs came to mind, and I flushed.

He seemed to sense a change in the inflection of our conversation, and his eyes dropped over my cotton-clad body. Neither of us spoke for several seconds. Finally, I cleared my throat and turned away with a nervous chuckle. "That's the worst Old West impression I've ever heard."

He gestured to the collection. "You should know, being an outlaw connoisseur."

"Actually, those were all gifts from my neighbor, Linus. He's a descendant of Jesse James. He's the connoisseur."

"Jesse James is from here, right?"

"Actually, from Kearney. His home is still there."

Lane nodded. "Must be a thrill, having the relative of your hero living close by."

"He's not my hero, but yeah, it's fascinating. Linus is a character. Pretty much everyone from Missouri claims to be related to Jesse James, but Linus is the real deal."

"Sounds like an interesting guy. I'd like to meet him someday."

It was said as if he planned to be around for a while. A little thrill traveled through me at the thought. Then reality chased the thrill away. *Married.* He's *married.*

I rubbed my free hand up and down my arm—scouring away the notion of a romance with Mr. Dark and Off-limits.

"Was there something you needed to see me about?"

"I wanted to follow up on Josephine Detweiler. Have you spoken to her lately?"

I dropped my gaze.

"Miss Donovan?" he prompted.

I sighed and raised my head. "Yes. She was here."

His brows rose again. "Did you tell her we wanted to speak with her?"

"Yes, I gave her your card," I responded slowly, not admitting I waited two days to do so.

"And?" He brushed his jacket back, once more resting his hands on his hips, giving me a view of his holster, his gun. Reminding me who he was.

"And... I assume she didn't call?"

"No, she didn't. Is there a reason why *you* didn't?"

"Didn't...?"

"Didn't call us and let us know she was in town?" His lips tightened, and I could tell he was losing patience.

"Didn't call and turn my best friend into the police?" My tone suggested the thought was preposterous.

"She's not wanted for a crime, but if she were, you do realize I could charge you with aiding, abetting, harboring, etc?" His gaze swept over my Jesse James collection and back to me with an expression that implied I was all about harboring fugitives.

I sighed and clenched the hair on top of my head in my fist. "You're right. I'm sorry. It's just that when she got here, she was..." I cleared my throat. "...ill. I felt she needed a few days to recover. Then, when I told her about it, I thought she would call. When I got home yesterday, she was gone—"

"A few days?"

"Huh?" My eyes went to his.

"A few days to recover? When did she get here?"

I released my hair and lifted my hands, palms up. "Thursday night."

The blue in his eyes deepened to a shade just darker than a storm cloud. "Thursday night?"

I nodded.

"So, she was here when I ran into you on Saturday?"

I nodded again, feeling guilty and miserable.

"I see." It was his turn to nod. "Well, Miss Donovan. Although your friend's not wanted for a crime, she's a known associate of a man who's wanted for questioning in a homicide." Anger sparked in his gaze. "If you speak with Miss Detweiler again, we would very much appreciate it if you'd let us know."

He went to the door and stopped, reaching into his jacket pocket. "Here." He slapped a business card into my hand. "In case you lost my number."

"I didn't—"

"If you don't contact us next time, Miss Donovan, I'll assume you have something to hide."

I nodded but didn't speak as he stalked out of my house and into the mist.

After closing the door, I leaned my forehead against it, clutching his card in my hand.

I just *thought* I couldn't feel any more miserable than I had when I woke this morning.

Chapter 7

The mist was starting to lift as Lane merged onto I-35 from I-29. Between the shedding branches along the highway, houses and towns peeked through. When he'd first moved to Missouri years ago, it had been spring and the trees were thick and leafy. He'd wondered where Missourians kept their cities and towns because, along the highways, there was nothing but trees. As the leaves had started to fall, he'd realized the towns were there, just hidden behind the thickly blanketed branches.

Lane dialed the cell number he'd gotten for Murray Bay, the single guest at the inn.

"Yes?" Bay answered, sounding wary.

"Mr. Bay?"

"Speaking. Who's this?"

"Detective Brody with the KCPD. I wondered if I could take a few moments of your time. I have some questions."

"Questions about what?" More wary.

"It has to do with a homicide."

"Homicide? I know nothing about a homicide. You've got the wrong guy."

"Please, Mr. Bay. It will only take a few minutes. Can I come to where you are now?"

A put-out sigh. "Yeah. I guess. I'm at the office but was just heading to lunch. Meet me at Ressler's Grill. You know it?"

"I do. I'll be there in fifteen minutes."

Lane hoped Bay was more forthcoming than Monroe Donovan had been. It rankled that she hadn't told him Detweiler was in town. In fact, he felt betrayed, which was absurd. Donovan was nothing more than a witness. A witness who'd withheld information. Wasn't like it hadn't happened a thousand times before. Trust was something he couldn't expect as a cop and hadn't. Until now. Normally, he didn't let the two mix, and starting to with Donovan made him feel uneasy.

The restaurant was packed, but the hostess led Lane to where Bay was seated at a corner table. He had already gotten his food and was eating. He stood, still chewing, and shook Lane's hand, indicating a chair across the table from him. Lane sat and ordered an iced tea when the waitress came around.

Murray Bay was around fifty, fleshy, with graying hair that was thick everywhere except for a spot right on his crown.

Lane pulled his notebook out and flipped it open as Bay continued to shovel bites of a club sandwich and french fries into his mouth.

"I understand you were a guest at the Highland Lily Bed and Breakfast on Thursday, October twenty-third," Lane said.

Bay stopped eating and his eyes went to stone for a brief moment. He slowly resumed chewing and swallowed, then took a sip from his tea before responding. "What's this about?"

"We're investigating a homicide. The night desk clerk at the bed and breakfast."

"I know nothing about any murder, like I told you on the phone."

"We're speaking to all the guests. Just trying to learn if anyone saw something that might aid in our investigation. You were there that night, so…"

"Why do you think I was there?"

"I don't *think* it. I know it. I need you to tell me if you saw anything unusual that night."

Bay pushed his plate aside, even though he'd only eaten half his sandwich. He rubbed the bridge of his nose with an index finger and briefly shut his eyes. When he opened them, they looked afraid.

"Yes. I stayed there. No, I didn't see anything unusual."

"Were you awake at around ten-thirty or eleven p.m.?"

His gaze shifted to a point somewhere to his right as he answered. "No. No, I don't think so. I really don't remember what time I went to bed."

"Who stayed in the room with you?"

"No one." A quick head shake. "My wife was out of the country."

"You were at a bed and breakfast alone?"

"Alone." His chin jutted out. "Why is that so hard to believe?"

As he spoke, he picked up a french fry and used it to poke at the others on his plate. Lane noticed that the french fry trembled slightly.

"I just find it a bit out of the ordinary that a man would check into a bed and breakfast, one within five or ten miles of his home, alone. You can understand that, can't you?"

"Not really. I wanted a little peace and quiet."

"Who lives in the house with you and your wife?"

"No one. Our children are grown."

"You said your wife was out of the country. Sounds like you could have found plenty of peace and quiet at home."

The french fry gouging stopped. Bay moved the plate away and twisted his hands together on top of the table. "You have your way of relaxing, Detective. I have mine. Free country, right?"

Okay, so he wasn't any more honest than Monroe Donovan.

"Mr. Bay, we're not interested in your personal life as a matter of idle curiosity. This is a murder investigation, and I need some straight answers. If you're cheating on your wife, that's your business." He wanted to add, 'Although it does make you an asshole,' but antagonizing a witness wasn't the way to gain cooperation. "We'll do our best to keep your personal life out of this, but I need you to be straight with me."

Bay flinched and once more looked away, this time at his white knuckles.

"I'm not seeing another woman," he said, slowly enunciating each word.

"So, you were alone when you checked in."

"I was."

"Did you speak with Mr. Hebringer?"

"Only briefly. You know. Checking in."

"Did he seem nervous to you? Afraid? Anything about him you can recall that seemed out of the ordinary?"

"No, nothing. I don't know the guy. I've just seen him when I've—" He gulped, his eyes widening.

"So you've stayed there before?"

Bay looked like he wanted to snatch the words back out of the air.

"I've stayed there a couple of times."

"Alone?"

Bay nodded jerkily.

"Mr. Bay, being totally truthful with me is very important. I'm not trying to ruin you, but I will dig up whatever I can find. It might be better if you were honest with me now so my digging doesn't toss any unnecessary dirt on you."

His jaw went slack, and his face paled. He slumped in his chair, his voice subdued when he spoke. "When I met Althea, I was working in one of her father's warehouses. I lived in an efficiency apartment and drove a fifteen-year-old car. I still couldn't make the bills most months. To this day, I don't know why Althea fell in love with me. We were married a few months after we met, and I haven't wanted for anything, material-wise, since."

He was silent for a moment. So was Lane.

"We had two children together and three grandchildren," Bay continued. "Still, after all these years, Althea holds the power. The financial power. One wrong step, and I'm that guy in the warehouse again, only now I know what it's like to not be that guy. And I can't go back to that. *Won't* go back to it."

Lane waited, wondering if Bay had him mixed up with a shrink.

Bay lifted his head and stared wearily at Lane. "I spent the night alone, Detective Brody. And that's my final answer."

****

Back in his car, Lane called Webber. "You get anything from your couple?"

"Not a thing. They stayed holed up in their room. Saw Hebringer at check-in, but not after that. Heard

103

nothing, saw nothing. You know, like Sergeant Schultz of *Hogan's Heroes*."

"Yeah, same here. Only my guy is lying. Clearly, he was not there alone."

"You're not buyin' what he's sellin?'"

"Would you check into a bed and breakfast, alone, when your wife was out of the country?" Lane tapped his fingers on the steering wheel and stared out the car window where people were passing by, hurrying quickly along the sidewalks, heads ducked against the biting wind.

"Ex-wife, now," Tony corrected. "But, when I was married? No way. Me and Rosie Palm and her five sisters would be hangin' at the house."

"Exactly. You know how it goes. Everyone has something to hide."

"Yep," Tony said. "That's about all we run into. Crooks and liars."

"Can't swing a dead cat without hitting one."

"So, you think he was with another woman?"

Lane considered for a minute. "I think he was with another *somebody*."

"Hmmm. Switch hitter, huh?"

"Just a guess. But he only said he wasn't seeing another *woman*."

"Curiouser and curiouser. The mom's plane is due to arrive this evening. I'll pick her up at the airport. If you want to talk to her, you can meet us at the station."

Lane started the car and pulled out onto the street. "I might do that, if I can get loose. I'm going to do some more digging into Bay's story."

"Sounds like a plan. Later, Huck."

****

I drove toward the theater at Legends, feeling a little pathetic for going to the movies alone on a Tuesday afternoon. But, I was worried about Josie, feeling restless, and not really in the mood for company. Besides, everyone I knew was at work, not playing hooky as I was. I also felt like a sloth for blowing off the job search, but my heart wasn't in it. To keep from feeling totally worthless, I'd called the *Star* and left a message for my old boss. He was on vacation and wouldn't be back for two weeks. I was sure he'd call when he returned, and I'd ask him if he had anything for me. That was *sort* of like job hunting.

"Suspicious Minds" by Elvis came on the radio and I turned it up, feeling my spirits lift. I had inadvertently become an Elvis fan in college while doing a paper on the impact of celebrities on society. Whether or not one appreciated Elvis' talent, there was no denying he was a phenomenon, the likes of which had never been seen before and would probably never be seen again. Not only did I find I loved his music, I'd discovered why he had the impact he had. He had this boyish, southern charm, but at the same time, a deeply embedded raw sexuality that was powerful and intoxicating. It was fortunate that he only used that power for entertainment. If he'd been a terrorist or a cult leader, he could have easily taken over the world. I was only six when he died, a few years younger than his daughter. Had I been ten years older, I was certain I'd have been a part of the frenzied, screaming masses, fainting and tossing my panties up on stage.

I was still irked over Adam's invasion of my cabin, but my anger had dulled some, and I was once more on the 'worry about Josie' band-wagon. I knew I should stop, but I couldn't make myself do it. It was worse this time, like some sixth sense was telling me something was wrong.

Had Matt done something to her because he feared she'd spoken to the police? Had she disappeared this time because she *did* know something about the murder? If so, I let her slip away without learning what she knew, without making sure she answered the detectives' questions. At best, I'd impeded an investigation. At worst, I'd endangered Josie's life.

Detective Brody hadn't been pleased with me. His suspicion, his distrust, was evident in his eyes when he'd stood in my living room, looking at me as though I were Mata Hari incarnate. That bothered me a little more than it should. *He* bothered me a little more than he should.

I took the State Road exit and curved around toward the mall. I was pulling into the parking lot when a familiar figure coming out of McDonald's caught my eye. Tall. Reddish-brown hair pulled back in a ponytail. Threadbare jeans and a Harley jacket.

Matt.

He was getting into a silver Nissan. I peered at the rear of the car, trying to catch the tag number, but I was too far away to make it out.

Keeping one eye on the direction the car went and one eye on my driving, I rummaged in my purse for my cell phone.

I located the phone and Detective Brody's card at the same time, then found a parking spot. I dialed Brody's number as I walked alongside the mall shops toward the theater.

****

Garrett Ramirez inhaled deeply, ecstatically. Of all

his vices, he would have to say smoking crack was his fave. Screwing a married man was probably second, simply because it was *verboten*, but crack definitely beat tapping Murray's flabby ass.

Crack. He giggled. Technically, they were *both* crack.

He curled his nose as the unpleasant odor of the street people leaning beside him against the building wafted to him. One of the dudes had spittle hanging from his mouth and a slut with filthy clothing and canker sores kept scratching at her crotch. Disgusting, the company you had to keep when indulging in secretive, illegal, pleasures.

Ah, but the lovely, lovely crack.

The low hum of a car caught his attention. A cop. Cruising slowly by. Garrett quickly slid the pipe behind his back.

Was the cop maybe looking for him? Did he want to question him about the dude at the B and B who bought it? That couldn't be it. No one knew he'd seen anything.

A little shiver of fear and excitement trickled through him. Did what he'd seen have anything to do with the murder? Oh—my—God. He bet it did. He felt his penis start to tingle. *Delicious.*

"I witnessed a murder," he blurted, not realizing he was going to speak until he had. The chick with the mouth sores lifted her head and almost focused on him, her eyes rounding a little in curiosity. The others acted as though he'd said, "I ate a jelly sandwich for lunch."

Now that the cat was out of the bag, he felt an intense, overwhelming compulsion to talk. No matter that what he said was filled with half-truths and exaggeration. He had a captive audience, one that was unlikely to go to the cops and, even if they did, so what? Murray was the one who insisted their affair be kept secret. He didn't give a flying rat's ass, other than that it might end the goodies he received from Murray. Might put a kibosh on the bling. Oh well, there were plenty of fish in the ocean. Or *whales* in Murray's case.

"It was Thursday night, and I was at the Highland Lily Bed and Breakfast." The chick was still the only one looking at him. One of the guys was picking something imaginary off his jacket sleeve. The other two were leaning against the side of the building, eyes closed. Okay, so a captive audience of one. What the F, an audience was an audience.

"I saw the desk clerk taking the trash out when I went outside for a smoke." That part was true. The guy hadn't seen him, and Garrett was going to call out to him. The desk clerk was smoking, too, and he thought they might bond. Besides, he was cute. But Garrett's cell had vibrated. Murray had woken up, wondering where Garrett had gone, demanding he come back to the room. Garrett headed back, but before he went inside, he thought he saw another figure moving in the darkness out on the grounds. He didn't stick around to find out. Then, he heard about the guy getting killed, and he just *knew* the person he'd seen had to be the killer.

"He was heading for the dumpster when these two men came up behind him and grabbed him." He didn't really see that part, but he figured most of the time, two people were involved in crimes. "One of them had a gun. The desk clerk started begging, and the one guy stuck the gun right in his mouth."

Garrett sucked on the crack pipe, long and hard. Another chick, this one a little cleaner and better-looking than the first, wandered up, wordlessly reaching out for the pipe. Garrett handed it to her and inwardly smiled. Now, an audience of two.

Yes.

This was *so* double-*d*-licious.

****

"Detective Brody," a husky voice answered.

My mouth went dry, and my stomach tightened. For a moment, I couldn't speak.

"Hello? Anyone there?"

"Yes. Sorry. It's Monroe Donovan."

Silence, then, "What can I do for you Miss Donovan?" His tone was reserved, bordering on unfriendly.

"I saw Matt. He got into a car. A silver Nissan."

"Where? Did you get a tag number?" Now there was interest.

"No. I couldn't get a good look at the tag. I saw him leaving from the McDonald's at Legends."

"Did you see which way he headed?"

"He was heading toward 435. I don't know which direction he went, or if he even took the highway."

I retraced my steps, deciding against the movie. I was no longer in the mood. I made my way back to the parking lot, phone pressed to my ear.

"I appreciate the information. We'll put out an APB on the Nissan, but it's not much to go on."

"I know. I just thought I should tell you."

"Yeah." Unspoken were the words, *like you should have told us Josie was in town.* "Have you talked to your friend again?"

"No. I'm sorry. I wish I could find her, too. I'm worried about her."

"You should be. She's running with a rough crowd if she's seeing Matt Lovell."

I was now on the sidewalk near the Holiday Inn that shared a parking lot with the mall. A taxi pulled up and my brother, Coburn, emerged. I wanted to call out to him, but didn't want to shout in Brody's ear. His opinion of me was low enough as it was.

I picked up my pace, heading toward the taxi. Maybe Coburn was having lunch at the restaurant in the hotel. I could join him, get a free meal, and the day wouldn't be a total waste.

I lifted my hand to wave, but he didn't notice me. I hurried toward him, continuing my conversation with Brody. "I know she's running with a rough crowd. I've always worried about her. Especially now. With the murder and all."

"I don't think it has a lot to do with your friend. Her boyfriend is only wanted for questioning as a witness."

"I hope that's all it is."

When I was perhaps fifteen feet away, another taxi pulled up behind Coburn's and stopped. Coburn went to the door and, opening it, he bent inside. A woman stepped out, her hand holding onto Coburn's. The hair was silvery blonde, not the red tresses of my sister-in-law. I watched as the two of them shared a passionate kiss before disappearing inside the hotel.

I halted in stunned amazement, then realized Brody was speaking.

"I'm sorry," I said, shock making my voice breathy and strained.

"Is everything okay?" Brody asked.

It took me a few seconds to answer. "Yes. Fine. I'm sorry I couldn't be more help." I said goodbye and ended the call. My mind was a cauldron of turmoil. Coburn was having an affair.

His wife was pregnant with their first child, and my flawless, saintly brother was screwing another woman.

****

"How are you feeling?" Adam asked me on Wednesday morning. He seemed exasperated. I was certain he was more angry at me for missing work than he was concerned about my health.

"Better," I said shortly, not sure if I wanted to confront him about the cabin.

"You know, you should come in to work unless you're really, really ill. Are you sure you didn't just do it to punish me about the promotion?"

A cold rush of fury swept through me, and I couldn't hold back. "It wasn't to punish you about the promotion, Adam, but I will admit, I had a rough night."

"Oh?" His brows rose.

"Yes. I spent half the night looking for Josie and ended up at the cabin." I waited. No reaction. "Guess what I found?"

"Josie?"

"No," I gritted, my anger increasing with every word. "I found handcuffs and condoms."

His eyes rounded, and his cheeks reddened. He didn't speak.

"You have any idea how they got there?"

He shook his head, but I could see the truth in his eyes.

"None at all?" I crossed my arms and glared.

He blew out a breath and said, "Yeah. I guess I do. Sorry."

"Sorry? Sorry you and the woman you cheated with

broke into my cabin and screwed in my bed? What the hell were you thinking? Did you purposely leave the evidence behind so I'd know? Just to rub it in my face?"

He shook his head, his expression miserable. "I didn't mean for you to find out." He rubbed a hand over his chin. "Tabitha was supposed to get the stuff. She must have… forgotten."

But I knew better. "No. She didn't forget. She did it on purpose."

He didn't confirm or deny. I turned and went to my cubicle, trying to concentrate on work, but kept thinking about Adam. Josie. Coburn.

Shit. What a week it had been.

At lunch time, Asia and I were sitting in the break room, she with her leftover chicken cacciatore and me with my cold ham sandwich. The only other employees there were Beth and Carl, who sat at another table. The TV suspended in the corner was showing *Days of Our Lives*. I'd watched the soap opera fanatically when I was in my twenties, but hadn't seen it in years. I was surprised to see several familiar faces on the show. Characters I assumed were long gone.

"Didn't Stefano die?" I asked Asia, whose eyes were glued to the screen.

"Yeah, several times," she said.

"And Tony? Roman?"

"They've all been back and forth."

"Hmmm," I said, my interest piqued in spite of myself. Especially when one of my past favorites, Steve "Patch" Johnson, appeared.

A commercial came on, and Asia turned her attention back to me. "So, what were you and Asshole going at it about?"

I explained the cabin discovery.

"*Asshole*," she exclaimed. "Can you believe him? Like he hasn't done enough to you already? What's next, he'll sell your organs?"

I smiled grimly. "Wouldn't put anything past him."

Wanting to tell her everything that had happened the past few days, and wanting to get it in before her soap came back on, I blurted, "Coburn's cheating on Naomi."

She arched an eyebrow. "Yeah? How'd you find out?"

"I saw him go into a hotel with another woman."

She nodded, taking a bite of her chicken.

"You don't seem all that surprised."

"I'm not. For one, he's a man. For another, he's hit on me before."

"What?" I nearly screeched. As far as I knew, Asia and Coburn had barely been around one another.

"At your birthday party."

We'd gone to a bar that night, my brothers, Naomi, Asia, and I.

"How? In the club?" I asked, trying to assimilate this startling revelation.

"Yeah. At one point, we wound up being the only two at the table. He slipped a hand along my thigh. Asked me if I'd ever thought about getting with another man. A white man."

I no longer wanted the sandwich. I pushed it aside. "What did you say? Why didn't you tell me?"

"I told him I'd been with white men and wouldn't be with *him* if his dick was made of pure gold. I didn't tell you because I didn't want to upset you."

I shook my head and downed the last of my Diet Pepsi.

Adam. Coburn.
Men.

****

"I'm Nathaniel," said a tall, thin, man wearing shiny clothes and too much jewelry. He rested his hands on his hips and smiled down at D.J. "You look lonely."

D.J. cringed. What was he thinking, coming into a gay bar? Being hetero in a gay bar was *not* the way to keep a low profile.

"I'm seeing someone," D.J. faltered, wondering if he should have made his voice more feminine. But not all gay guys talked that way, right? He'd always wondered about that. Did they cultivate the manner and high voice once they discovered their sexuality? He didn't think it was genetic. Since they were supposedly gay from birth, their affectations should have been with them since the beginning. He didn't remember any boys in his grade school talking like Carol Channing and twitching their asses like runway models.

No matter. That was a quandary to ponder at a later date. For now, he had more pressing issues.

The guy pouted and the lips curved into what was probably supposed to be a provocative smile, but D.J. just couldn't think of a guy as 'provocative,' even when he was wearing eyeliner and lip gloss.

"Well," he purred, "then he's a fool for letting a dish like you out on your own."

Nathaniel sauntered away and D.J. let out a breath. Goddamned Garrett Ramirez. He'd been following the little prick for twenty-four hours and still hadn't caught him alone. The guy was quite the social butterfly, quite the flirt, too, from what D.J. had observed so far.

Flirt, hell. He was a whore. In the two hours D.J. had

been in the bar, he'd seen Ramirez disappear outside three different times with three different guys. Could have been stepping out to do drugs, but from the expressions of secret gratification on his companions' faces, D.J. would guess there was a little cock-sucking to go along with it.

D.J.'s focus on Ramirez had been a last-minute development. The planning and work he'd put into the others wasn't necessary with Ramirez. He wasn't part of the original plan. He'd become an unwanted complication that had to be hastily dispatched.

He'd seen something at the bed and breakfast, though not exactly what he'd claimed. There hadn't been two men. D.J. worked alone. Whatever he'd seen had to be kept quiet. D.J. couldn't have his plan thwarted before it was complete.

He was likely to get caught eventually, but he would make sure it wasn't until after he'd finished them off. One by one, they'd pay.

D.J. had intended to stay as invisible as possible. Seemed like a gay bar would be a good place to do that, but maybe not. Would the pouty guy pose a problem? D.J. didn't think so. The guy was probably working the room, likely wouldn't give D.J. a second thought.

Ramirez was who D.J. needed to focus on. D.J. saw him go out with a fourth man and it gave him an idea of how to get Ramirez alone. The thought made his stomach churn, and he took a long drink of the whisky. *Chill out,* he told himself. *You don't actually have to do the guy. You only have to entice him outside.*

Well, he'd *do* him. Just not in the manner Ramirez would want.

The thing was, coming onto a man, period, even in

pretense, was repugnant to him. Not that he was homophobic, but he was most definitely, thorough and through, forever straight. But he was tired of waiting for an opportunity that never came. Ramirez had two roommates and a horde of friends. Stalking a homo was not at the top of his list of favorite things to do, and he wanted it over with.

The waiter came around and he ordered another drink. In a few moments, Ramirez came back in. D.J. downed the whisky, then headed over to where Ramirez was draped against the bar.

"Looking for some action?" D.J. said, leaning in so only Ramirez could hear.

Ramirez pursed his lips and took a drink of something tall and orange. He was slightly built and wore tight, white pants and a blue shirt with half the buttons undone, showing his scrawny, shaved chest. His ears held more rings than the Olympic symbol.

"Want to go outside?" Ramirez asked in a low, womanish voice.

"You go first," D.J. said. "I'll be out shortly."

Ramirez's neatly trimmed brows drew together. "You embarrassed, sweetheart?"

D.J. jerked his head toward the crowd. "I have an unwanted admirer. Don't want to hurt his feelings."

Ramirez smiled and took another sip, eyeing D.J. over the rim of the glass. "I'll see you in five."

D.J. waited a few minutes after Ramirez left, then looked around the bar. No one seemed to be paying attention. He strolled toward the back, then quickly slipped out the same door through which Ramirez had disappeared.

It led to an alley. Dark. Lit only by the meager glow

of the lights on the outer streets.

Ramirez was waiting for him next to a dumpster. Nice. The guy was all romance.

D.J. wasn't sure how to begin a make-out session with a dude. He walked up to him and halted, letting Ramirez take the lead.

Ramirez reached out and ran a hand along D.J.'s crotch. A rush of revulsion surfaced, along with a slight twinge in his groin. Brief panic fluttered through him. Jesus. Was he turned on by the touch of a *man*?

No. It was just a physiological reaction to the danger and anticipation. He'd heard somewhere about how different emotions could induce arousal. That was it. Yeah. Had to be.

He wasn't about to find out, though. When Ramirez's free hand reached for D.J.'s zipper, his own raised. Ramirez let out a surprised grunt as the knife slid into his gut.

Chapter 8

Lane poured a cup of coffee and took it to Tony's desk. Propping a hip on the corner, he sipped from the cup. Tony was leaned back in his chair, tossing a Koosh ball from hand to hand.

"Let's see," Tony said reflectively, "no murder weapon. No eye witnesses. No DNA matches. No vehicle ID." He looked at Lane. "What exactly *do* we have?"

"Not a hell of a lot. The sum total of our evidence would fit on the head of a straight pin."

Tony pursed his lips and frowned. His phone rang and he answered, still tossing the Koosh up in one hand.

He listened for a while and his brows rose. "Yeah?" Tucking the phone under his chin, he said to Lane, "They got a guy in lock-up. Said a gay crack-head was shooting off his mouth about a murder. Said he saw something. He was staying at the inn." Into the phone, he said, "Got a name?" He wrote on a notepad. "Your guy know where Ramirez is?" Listened again. "Thanks, man." He hung up the phone.

"What'd this guy see?" Lane asked. "Who is he?"

"Dupree is the guy in lock-up. Said a dude named Garrett Ramirez claimed he was staying at the inn the night of the murder. Went out for a smoke and saw a couple of guys with a gun."

"A couple? Everything points to our guy working

alone."

"Yeah, but Ramirez swears he was there. Wouldn't hurt to talk to him."

"Does Dupree know where we can find Ramirez?"

"Nah. Just hangs with him on the streets from time to time."

"I bet Ramirez is the mystery guest Bay entertained that night. Run Ramirez through the database. Get an address. Might as well check NCIC while we're at it."

Tony dropped the Koosh ball and turned to his keyboard.

"Did I hear you say Garrett Ramirez?" a female voice said.

Lane looked around to find Lucinda Rochester standing behind him.

"Yeah. Why?"

"Gay guy?"

"Yeah," Tony said. "Whatcha got?"

"I got *him*. Murder victim. Last night at Ziggy's."

"No shit?"

"Absolutely no shit."

Lane looked down at Tony. "Ramirez runs his mouth about the B and B murder. Now he ends up dead? The head of the pin just got a little more crowded."

"Yep. Not likely a coincidence." Tony turned to Lucinda. "What's the story?"

"Bar patron found him last night in the alley behind the bar. Stab wound to the mid-section. Dead at least twenty-four hours. We confirmed he was at Ziggy's Wednesday night. Went in and out with several different men throughout the evening. No suspects thus far. No eye wits. We talked to his roommates. Two straight women. They were pretty shaken up, but no help. Why are you guys interested?"

Lane explained the connection to the B and B killing, that Ramirez had been a guest the night Hebringer was murdered.

Lucinda nodded. "Might put a whole new light on both our cases."

"If this guy was killed because of what he saw, how did the killer find out he saw anything?" Lane asked.

"Good question," said Tony. "Unless he's into the dope scene, too? Word got back to him?"

"Possible," Lane mused. "We need to talk to the guy in lockup. Can't talk to Ramirez, might as well see what else this guy knows."

"After, you want to head over to the scene and see if anything grabs you?" Lucinda asked.

"Yeah," Lane said. "We also need to talk to the employees at the bar. Give us an hour and we'll meet you in the alley. Unless you want to come along while we talk to the people in Ziggy's?"

"Nah," Lucinda said. "I'll just meet you outside. Depresses the hell out of me to be in a room full of hot guys, knowing they'd rather have another hot guy than me. Tough enough to keep up the self-esteem as it is."

****

Johnny Dupree was pale and thin, with long fingers that tapped continuously against his thighs. He had blond, close-cropped hair and a triangle-shaped head that God no doubt intended to be covered by a hat.

Lane and Tony sat across from him in the interview room.

"So," Lane said. "Where do you know this Ramirez guy from?"

Dupree shrugged. "The streets, man."

"When did he tell you about the murder?"

"Didn't."

"Didn't?" Tony cut in. "Thought he was shooting off his mouth about a murder at a bed and breakfast?"

Dupree's head nodded vigorously. "Yeah, but not to me."

"To who then?" Tony asked.

"Crack whore named Teresa."

"Teresa told you about the shooting?"

"Yeah. Said this guy was staying at the bed and breakfast, went outside for a smoke and saw these dudes with a gun. We thought it was kind of cool Ramirez saw it since the dude really got popped."

"Yeah, cool," Lane said. "Do you know where we can find Teresa?"

Dupree shook his head. "She's around, man, you know? Just... around."

"What does she look like?"

Another shrug. "Like a crack whore. Skinny, shriveled up. Herpes on her mouth. Thin, brown hair."

"Got a last name?"

"Nope."

"Did Teresa say who else was around when Ramirez told about the shooting?"

Dupree squinted, rubbing a finger along the side of his nose, as if anticipating the coke that would be inserted later. "No, man. She just said Ramirez was this fag who saw some dude get popped."

"Thanks." Tony said, his tone heavy with sarcasm. "You've been superfluously helpful."

Dupree looked up, a spaced-out grin on his sallow face. "That's good, right?"

****

Friday was Coburn's birthday, so an unscheduled dinner was being held in his honor.

The house smelled of pot roast and chocolate cake. Dad and my brothers were sprawled in the living room watching the World Series of Poker on ESPN.

On the rare occasions when there were no televised pro or college football, baseball, basketball, or hockey games, and no UFC championship fights, the men in my family tuned into whatever competitive fare the sports network offered. After all, their very survival was dependent upon observing some type of competition, preferably of the sweaty, testosterone laden nature. When that wasn't possible, watching an edge-of-your seat, tension-racked card game would do.

Recently, I'd seen this event called rodeo poker. Spectators had the opportunity to play a card game in the middle of the ring. They would release a bull and the player to stay the longest at the table without fleeing in fright was declared the winner. Now *there's* a card game worth watching. Release a thousand pounds of horns and fury in the middle of the World Series poker tournament, and I'm all over it.

"I'm going to help Mom in the kitchen," I told them. "Keep me posted."

I received a few non-committal grunts, which didn't leave me optimistic about my odds of receiving updates.

Naomi was in the kitchen, looking content and radiant in a blue dress and one of Mom's aprons that barely hid the bulge in her tummy. She was about my height, but slender with naturally curly red hair and hazel eyes.

Naomi greeted me in her usual friendly manner, and my mother said, "You look nice, dear."

"Thanks, Mom," I said when I had sufficiently recovered from the unexpected praise. I'd worn champagne colored slacks and a long, green tunic style blouse. I'd made more effort than normal, feeling guilty about my previous slovenly appearance. I was dubiously pleased at the compliment. I'd grown accustomed to her ignoring the positive and accentuating the negative.

Then, she said, "I don't see how you can afford nice clothes since you didn't earn that promotion. Still, it's good to see you looking somewhat feminine for a change."

And the planets of my world were once more aligned.

"Monroe, will you chop the salad?" she went on. "Be sure to cut up radishes. Coburn absolutely loves them."

"Yeah," I said as I headed to the sink. "Coburn loves a lot of things."

Both women looked at me quizzically. My voice must have conveyed the double intender, but neither of them commented. I let a relieved sigh escape. If I were going to tell them, I'd break it to them gently. I wouldn't do it with snide innuendos.

But I wouldn't tell them. Even though Coburn didn't deserve my loyalty, I couldn't hurt them like that. Not even my mother. I never found out for sure, but when I was in my early teens, I suspected my father had been unfaithful to my mother. Once, when he was out and hadn't gotten home when expected, I walked into their bedroom and caught her sobbing, holding her wedding album. I wouldn't say anything now because I didn't want her to feel betrayed by yet another man in her life.

I washed my hands, then began rinsing vegetables

while Coburn's fan club chatted behind me.

I focused on the clock above the sink, trying to tune them out, but my irritation only increased. The clock was festooned with brightly colored fruit—although over the years, the colors of the fruit had faded—and hadn't worked for more than half of my life. The hands perpetually declared the time to be two-thirty-seven. At least it was correct twice a day.

It had always bugged me that the broken clock still hung uselessly in the kitchen. I mean, what was the point? It wasn't as if it enhanced the décor. It was hideous. The microwave and stove both had digital clocks, yet my mother kept that monstrosity on the wall.

I wanted to turn and scream at my mother, "Take the fucking clock down, already! By the way, your golden boy is a lying sleaze." Then, to Naomi, "your perfect husband is a cheating dick-head." Instead, I continued rinsing and chopping until I heard my mother triumphantly proclaim that dinner was ready.

We sat down to a feast of pot roast, new potatoes, squash, and homemade dinner rolls. For dessert there would be double-chocolate layer cake. All of Coburn's favorites. Well, all his favorites except 'slutty blonde bimbo.'

"When do you leave for Miami?" my mother asked Coburn.

"Monday morning," Coburn said.

"You're going out of town?" I asked.

"Yeah. A medical convention."

"Is Naomi going?"

Coburn had been reaching for a dinner roll, but stopped in mid-motion. "No," he said quickly.

"You really should." I turned to Naomi. "You'd

enjoy getting away and you guys could treat it like a second honeymoon before the baby comes along and there's no more alone time."

Coburn looked at me as if I'd suggested he dunk his head in a toilet.

"True. It would be lovely to go to Miami," Naomi said, sounding hopeful and doubtful at the same time.

"That's not a good idea," my mother said firmly. "It wouldn't be good for the baby. Naomi needs to stay here near her doctor and take care of herself and the baby."

Coburn gave her a pathetically grateful look. Without even knowing it, she'd come to the aid of her special boy once again.

After dinner, I offered to clean the kitchen by myself, insisting that Naomi and Mom should relax since they'd done most of the cooking.

I really just wanted to be alone.

When I finished loading the dishwasher and wiping down the counters, I stepped out on the back porch and stood in the blissful stillness of the cool night air.

The door behind me opened and I turned, relieved to see that, of all the people it could have been, it was Gable.

"There you are," he said, coming to stand beside me. "You better come inside. You'll miss out on the bestowal of gifts."

"Wouldn't that be a shame," I replied.

"It would. The wise men are due to show up any second."

I laughed. Gable liked to align himself with me in a 'we're in this together' sort of way, as if we were on the same level in my mother's eyes. Truth was, although Coburn was her obvious favorite, Gable and Mitchum tied for a very close second.

I looked above the tree line to where the moon was a narrow silver parenthesis in the inky black sky.

"Remember when Dad used to tell us that was his big toenail he lost?" I said.

"Yeah. I believed it, too."

"So did I."

"Remember before the days of pre-moistened towelettes when Mom would 'can a washcloth' to take with us on trips?" Gable laughed and shook his head. "And, what was with heating a towel in the oven for earaches? I mean, there were heating pads, right?"

"I think it was more labor-intensive to do the towel thing. Showed she cared more than sticking a plug in an outlet would have done."

"To tell you the truth, I liked it when she did that. It felt good. All toasty and cozy. Made me feel secure for some reason. I even liked the way it smelled." He lowered his voice conspiratorially. "Don't tell anyone, but sometimes I faked an earache, just to get the baked towel."

I smiled. "Ooooh, how many hail Mary's did that one cost you?"

He smiled back. "Not nearly as many as you might think." Reaching out, he gave my arm a gentle squeeze. "Have you heard from Josie?"

I shook my head. "Not a word."

"Saturday, I visit the local shelters. I'll ask around a little, keep my ears and eyes peeled."

"Thanks," I said, putting my hand over his and squeezing back.

"Now, let's go inside and pay proper homage to the Chosen One."

****

Ziggy's didn't look like a gay bar, in that the walls weren't painted in rainbows and there were no photos of Liberace or Lady Gaga. There was, however, a disc jockey playing a duet of Elton John and George Michael singing "Don't Let the Sun Go Down on Me."

Tony motioned for the bartender, who finally spotted them and made his way to where they waited.

"What can I get you?" he asked, but he eyed them like he knew they weren't here for the same reason as his other customers.

"Were you bartending Wednesday night?" Lane asked, showing the bartender his shield.

"I bartend every night. It's my bar."

"You Ziggy?" asked Tony.

He shook his head. "Don Walsh. Ziggy is my favorite cartoon." He leaned his hands on the edge of the bar. "Anyway, like I told the other cops. I was here Wednesday night."

Tony reached into his jacket pocket and pulled out a photo of Garrett Ramirez, extending it toward Walsh.

Walsh didn't spare it a glance. "Guy was killed right outside my door. He was a regular. You think I need a picture?"

Tony slid the photo back in its place. "So, you noticed Mr. Ramirez here on Wednesday night?"

"Garrett's in the room, you can't *not* notice."

"Why's that?"

"Look around you, Detective. You got all kinds of people." Lane glanced around the bar to where same-sex couples, mostly men, either sat at tables, some with their arms draped loosely over one another, or swayed together out on the dance floor. Many of them wore

127

Halloween costumes. One group of men even went so far as to dress as the Village People. "Not every homosexual looks like an extra in a cabaret show. I mean, do I look gay?"

He didn't. He was solidly built with a Fu Manchu mustache and thinning hair. Looked more like a teamster than a bartender at a gay bar.

Not waiting for a reply, he continued. "Garrett was a stereotypical flamer. Flamboyant, loud, feminine. Kind of a little bitch sometimes."

"You're saying he stood out?"

"Stood out. Put out. Went out." Walsh jerked a head toward the back of the bar.

"Went out?"

"Garrett liked to… entertain, for lack of a better word, out back. Any given night, you'd see him go outside with anywhere from three to ten men. All different."

"He did that on Wednesday?" Lane asked.

"Every night he was here."

Lane took out his notebook. "Do you know the guys he went out with? Names? Especially the last one you saw with him?"

"Don't know any of them."

"Is there a camera on the back door?"

Walsh sighed, straightened up. Crossing his arms, he said. "Let me speed this up for you, Detective. No cameras on the back door. No cameras in the alley. Don't know with who or what time he went out the last time. Don't know the names of anyone he went out with that night, or any night. Don't know who he hung out with when he was here. Don't know the guy who found the body. I told you everything I know. Period. Just like the other cops. Now, it's Friday night, fellas. I need to get back to work."

"One more question," Tony said as Walsh started to turn away. "And this is just for my own curiosity. Did you every hook up with Ramirez?"

Walsh snorted a laugh. "I like my men a little more masculine. If I were going to go for someone as feminine as Ramirez, I'd have saved myself a lot of headaches and just stayed straight."

****

Lucinda met them in the alley behind Ziggy's. She'd changed clothes since they'd seen her at the station. She wore tight black pants and spike-heeled boots. Her black knee-length coat was open, showing a silky cream-colored blouse, unbuttoned to nearly nipple depth.

Lane had to force his gaze away. It had been a very long time since he'd had a woman.

Tony's eyes rounded and a low whistle escaped between his clenched teeth. Lucinda pretended not to notice, but Lane saw a smile curve her lips.

"The body was found over here." She led them to a dumpster. "One stab wound in the mid-section, then a slice upward. A bar patron found him last night when he came out for some fresh air. Not the best place to go for fresh air. I suspect he came out here for something a little more stimulating. Ramirez was killed the night before."

"What about the guy who found him? You run a check on him?"

"Yeah. We cleared him. No priors. Tight alibi for the night Ramirez was killed. From all we can gather, never laid eyes on Ramirez until he was dead."

Lane searched all sides of the dumpster, then the wall along the alley, checking carefully in the area where the body was found.

"Were any messages found at the scene?" he asked Lucinda.

"Messages? You mean, like, did the killer leave a note?"

"Right."

Lucinda shrugged. "Nothing we found. But maybe we should check the dumpster for the paper? It coulda gotten mixed up with trash."

Lane shook his head. "No. Probably not paper. At our scene, the words, 'Partners in Crime' were painted in red on a tree near the body."

"Blood?"

"Spray paint."

"Nothing like that around here, but we can have the techs go over it again tomorrow when it's light."

"Good idea." Lane shoved his hands in his jacket pockets and made one more sweep through the area. "Guess we've done all we can do here," he said when he returned to where Tony and Lucinda stood.

The three of them headed around the side of the building to the parking lot. When they reached Lucinda's car, she looked up at Lane. "Can I talk to you for a second?"

Tony grinned. "Yeah, I'll just call in to the... uh... thing for the... you know."

He sauntered away, slid into his car and started it. After a few minutes, Lane could hear, "Feel Like Making Love" by Bad Company blasting from the vehicle. Not a coincidence, Lane was certain. *Asshole.*

"How are you?" Lucinda asked, stepping closer so Lane got a whiff of her perfume.

"I'm good."

"Are you really? How's the situation with the wife?" The last word was said with an edge. Everyone at the station knew his story. Not the dreadful, pathetic details, but they knew the highlights. It was difficult to keep a secret around cops. Especially when it involved betrayal and murder.

"Nothing's changed."

"Yet you still remain faithful?"

"It's complicated."

"Why complicate it? What you need is pretty basic. You deserve to feel pleasure."

"It's kind of a mess right now. I don't want to add to the turmoil by…" he shrugged as if to say, 'you get the message.'

She stepped closer, and her throaty voice purred, "Can I ask you one thing? When you do decide to give in to your urges, and trust me, one day you will, promise that I'll be the one."

Thoughts of Monroe flashed through his mind, and he closed his eyes briefly. Opening them, he looked down at Lucinda. "I'll keep that in mind," he said, not making any promises.

Lucinda leaned slightly forward, giving him a birds-eye view of the cleavage. She ran a hand down his shirtfront. "I would take very good care of you," she whispered. "Let me know when you're ready to feel extraordinarily satisfied."

"I will," Lane said, his voice coming out strained.

He dragged himself away and opened her car door. "Goodnight, Lucinda."

"'Night," she said, sliding in, then driving away with a final wave.

Lane took a deep, cleansing breath and released it

slowly. He climbed in beside Tony.

"Hey, you shoulda gone with her," Tony said with a grin. "I wouldn't have minded you blowin' me off. Especially if it was so you could *get* blown."

"How about you blow me, asshole?" Lane said irritably. "Just drive."

****

On Saturday night, Asia and Darion invited me to dinner, but I declined. The week had been a bit too exciting. All I wanted to do was be alone and unwind.

I put on a Lifehouse CD and poured a glass of wine. I sank down in my recliner and closed my eyes, trying to clear my mind of all the bullshit that had gone on in the past week. It almost worked, but the wine and music couldn't quite chase away my dark thoughts.

When the CD ended and the glass was empty, I called Gable to see if he'd learned anything at the shelter. He hadn't. I hung up after he promised to let me know if anything came up.

In the bathroom, I stripped off my clothes and turned the shower on full blast. I stepped under the hot spray, enjoying the almost painful sting of the water.

I shampooed my hair and scrubbed with ginger-citrus body wash, staying until the hot water was almost gone.

Toweling off, I stood in front of the mirror, naked, and partially blow-dried my hair. As I reached for my robe, I heard a thump, then a scraping sound, and froze.

My legs went weak and a tremble worked its way from my toes through my chest.

What was that?

Even living alone, I wasn't prone to being skittish or imagining noises. I seldom became frightened. Wasn't the least paranoid.

That had been something, though. Some noise inside my house.

I pulled the robe over my still-damp body and belted it.

I didn't have a weapon in the bathroom, or in either bedroom. There was a gun in the living room and knives in the kitchen, but in this part of the house, nothing. My phone was in the front room, too. Although, what would I do if I had it? Call 9-1-1 and tell them I thought I heard a noise?

I rummaged through the cabinets beneath the bathroom sink and came up with a spray bottle of Tilex. Tough on mildew, had to be tough on exposed eyeballs.

Slowly, I eased the bathroom door open and crept to the front of the house. The living room was empty.

I made my way carefully to the kitchen and pushed the door open.

My hands tightened on the spray bottle and I gasped, drawing the attention of the man seated at my dining table.

Chapter 9

Lane had been trying to catch Murray Bay at home for most of the day. So far, no luck.

Each time he called, the housekeeper politely informed him Mr. Bay was not at home but was expected later. She always asked if she could take a message. Lane always said no.

He didn't want Bay to know he was coming. Wanted to catch him off-guard.

At around seven o'clock, on his fifth phone call, Lane's persistence paid off.

The housekeeper told him—a bit frostily—that Mr. Bay had arrived home. May she tell him who's calling? Again, Lane declined. He drove half a block and was on the porch ringing the doorbell in a matter of moments.

"Murray Bay, please." Lane said and, before she could offer to 'tell him who wished to see him,' Lane showed her his shield. "I'd appreciate it if you'd just take me to him."

The woman's lips tightened, but she nodded. "Right this way."

She led him through a marble-floored foyer into a massive room. A skylight in the center of the vaulted ceiling gave the elegant room a muted glow. At the far end of the room was a fireplace with a marble mantel. Paintings on the wall and statuettes placed randomly on tables and shelves were so indecipherable and so unappealing, they must have cost a fortune.

Murray Bay stood at a bar that took up most of one wall. Behind him was enough liquor to keep ten fraternity houses happy for at least a week. He wore a tux and was pouring something clear out of an Indigo-colored bottle.

A woman in a pearl-studded black evening gown rose from a white satin-covered sofa. She was about Murray's height and age, but slender, with short gray hair and a pencil-straight spine.

Murray Bay said, "Detective?" at the same time his wife said, "What is the meaning of this?" directing her question more to the maid than to Lane.

"The gentleman insisted I bring him straight back."

Althea Bay dismissed the woman with a quelling glance and turned to her husband. "You know this man?"

Bay nodded jerkily and gulped from the stemmed glass.

"I spoke to Mr. Bay a few days ago about a case I'm working on." Lane rescued him momentarily. "There's been a new development I'd like to discuss." He looked at Bay. "You're a difficult man to catch at home."

"We were at a charity function," Bay said. "This is Detective Brody, dear. Detective, my wife, Althea."

"How do you do?" The woman said politely. Then to her husband, "What case is he referring to?"

Murray stared at Lane blankly for a few seconds, then said, "There's an embezzlement case involving a business associate. Detective Brody is speaking to some of the companies they do business with."

"Yes," Lane agreed. "Should we talk in here or—"

"No," Bay interjected loudly, then his face turned a shade of pink, and he went on in a more modulated tone,

"My study. I have paperwork we may need to look at."

Bay refilled his glass and led Lane from the room after giving his wife a quick peck on the cheek.

They went into a darkly-paneled, masculine room with bookshelves running the length of one wall and a large desk in the center. Bay sat behind the desk and Lane took the chair facing it without an invitation.

"You had to come by my house?" Bay asked, his fingers strangling the glass.

"As I said, there's been a development." Lane pulled out a notepad, pretending to consult it. "Do you know a Garrett Ramirez?"

Bay's eyelids flickered. "No. Doesn't ring a bell. Why?"

Lane frowned as if perplexed. "Well, we think he knew something about the murder at Highland Lily, but we can't ask him."

"Why not?"

A slight hesitation, then, looking directly at Bay, "Because. He's dead."

Bay's face paled, and he blinked rapidly a few times. The flesh on his cheeks quivered. An anguished cry tore from him, and he clamped both hands over his mouth. The eyes above his white-knuckled grip were tormented.

"I guess you just now remembered him?" Lane said quietly.

Dropping his hands, he whispered, "What happened?"

"He was murdered. They found the body Thursday night. You didn't read about it in the paper?"

He shook his head, not speaking.

"We think it had something to do with the killing at the bed and breakfast. It appears Mr. Ramirez saw something that night."

"No. He didn't see anything."

"You sound certain."

"I am."

"How do you know?"

Silence.

Lane shifted forward in his chair, leaning toward Bay. "Look. The time for bullshit is over. You already lied to me and it might have cost your... friend... his life. I know he stayed with you that night. I have two murders to solve, and you don't want your wife to know you had a lover. I personally don't care who you have sex with, Mr. Bay. I just want to catch the killer. I'll get the information one way or another. If I have to involve your wife, I will. If you come clean with me now, we might be able to keep it between us." Lane slapped the notepad against the edge of the desk and Bay jumped. "I don't like being lied to. You get one more shot."

Bay sighed and took a long swallow of his drink. His voice subdued and thick with tears, he said, "That Thursday night, I woke at around ten-thirty. Garrett was gone. I called him and, in about ten minutes, he came back to the room. He'd been outside smoking. He never said a word. Acted like everything was perfectly normal."

"Maybe he just didn't want to tell you about it."

Bay smiled, his eyes getting a misty, faraway look. "Garrett loved drama. Craved it. Craved attention. Believe me, if he'd seen anything, he'd have been bursting to tell me about it. Also, Garrett found me somewhat tedious. He'd have done anything to liven up one of our evenings together."

"He told some people that he did see something.

Maybe he just didn't want to worry you."

Bay shook his head. "After you came to see me, I told Garrett about it. He got this gleam in his eyes and told me how he'd seen the desk clerk outside when he went for a smoke. He was excited that it was probably not long before the guy was killed. I told him to keep his mouth shut, that he didn't know anything, anyway." A small smile touched his mouth. "He probably kept building it up in his head and came up with this fantasy about seeing something. But, he didn't. Believe me."

"Looks like someone believed he did. Might have gotten him killed."

"Oh, God. He's gone." Bay's face scrunched and the sobs came again. This time, his entire body shook with them.

Lane stood. "Let me know if you think of anything that might help us find who did it."

Bay nodded, but Lane could tell his mind was somewhere else.

On the way out, Lane passed Mrs. Bay. "Good evening," he said, wondering how her husband was going to explain sobbing over a business associate's embezzlement.

Lane's phone rang as he walked across the street toward his car.

"Tony," he said into it, "I was just going to call you."

"Get something from Bay?"

"Just that it appears Ramirez didn't know shit after all."

"Why did he run his mouth?"

"According to Bay, he was into drama."

"So, making shit up got him dead. Ain't that a bitch."

138

"That is indeed a bitch. So, why were you calling me?"

"Cobra called. Said he was at a party and Lovell and his girl were there."

Cobra—creatively nicknamed because of a snake tattoo that covered most of his neck—was a snitch they used from time to time.

"No shit?" Lane said, pumped that they might finally find the bastard. "Where? When was this?"

"Downtown. Earlier this evening."

"Get an address?"

"He couldn't remember. Probably too stoned. He said they're not there now, anyway. Got into a huge argument. Lovell beat her pretty good. Started screaming at her about her big mouth friend poppin' off to the cops and how it was gonna get her killed. Lovell started ranting and breaking things. Said he'd shut that crazy bitch up for good. Then he took off with the Detweiler chick begging him not to hurt her."

Lane had reached his car and was fumbling in his pocket for his keys. He stopped, freezing as the implication sunk in. "Monroe Donovan," he breathed.

"That's what I was thinking. You might want to head over there."

"Where are you? You close?" Finally pulling his keys out, he unlocked the car and jumped in.

"No. I'm nearly to Wichita. Gotta pick up the kids."

"Shit." Lane's heart pounded hard against his chest as he pushed the car past the speed limit. At that moment, he knew how Murray Bay felt. "I'm heading that way. I've gotta go. I'm going to call her."

"Let me know—"

Lane disconnected and dialed Monroe's number. It

rang until it went to her voice mail.

Shit.

He was half an hour away. He stepped harder on the accelerator.

****

When he saw me, Matt Lovell came to his feet. His eyes were wild, Manson-like, his hair frizzy and tangled, making it look as though a tumbleweed surrounded his head.

"What the hell are you doing here?" I demanded, trying to keep the tremor from my voice.

He started toward me. "Thought it was time me and you had a little chat."

I pulled the spray bottle out and pointed it at his face. "Stay back."

He threw back his head and laughed. "You think I'm scared of a—"

I extended the bottle and pressed the trigger. Nothing happened.

The damn nozzle was turned to Off. Why didn't I think to check? Before I could switch it to On, Matt slapped the bottle out of my hand.

He grabbed my arm and dug his fingers into the soft underside. I yelped, and tears sprang to my eyes. My arm went numb, then a burning, sharp pain coursed from my fingers up through my shoulder.

He smelled of stale booze and cigarettes and body odor. I tried not to breathe in.

"What do you want?"

"Tell me how much the cops know."

"I have no idea."

He dug his fingers in deeper. "Don't lie to me."

"I'm not lying. God. Let me go." I tried to pull free

but couldn't. "How would I know how much the cops know? You think they run their evidence by me?"

"What have you told them?"

"Nothing. I don't know anything to tell them." I lifted my chin and said defiantly, foolishly, "Trust me, if I knew something, I'd tell them."

He pulled me closer, breathing his toxic breath into my face. "You need to be taught a lesson."

"Like you taught Josie? What has she learned? To stay wasted so she doesn't have to see what a loser you are?"

He released my arm and punched me in the face. The blow slammed into my mouth and jaw, sending me flying backward, and I landed hard on my butt. Blood trickled from the corner of my mouth, and I reached a hand up to wipe it away.

"You better not say shit, bitch." He slowly came toward me. "You better leave Josie out of it, too. She don't need you."

My cell phone rang and I looked to where it lay on the dining table.

"Don't even think about it," he warned. "You and me ain't done yet." He reached for the snap on his jeans, still coming toward me. "I think what you need is a man."

"No!" I crab walked backwards, trying to get away from him, but he kept coming. "Just leave, and I won't say anything."

He laughed. "That's right you won't say anything. Nothing except 'Oh, Matt, give it to me again,'" he said in a mocking falsetto.

Reaching down, he grabbed me by my hair and yanked me to my feet. I stumbled against him, then recoiled, gagging. He now had his pants undone and I could see the filthy underwear he wore.

He reached behind him. When his hand came back around, he was holding a knife. I let out a scream. His hold on my hair tightened. "Shut the fuck up." He ran the tip of the knife down my cheek and I felt blood again. It wasn't deep, not a gusher, just deep enough to break the skin.

Tears welled and I jerked at his hold. "Get the fuck out!" I screamed.

"After I have a little fun, I'm gonna fuck you up. I'll fuck your whole family up."

I laughed, a tearful, desperate sound. "My brothers will kill you. After they make you cry like a little girl."

He shoved me back and reached out to grab the front of my shirt, but I careened out of his grasp. Losing my balance, I once more landed on the floor, this time on my hands and knees.

A sound at the door caught my attention, and I looked up. Help had arrived. In the form of my eighty-two-year old neighbor.

"Marilyn? I heard—" Linus noticed Matt and his face became a thundercloud. "Hey, you listen here. I'm calling the—"

"You ain't calling shit, old man." Matt lunged toward him.

My fingers found the bottle of Tilex. I snatched it up and twisted the nozzle, coming to my feet.

"Hey, you shriveled-dick piece of shit," I screamed.

Matt whirled, the knife held out in front of him.

I aimed at his eyes and squeezed the trigger. He dropped the knife, his hands going to his face, and let out an agonized yell. The room filled with a noxious odor. I squatted and scrambled for the knife. My fingers closed over it as Matt lurched toward me.

"You fucking cunt! My eyes..." he made a retching sound and stumbled blindly in my direction.

He removed his hands from his face and blinked rapidly, his gaze roaming over the floor, probably looking for the knife. When he didn't find it, he lifted his head. His eyes were blood-red and pouring liquid, but they managed to focus on the knife I held toward his chest.

"Linus, you okay?" I asked.

"Yeah," he panted. "You?"

"I'm fine. Call the police."

Matt swiped at his face with his sleeve, then backed away. He kept backing until he was at the door that led outside, grappling for the knob.

"I'll see you again, bitch," he rasped, then opened the door and fled.

I heard Linus talking to the police, and I let the knife fall from my fingers. I was just now starting to feel the effects of my injuries. My jaw ached and my face felt as though a thousand bees had embedded their stingers. Not to mention, my rear-end was throbbing.

"You all right, honey?" Linus came toward me, holding a kitchen cloth. Gently, he dabbed at the blood on my face.

"I'm okay. Are you sure you're okay?"

"Yeah. Punk like that. I'da made mincemeat out of him. I was just about to when you sprayed him."

I smiled, tears once again filling my eyes, coursing down my face. I hadn't realized how frightened I was until that moment. Matt Lovell was a lunatic.

"Monroe? God. Are you okay?" I turned at the

voice.

Lane Brody stood in my doorway.

****

Monroe's hair hung free and tousled around her shoulders. She wore a pale pink robe, loosely belted. It appeared she was nude underneath. Lane tried not to think about that as he rushed over to her. "What happened? Lovell?"

Monroe nodded, her face battered and tear-stained. Tight, hot rage expanded in his chest. He had never wanted to kill so badly in his life. Not even when he'd found another man fucking his wife.

The old man with the hand towel said, "Bastard ran out the back door. Cops are on their way."

"Stay with her," Lane said, then headed outside. Monroe's yard wasn't large. There were a few trees, but not many hiding places. He searched quickly, along the fence line, even as far as to the cemetery. Not a sign of him anywhere. Lovell was long gone.

By the time Lane went back inside, a patrol car and ambulance had arrived. An EMT was seeing to Monroe and the old man.

A patrol cop stood in her living room, notepad in hand.

Lane nodded to the cop, then said to Monroe, "What was Lovell wearing?"

She told him, and Lane keyed his walkie-talkie. When dispatch answered, he said, "I need you to broadcast a pickup for a Caucasian male, Matthew Lovell." He gave the description. "Lovell was last seen in the vicinity of Tenth and Patrick. Might be on foot or might be driving a silver Nissan. Plate number unknown."

When he hung up, the EMT was speaking to Monroe. "Everything checks out. Nothing broken, but you might want to go the hospital just to be sure. You could have a slight concussion."

Monroe shook her head. "I'm okay."

"Please," Lane said. "Let a doctor take a look."

"No. I'm okay. Really."

Lane nodded at the ambulance attendant, and he left.

"This is my neighbor, Linus," Monroe said. "Linus, Detective Brody."

Lane shook the man's hand. His grip was surprisingly strong. "Thanks for coming to her rescue," Lane said.

"Little lady handled herself pretty good." Linus gave Monroe an affectionate smile.

"I want a car on them tonight," Lane said to the patrol cop. He turned to Monroe. "You two should stay together. It's easier to keep an eye on just one house."

"Linus can stay here," Monroe offered.

"I got my pooch at home. And my meds. Why don't you come stay with me?"

"No. I'm fine, really. I'll lock up. The car will be right outside. Our houses aren't that far apart. Matt doesn't know which house is Linus's, so he's probably safe. I doubt if the chicken shit will even be back. He's terrified of going to jail. Besides. Linus and I both have guns." She smiled, then winced and put a hand to her cheek where a white bandage covered her wound.

"Okay. But call if you need me." Linus gave Monroe a quick kiss on the forehead, then headed to the door.

"See him home," Lane told the officer.

When they were alone, Lane stared at Monroe silently, attempting to push back the fear and stay

145

focused. Like a cop.

"How did Lovell get in?" he asked.

"I'm not sure. I was in the shower." As if just realizing she still wore a robe—only a robe—she tightened the belt and crossed her arms over her middle. "When I came out, he was in my kitchen."

Lane clenched his jaw, picturing that asshole invading her home. Waiting for her when she came out of the shower... vulnerable, half-naked. He cleared his throat and said sharply, "Weren't your doors locked?"

"I think so. I usually lock them."

Lane shook his head. "And you couldn't have called us? Called *me*, as soon as you saw him?"

Her bottom lip quivered. "I wasn't... my phone was... I'm sorry. I couldn't get to my phone." She looked up at him, tears pooling in her eyes, making them look like liquid chocolate. "I'm sorry he got away."

She thought he was angry because Lovell escaped. Good. Let her think that. Safer that way.

"Did he give you any indication of where he was staying?"

"No. Nothing. He wanted to know what the police knew. What I'd told you."

"How would he know we'd even talked to you?"

Monroe shrugged.

"Unless your friend told him?"

"Josie wouldn't do that. She might have told him you were looking for him, but she wouldn't have told him I'd talked to the police. She wouldn't."

Lane didn't think Detweiler deserved Monroe's trust or loyalty, but he let it slide. He hoped he was right, though, that Monroe was mistaken, and that her friend *had* told Lovell the cops had asked Monroe about him.

The only other logical way Lovell would know Monroe had spoken to the cops was if he'd been following her.

"Did Lovell say anything to you at all that will help us locate him? We really need to find him. You understand that, right? Especially now."

"No, he didn't," she whispered, lowering her head. "I'm sorry."

A slight tremble shook her shoulders. It took all Lane had not to draw her into his arms and still her shaking, to make her tremble for another reason.

Jesus. What was wrong with him? Sexual thoughts at a time like this?

"You might want to put some clothes on," he barked.

Her head flew up and they met eyes. "Aren't you leaving? I'd like to go to bed. And, I apologize, Detective, but I don't wear clothes to bed." Her face colored and she added quickly, "I mean, I wear pajamas. Not clothes."

Lane sighed, feeling like an ass. "I'm sorry. Yes, I'm leaving. Just wanted to stay for a little while. Make sure the squad car's in place and that you're okay."

She nodded. "Would you like something to drink?"

"No, thanks. I'm fine. Can I get you something?"

"No. But I think I need to sit for a minute."

"Of course."

He held gently to her arm and led her into the living room. She lowered onto a sofa and he took the chair across from her. Even with the fumes of the Tilex in the air, he could smell her scent.

The room was dim, lit only by a small lamp on the table next to her. They sat in silence for several moments. An odd, warm intimacy settled between them. Lane tried to think of something to say, but couldn't. He just wanted to sit with her. Be with her. Know she was safe.

She sat with her back straight, her hands crossed and resting in her lap. She seemed tense, on edge.

"Hey," Lane said, scooting forward in his chair and reaching out to place a hand over hers… foolishly touching her. "Are you sure you're okay? You need to relax."

Without thinking about it, he began to lightly brush the skin on the back of her hand, marveling at the velvety softness of it. Unable to stop himself, he compared Catherine's dry cool touch to Monroe's warm, silky one.

Monroe's posture loosened, and she smiled tentatively. "I guess I am a little tightly wound."

"That's understandable after tonight." His voice was hoarse. He cleared his throat.

She nodded and unclasped her hands, turning them so that his fingers brushed her palms. Her breath hitched, and his breathing slowed, became labored.

Not speaking, they sat that way for several seconds, her staring down, him looking at her bent head. He didn't think she was even aware of it, but her knees parted slightly beneath their hands, revealing a strip of flesh along her thigh. He was mesmerized by that glimpse of skin, knowing it would be as soft, maybe softer, than that he was touching now. It made him instantly hard.

"Monroe?" His words came out an intimate whisper.

"Hmmm?" she said without lifting her head.

"I think I'm in trouble here."

Now she looked at him. "Why's that?" she asked softly.

His gaze dropped to her mouth where the full lips were marred only by the small cut at the corner.

"Because, all I can think about is what it would feel like to kiss you."

Her eyes rounded slightly, as if she were surprised at his words. Didn't she know what he'd been thinking, almost since the instant he'd met her? Wasn't his desire for her blatant? Couldn't she sense this overwhelming tug of attraction he was feeling?

She regarded him for a moment, then gave a small, knowing grin. "And you being married is where the trouble comes in?"

Lane barked a humorless laugh. "Yeah. That just about sums it up."

"So, this is sort of like the trivia. One of those useless facts you gather? What would it feel like to kiss Monroe Donovan?" Her smile was teasing.

"No," he said huskily. "Trivia facts are things I *know*. Kissing you, I can only imagine." *And have*, he added silently.

Neither of them spoke. Lane stared at her mouth, fighting the urge to taste it. She leaned slightly forward, that teasing smile still in place, her gaze still locked on his, and he nearly groaned in anticipation.

Suddenly, the smile dropped from her face, and she jumped to her feet. Her breasts momentarily swayed in his vision, and he had to suppress a gasp.

"I'm sorry. I don't know what's wrong with me." She moved away, turning her back to him and clenching the hair on top of her head. "I shouldn't have…"

He sighed deeply, hating himself for being an idiot.

Hating her for putting a stop to what had been about to happen.

"It's the adrenaline," he said tightly. "After the danger, it's natural. I'm the one who should apologize."

She faced him, but he spun toward the door.

"Lock up behind me," he said over his shoulder. "Don't open up for anyone except a uniformed officer."

He didn't need to add, 'or me,' because he damned sure wouldn't be back. "Try to get some sleep," he bit out. Even as he said it, he knew *he* wouldn't.

"Thank you," she said, but he was already heading out the door.

Chapter 10

My ringing phone dragged me from sleep hours before I was ready. I brought it to my ear and said hello, or something resembling the word.

"Monroe, dear? Did I wake you?"

Katie's mom, Corrine. I sat up and swiped a hand over my face, wincing when the pain in my jaw protested the action. "No, you didn't wake me."

"Can you come over? Right away?"

Straight to the point. No, "How are you, hon, how's the love life, the family?" All the usual chit chat before the inevitable, "Have you learned anything about my Katie?"

"What's wrong?" Monroe asked as she suppressed a yawn.

"I need to see you. Please. I'll cook breakfast."

So, she really meant *now*. Something had to have happened. But what? Couldn't be a development in Katie's murder—Corrine was no Jessica Fletcher—so what could have her so worked up?

"I'll be there as soon as I can."

I hung up the phone and crawled out of bed, crying out at the sharp pain in my tail bone, my knees, my head, pretty much everywhere.

I started the coffee and took a quick shower, then filled a travel cup and went to my car. The officer was still there, his squad car parked along the curb between my house and Linus's. He waved at me as I pulled out of the driveway. It was seven a.m. Linus would be awake. I dialed his number from my cell.

"Hello," he answered, sounding kind of perky for an eighty-two year old who'd nearly been attacked by a violent drug addict less than ten hours ago.

"Hey, Linus. It's me. You okay?"

"I'm good. How about you? What you doing up so early on a Sunday morning?"

"A friend called and needed to see me. I'm heading over there now."

"Everything all right? You're not messing with that Josie girl so soon after her punk boyfriend pulled that stunt, are you?"

"No. A different friend."

"Promise?"

"Promise."

After Linus extracted another promise that I'd be careful and that I'd let him know if I needed anything, we ended the call.

As I drove, I pondered Corrine's call. I couldn't imagine what it was about. Corrine and her husband, Vic, still held out the hope, even after all these years, that their daughter's killer would be found. Ten years ago, we'd pooled our money and hired a private detective. A year passed and he didn't find anything. The money ran out, so we had to let him go.

Since I was a journalist, Katie's parents thought I could solve the murder. I wanted to. I'd tried, but so far, not a clue. Not that the police had done much better. Although there'd been a suspect in both Katie's murder, and the one that happened the year before—a man who'd been released from prison after serving time for rape—

no arrest had been made. Apparently, there hadn't been enough evidence to file charges.

Corrine and Victor Broussard lived a mile from my parents, in the same house they'd lived in when I was a child.

I knocked on the door, and it opened to the smell of bacon and Corrine's embrace. Corrine was short, blonde, and pretty. She constantly wore a warm, beaming smile. The only time it had gone missing was in the years following Katie's death. It had slowly returned, but never had quite the same vitality. Since then, it seemed a little forced, brittle.

"My dear," Corrine said when she released me. "What happened to you?"

I knew she was referring to the bruise along my jaw line. I'd seen it in the mirror that morning.

"I fell," I said, uttering the standard cliché Josie, and most battered women, used.

"Come in. Vic's in the kitchen."

We walked through the living room where I tried to avert my eyes from the neon orange scrap of material draped over an easy chair. It was Katie's jacket. She'd slung it over the chair, probably just a few days before she died. Corrine hadn't gotten rid of it. Nor had she taken anything out of Katie's room. I'd been up there a few times since Katie died. Clothing was still scattered on the floor, although Corrine moved it from time to time to clean. Posters of a young Matt Dillon and Van Halen hung on the wall. Katie's favorite sparkly lip gloss still sat atop her dresser. I found it both endearing and worrisome.

Vic stood when I entered the kitchen and wrapped me in a bear hug. Out of our group of friends, Katie's dad had been the 'fine' dad we'd all had a bit of a crush on. He was tall and dark-haired with hazel eyes and the 'aquiline' nose and broad shoulders of the heroes in the category romances I read at the time. Now, although only in his mid-fifties, the looks were gone, worn away by time and grief. The height had given way to stooped shoulders, the hair gone gray, the hazel eyes marred by hopelessness.

"How do you want your eggs?" Corrine asked after I'd taken a seat at the Formica table.

"Scrambled."

She brought over a plate filled with eggs, toast, and bacon and set it in front of me, along with a glass of orange juice.

"Aren't you guys going to eat?" I asked.

"Already did," said Vic.

"We've been up for a while. Just waited to call so we didn't disturb you too early."

I almost asked what her definition of 'too early' would be on a Sunday after the hell night I'd had, but didn't.

The breakfast was good, and I was hungry. "So," I asked after I'd cleaned my plate, "what's this about?"

Corrine reached into the pocket of her slacks. She plunked down a penny on the table in front of me.

When no explanation followed, I looked up at her. "Yes?"

"Look at the year."

I did. 1971.

"Okay."

"That's the year Katie was born." I waited. "I found it on the day of her funeral. In her room. I've kept it close to me since. It brings me comfort."

Corrine had never told me this before. I didn't know why she was telling me now. I nodded and waited some more.

"You know the pennies from heaven story, right?"

"Yes. I read about it in Ann Landers. How people find pennies after losing a loved one. Pennies with a significant date. They feel it's a message from beyond the grave."

"Right."

"Okay. So, you waited twenty-five years to tell me you've been holding onto a penny from the year Katie was born?"

"It's not that," Vic said.

I glanced at him. Until now, he'd been sitting quietly, listening to his wife.

When he didn't offer more, Corrine spoke again. "I went to visit Katie's grave this morning."

"How early was that? You called me before seven." I felt guilty as soon as I said it. Didn't matter, though. Neither of them seemed to notice.

"I found this on her grave." She placed another penny in front of me. Without being told to, I picked it up and looked at the date. 1983. The year she died. I admit, it gave me a little chill. "Then, as I was leaving, right next to her tombstone—" Corrine stopped, her voice choked with tears. I didn't offer a hug. I knew if I did, that'd be it for both of us. We'd be lost in a torrent of sobbing. "Right next to her tombstone, was this." Another penny appeared.

I looked down, for some reason not wanting to touch it. She'd placed it head's up so I could still see the date. 1969.

"Okay," I said slowly. "So…?"

Her face paled. She wrung her hands together, staring down at the penny. "It wasn't there when I arrived," she said in a whisper. "I'm sure of it. I always clear everything around my little girl's resting place. I would have seen it."

"A penny is pretty small, maybe—"

"I would have seen it," she cut in sharply, stunning me into silence. "I'm sorry. But I *know*. This is a sign."

"What kind of sign?"

"About her murder. I'm not sure exactly what it means. Maybe the killer was born in 1969."

I quickly did the math. "So, you think a fourteen-year-old boy killed Katie?"

Of course, it wasn't impossible. Kids younger than that committed murder. It was less common in 1983, but not unheard of. Still, it didn't seem right to me. In my mind, I'd created an image of the killer. He was huge and mean and dirty and dark, with harsh features and menacing eyes. It didn't jive with a fresh-faced, pimply adolescent.

"It could have been," Corrine insisted. "There were some rough boys in the neighborhood."

"Rough boys?"

A nod. "The Simpsons, for one." She ticked it off on her finger like she was going to name more but didn't.

"The Simpsons?" I almost laughed, but this wasn't the time for amusement. The Simpsons were three brothers, Eric, Josh, and Steven. They were around mine and Katie's age, although the oldest one might have been fourteen, which would match the date of birth on the penny. They ran the neighborhood all hours of the night and were notorious for practical jokes. The worst thing I knew of them doing was lighting a bag of excrement on

Mr. Gruber's porch, hiding, and watching while the man rushed out and stomped on it. Not exactly saintly, but a far cry from murdering a twelve-year-old girl. Katie and I had thought it was funny.

"I'm not sure if any of this means anything," I said, then remembered something that might be relevant. "The suspect they had back then. Wasn't his first victim fourteen?" As I uttered the words, I realized it sounded as though I was actually buying into the 'pennies from heaven' angle.

Corrine nodded slowly, looking at me as though I'd parted the Red Sea. "You're right. You're so smart, Monroe. I knew I should come to you. This will help you figure it out."

"I'm not so sure about that, but I'll do what I can. You know I will."

Corrine nodded again and stared at a spot over my shoulder. "You know, we almost lost Katie at birth." I did know. I'd heard the story before about how Katie had been premature, her lungs not fully developed, and the doctors gave her a fifty-fifty chance of survival. I also knew that Corrine hadn't been able to conceive after. Katie was their only child and she'd been brutally ripped from them. "I'm not sure why God would take her from us when she was a miracle baby, but it's not up to me to question. I do, however, question why her killer would get by with it. Why he is free to live his life when my baby isn't." Tears welled, then spilled down her cheeks. "Every day, I expect her to walk through the door, to tell me it was all some kind of horrible joke and she's home for good. Funny thing is, even though it was twenty-five years ago, I expect her to still be twelve." She looked at me now and her voice dropped to a tortured whisper.

"She'll always be twelve."

I nodded, unable to speak around the lump in my throat.

"We can't rest until the person who did this is caught. Until he pays for taking my baby girl." She put a finger on the penny, pushing it toward me. "Take this. It might help."

I regarded it as I would a brown recluse spider. "I don't need it. I'll remember 1969."

She shook her head vigorously and said, "You keep it. I don't want it in my house."

****

Cobra located Teresa, the girl who'd heard Ramirez shooting off his mouth. He set up a meeting at a tiny, dimly lit café on Troost Avenue. When Lane and Tony went inside, Cobra was already there, sitting at a table with an overweight Asian and a malnourished female who could have been any age from fifteen to fifty. The other four tables were empty.

The café held no food smells, only the odors of urine, unwashed bodies, and incense that did a poor job of covering the scent of weed.

"This here's Big Eddie," Cobra said after they'd taken seats around the scarred table.

Lane turned to the woman. "You Teresa?"

"No one talks to her less they go through me," Big Eddie said, his voice much softer than Lane would have expected, coming from such a large body.

Lane considered ignoring the command, then decided the quickest way to get information was to play along.

"You weren't there the day the guy was spouting off about the shooting, right?" Lane asked Big Eddie. When

Eddie shook his head, Lane said, "Then I need you to ask her about it. We need to know who else was around."

Big Eddie turned to the woman and repeated the question, as if she hadn't just heard Lane say the same thing. Lane wondered—if Big Eddie was her keeper, her spokesperson—how she had managed to be without him when she was hanging with Ramirez. Maybe the no speaking rule only extended to cops.

Teresa stared off for a few seconds, thin fingers picking at the scab on her lower lip. She turned dull, red-streaked eyes to Eddie. "Don't remember."

"You better remember." Big Eddie's soft voice rose to a menacing growl.

Eyes coming into focus long enough to appear frightened, Teresa squinted. "Some old guy. A few more... a chick came at the end." She shrugged. "Don't know names. They're just... you know... bodies and shit."

Big Eddie reached out and gripped her upper arm and Teresa flinched, her face showing pain, the first emotion Lane had seen her display.

"Hey, let her go, man," Tony said. "She's doing her best."

Big Eddie turned his mean, small eyes on Tony. "Don't tell me how to deal with my woman."

He lifted a large hand, clenching it in a fist and pulling back as if to punch her.

Lane's arm shot out and he gripped Big Eddie by the wrist. Big Eddie turned his piggish eyes on Lane. "What the fuck? You come into my crib and disrespect me?" He released Teresa and started to stand.

Before the big man knew what happened, Lane snaked his grip from Eddie's wrist to his throat, digging into the fleshy neck and squeezing. Eddie's hands grappled with Lane's as he dropped back into his chair, his face turning a reddish purple. He couldn't budge Lane's hold and, after a second, gave up, wheezing and staring at Lane with the eyes of a dying fish.

Bringing his face close enough to smell Eddie's rancid breath, Lane said, "We came here to talk to your girl. Don't want any trouble, but if you touch her, that's exactly what you'll get. Now, give the lady a chance to speak, show her some respect, and we'll be out of your hair. Screw with us, and I'll yank your larynx right out of your fat throat."

Big Eddie might not have known what a larynx was, but he nodded as vigorously as Lane's grip would allow, eager to please.

Lane let him go. Big Eddie massaged his throat with both beefy hands, glaring.

"In case you're thinking of teaching her a lesson after we're gone, my good friend, Cobra, here is going to keep an eye on you both. Word gets back to me you've so much as wrinkled her clothing, I'll be on you harder than a pit bull on a pork chop."

Although his eyes spewed hatred, Big Eddie's voice was conciliatory. "Sure, yeah. Just got a little carried away. Teresa," he looked at the woman, "anything you can remember to help these dudes… just say."

Teresa shrugged, looking from Lane to Tony, then to Big Eddie. "Told you all I can. Dude was running his mouth. Some freaks was around. 'sall I know."

"Thanks for your time." Tony looked at Cobra. "You hear anything, let us know."

"You got it." Cobra nodded. "You da man."

Tony and Lane left and as they slid into the car,

Tony said, "You know he's not gonna stop, right?"

"What?" Lane squeezed his eyes shut and rubbed the bridge of his nose with his thumb and forefinger. Being around dimwitted assholes always gave him a headache.

"Wailin' on the girl. You know your threat didn't mean diddly shit to him. It's in his blood."

"Yeah. I know."

"So, other than giving you a chance to exercise your machismo, that was pretty much a waste. Still have no idea if or how the killer got wind of Ramirez's bullshit."

Lane sighed and scrubbed his hands over his face, regretting it instantly when he once again smelled the stink of the café...of Big Eddie.

He pulled an anti-bacterial towelette out of the canister they kept in the Crown Vic and wiped his hands with it, then tucked it into the cup holder.

"Maybe she'll remember something later," he said without conviction.

Tony slid a stick of gum into his mouth and chewed. "Yeah, right. Bet it's been a while since that chick remembered anything."

Lane thought of her wasted body, her spaced out gaze, her perpetual confusion. "Yeah," he agreed. "Most likely a long while."

****

Although I was preoccupied with the thing with Matt, the thing with Josie, my looming unemployment, and the thing with the pennies, I remembered to do something I'd thought about since meeting Headphone. Well, I hadn't exactly 'met' him, but I still felt acquainted.

I dug out some of my CD's I seldom listened to and

took those, along with a sixteen-pack of double A batteries, with me when I left for work on Monday morning. There were no Elvis CD's in the batch, but I justified this with the idea that he probably didn't care for Elvis, rather than admit I didn't want to part with them.

Professor and Headphone were, predictably, sitting next to the fountain in front of the newspaper.

As I approached, I heard a song coming from Headphone's headphones, but couldn't distinguish which one it was.

After saying good morning to him and the professor, I extended the plastic Wal-Mart bag that held my gifts toward Headphone. He didn't look up.

"What's that you have there?" the professor asked.

"I brought him some CD's and batteries."

"Bless you," the professor said. "He plays this same tiring song over and over."

"What is it?"

"'Escape' by Rupert Holmes."

"Not familiar with that," I said.

"Oh, but I'm sure you are. Most people call it the "Pina Colada Song" and think Jimmy Buffet did it. But, they're incorrect."

"Right," I said. "Now I know the song. It's his favorite?"

The professor shrugged. "His current favorite. The previous one was some hootenanny country music CD. I never thought I'd say this, but I long for those days again."

"Hey," I said. "I like country music."

He grinned. "I promise not to hold it against you, my dear." He nodded toward Headphone. "He's played that continually since he got it. He told me some man who was passing by gave it to him. I'd like to give his benefactor a piece of my mind."

"He told you that?" I asked, unable to imagine the man speaking to anyone.

"He communicates from time to time." The professor took the bag from me. "I'm sure he'll enjoy these as soon as he's worn that one out. Or, as soon as I get sick enough of it that I rip it from the player and smash it to pieces." He smiled. "He'll certainly make use of the batteries. That's very kind of you. I'll thank you for him since he is either incapable or simply rude."

I grinned and said goodbye, heading into the office.

Asia went ballistic when she saw my face.

"What the hell happened to you?"

Sighing, I recounted the details of Matt's assault.

"That sorry little prick. Wait 'til I tell Darion. He'll pound his hippie ass to dust."

I had no doubt that Darion could do just that and allowed myself a few moments fantasizing about it before shaking my head. "No one can seem to find him. He comes and goes at will, then disappears into his hidey-hole whenever the cops come around."

"Speaking of cops. Lane Brody came to your rescue? How romantic."

I rolled my eyes, even though a thrill of warmth crept through me at the memory of his touch. "Didn't exactly come to my rescue. Linus did. The worst was pretty much over by the time Lane arrived."

"You have your version, I have mine." She smiled widely. "Mine is much sexier, believe me."

"Jesus, Asia, he's *married*. Let it go."

"Screw 'married.' I hear there's something wonky

about his marriage. His wife is mental or something. Besides, how married is anybody these days, really?"

At my raised eyebrows, she said, "Oh, not me. Darion and I are doing fine, in spite of my occasional fantasies. I just look around and, you know, marriage is pretty fleeting in most cases."

"You're preaching to the choir, my dear."

"I mean, take A-hole Adam's little woman. She screwed around on her man, left him for another guy, and now has a restraining order against him. Ask me, he's the one needs a VPO against that crazy bitch."

"She has a restraining order against her ex? Why?"

Asia shrugged. "Hell, why does anybody? Maybe he stalked her or maybe she just doesn't want him around. I can't figure out what crazy bitches are thinking."

"How did you even know about it?"

Another shrug. "What can I say? I know things."

"Is there anything that goes on that you don't know about?"

"Let's just say if I don't know about it, it ain't worth knowing." She looked over my shoulder. "Speak of the Devil Bitch."

I turned to see Tabitha come in with Adam, leaning her head toward him to listen intently to whatever he was saying. When Adam saw me, he left Tabitha's side and rushed over.

He peered down at me, his gaze trained on my jaw. "Monroe. Good God, what happened?"

I heaved a sigh, already weary of repeating the story. I did it anyway.

"Did the police catch the son of a bitch?" Adam asked, his voice sharp with concern.

"No. Not yet."

I glanced at Tabitha, who'd caught up to Adam in time to hear our conversation. I noted a glimpse of resentment on her face before it was masked. "That's just awful, Monroe. I'm so sorry."

"Sorry's right," Asia muttered under her breath, and I cut her a look.

"Thanks, Tabitha," I said.

"You know," Tabitha turned to Adam, "this is why you need to do something about those creeps hanging around outside."

"Creeps?" Adam said.

"Those nasty homeless people. You never know when someone might go off. I could be the next one hurt. You need to keep them away from here."

"It's a free sidewalk, hon," Adam said distractedly, still gazing at me with a look of sympathy. "Are you sure you're okay?" he asked.

"I'm fine," I said, a little uncomfortable at his attention, and peeved at Tabitha's remarks. "Those people out there aren't hurting anyone," I told her. "They're not dangerous."

Her lips curved. If she was trying for a smile, she failed miserably. But she would get an A plus if a derisive sneer was her aim. "With the company you keep, Monroe dear, I'm afraid you're not exactly the one to decide who is and isn't dangerous." She said this as if I'd been blithely, willingly entertaining Matt when something went horribly wrong.

Asia cut a look at Adam. "Yes, we're all guilty of slumming with the dregs of society from time to time." Her gaze went back to Tabitha. "No accounting for taste, right?"

Red dots of fury appeared on Tabitha's cheeks, but

Asia took me by the arm and swept me away to my cubicle before she could respond.

****

Lane pulled a chair next to Tony's desk and straddled it, waiting for him to get off the phone. Tony cocked his head and tugged upward with a clenched fist next to his neck, pantomiming hanging himself. Must be talking to the ex.

"No," he said patiently into the phone. "I did not call you a cunt. I would never do that. I *like* cunts." At her response, he flinched and held the phone away from his ear. Lane could hear Amy's high-pitched tirade but couldn't make out the words. Pulling the receiver back to his ear, Tony scratched his fingers along the mouthpiece. "Huh? Sorry, can't... bad sig... talk... later..." Drawing the phone away once more, he punched the end button.

Lane clapped his hands. "Bravo. Magnificent performance."

"Hey, I do what I can for the fans." Tony leaned back and linked his hands behind his head. "We've been going at it for months. She says I should only get the kids every other weekend, no holidays, and no phone calls between my visits. Hell, my kids moved to Wichita. You think I'm gonna not even call 'em?" Tony had two kids, a boy and a girl. The boy was ten and the girl was around thirteen or fourteen. She would soon be at the age where she no longer wanted to spend time with her dad, so Lane could understand Tony wanting to take advantage of every opportunity. "The ex wants the house but doesn't want to pay me my part of the equity. She wants to keep the truck and me to take the Cavalier. I told her I wasn't driving a woman's car. She also wants the boat."

"Jesus. You're going to pay out the ass in attorney fees if you keep going back and forth. Can't you make some kind of counter offer? Come to some kind of terms?"

Tony shook his head. "Nope. I don't negotiate with terrorists."

Lane chuckled. Oddly, he was envious of Tony's bitter, vicious, Ali-Frazier style divorce. It was preferable to the way his marriage had ended.

"How's Monroe Donovan?" Tony asked.

Lane shrugged. "Haven't talked to her."

Tony narrowed his eyes. "You haven't checked on her since Lovell nearly killed her? Jesus, Huck. Some knight in shining armor you are."

Lane let it pass. He'd given Tony a rundown of what had taken place, leaving out his near fatal hard-on.

"The bastard is slicker than greased bat shit," Lane said. "Faded right back into the woodwork. Can't get a bead on him. Not even a hint of where he might be."

Leaning forward, Tony picked up the file on the B and B killing. "Yeah, and we've got this one yanking our nads, too." He flipped through the paperwork, reading the notes aloud, even though Lane already knew most of what was there. "Ramirez's roommates knew nothing. Said, let's see… on Tuesday, the night before he bought it, Ramirez told them the same story he told the street people. Saw two guys approach Hebringer." He sighed. "Maybe we are looking for two shooters."

"Bay seemed certain Garrett was making it up. Nothing points to two shooters, other than his story. Hell, I'd settle for finding one shooter at the moment."

"If the same guy did Hebringer and Ramirez, he's not always a shooter. Likes knives, too."

"Probably uses whatever fits the circumstances. A gunshot outside of Ziggy's would have drawn attention."

Still flipping through the file, Tony said, "Ran a list of construction workers in the area, checking for anyone with a record. Plenty of hits, but not any with this guy's M.O. Not many to do with firearms at all."

"Did the footprint cast come back?"

"Yeah. Size ten and a half." Tony looked up. "My size. Whew! Case solved." He slapped the file closed. "We got shit, Huck. Diddly shit."

Lane tapped his fingers on the back of the chair, thinking. "Okay, we know what we don't have. Let's talk about what we do have. Construction dust at the scene. The message painted on a tree. Ballistics report confirms the weapon was a Smith and Wesson .38 special. Nothing came up through NIBIN." NIBIN was the National Integrated Ballistics Information Network that searched ballistics data for links to other crimes. The gun used in Hebringer's death didn't get a hit. "And, this homicide is possibly linked to the murder of a homosexual man who was a guest at the bed and breakfast the night Hebringer was killed—"

"Possibly?"

Lane shrugged. "If we're dealing with only what we know, it's just a 'possible' link. The murder weapon was different. No messages left at the scene."

Tony nodded. "And, since Teresa didn't know her own name, let alone who else was around at the time, we don't know how many people might have heard Ramirez's story. The killer could have been in the group, listening."

"Yeah. Or, the way word gets around on the streets, he could have heard it the same way Dupree did.

168

Through the grapevine."

"Limitless possibilities and no cold, hard, facts. No evidence, no eye witnesses." Tony's face took on an expression of rapturous delight. "This is starting to be my *most* favorite kind of case."

****

"Did they find the prick yet?" Asia asked.

Matt was 'the prick,' Adam was 'the asshole,' so I knew who she was referring to. Besides, unfortunately, Adam wasn't missing.

"Not that I know of."

"Any word from Josie?"

I shook my head, not looking at her. I was trying to get the last of the obits in before deadline and there were many. It seemed people had been keeping themselves busy dying lately.

"You know," Asia said. "If you weren't friends with her, this would never have happened."

I closed my eyes and sighed. "No lectures right now, 'kay? I'm kind of busy."

"Darion's been itching to get hold of the prick ever since I told him what happened."

"If I find him, Darion will be the first one I call," I murmured distractedly.

Asia said more, but I didn't catch it. My eyes were riveted on my computer screen. The obituary I was working on listed the date of death as November seventh. Today was the fifth.

Weird. In all the time I'd done this, I'd never received an obit with the wrong date. Now I'd gotten two within a couple of weeks?

A trickle of unease wound through my body, but I wasn't sure why. Nothing menacing about a typo.

I sent a reply email to the person who'd submitted the obit, letting them know they'd listed an incorrect date. The deadline was looming, though, so I didn't expect to hear back from them in time. I picked up the phone to call Adam.

"Hey, you listening to me?" Asia again.

"Sorry, actually, I'm not. I'm trying to get some work done. Maybe you should, too."

"Fine," she huffed. "I'll save my pearls of wisdom for someone who appreciates them."

She stalked away, managing to look regal even when she was pissed.

I dialed Adam's extension. "Yes?" he answered briskly.

"I received an emailed obituary with the wrong date listed."

"What? Another one?"

"Yeah. The date of death is listed as this coming Friday."

"Did you email them about it?"

"I did. But, just now. I just discovered it. I doubt we'll hear back before this has to go in. Want me to hold off or print it without the date?"

"Shit." I heard him sigh. "If you don't hear back, print it without the date. The family will be more upset if it doesn't go in than if it goes in without a date. They won't have much right to be pissed, since it's their error."

"Okay. I'll give them a few minutes. If I don't hear back in time, I'll send it through minus the date."

He hung up without saying goodbye. Geez. Like he was the only busy one around here.

I finished up the other obituaries and still hadn't heard from the Lohman family, so I removed the date and sent the obit through.

As I did, I wondered why my trepidation lingered.

Chapter 11

Rain lashed the living room window and pounded the roof, sounding like marbles dropping on concrete. Streaks of lightning burst through the cracks in the wooden blinds. An Elvis CD—*That's the Way it is*—played on the stereo, but it was struggling to compete with the crescendo of the storm.

I hoped the power stayed on, for many reasons, but mainly because I was on my computer.

Two years ago, when I'd been a crime reporter for the *Star*, a young girl, Maya Pittman, had been murdered, and I'd done the story. Her killing was vaguely similar to Katie's and Cassie Carthage's—the girl killed the year before Katie—but the police didn't link the crimes. Nor did they make an arrest. In Maya's case, her male teacher had been the prime suspect. They'd been having an affair. As far as I knew, the police were still investigating him, but apparently hadn't found enough evidence to make an arrest. At seventeen, Maya was older than Katie and Cassie had been, but the murder shared many of the same characteristics in that Maya was also choked and sexually assaulted, and her body was also found in a wooded area.

Over the past few years, I'd randomly researched murdered girls on the Internet—especially those whose cases were unsolved—hoping I could find something that would help me to solve Katie's. Or, at least, stumble across some kind of information I could take to the police so they'd reopen Katie's case. So far, nothing like that had occurred and lately, I'd been neglecting that task. After speaking with Corrine, my guilt had inspired me to renew my amateur investigation.

At the moment, staring at a photo of Brie Samuels, sadness weighted my heart. Brie had only been thirteen when she was murdered. Her killer had never been caught. She lived in a small town near Omaha, Nebraska, the daughter of divorced parents. She disappeared one weekend, but it took them several days to even realize she was missing. It was during the summer. Her father thought she was at her mother's, the mother thought she was with her father. Shortly after they discovered she was gone, her nude, stabbed body was found in a corn field by volunteers.

The information to be found on the Internet was limited, but I had to do what I could. Especially after my visit to Corrine and Vic. They were counting on me. Katie was counting on me.

I picked up the penny. I wasn't sure why Corrine thought I should have it, but I'd kept it on my computer desk since she'd given it to me. I didn't know if I believed in it or not, but from what I understood, the pennies from heaven thing was supposed to be about comfort. Not about being creeped out over a murder. I turned the penny over in my hand. 1969. Did it mean anything? Were these truly messages from Katie or was I getting as removed from reality as Corrine?

A thundering noise sounded, making me jump. At first I attributed it to the storm, then I realized that wasn't what it was. Someone was knocking on my door. And making a hell of a racket in the process.

Matt?

My heart thumped in rhythm with the beat of the pounding. This time, I'd be armed. I grabbed my .22 from the top of the closet in the foyer. I'd learned to shoot growing up with my brothers, and as a single woman living alone, they'd insisted I have a weapon for protection. In all these years, I'd never gotten it out. Until now.

I went to the door and peered through the peephole. I flipped on my porch light, but with the rain and the darkness, I couldn't make out anything but shadows. I shouted, "Who's there?"

The words that came back were muffled by the storm, but it sounded like he said, "Lane."

I took my chances and swung the door open.

Lane stood on my porch, holding a limp body in his arms.

"Jesus Christ. Josie," I whispered, stepping back quickly so he could come in.

I shut the door and whirled to face him. "Is she… dead?" My voice was strangled with fear.

Lane shook his head. "She's not dead. She's loaded out of her mind, though."

I realized then how stupid my question was. Like Lane would bring my friend's dead body here.

He glanced down at the .22, and I turned and shoved it back in the top of the closet, not offering an explanation.

"Here, come through here." I led him into the living room where he lowered Josie gently onto the couch. A black raincoat covered her. I was sure it belonged to Lane. "What…? How…?"

"Right now, you need to get her out of those wet

clothes and into something warm. Do you have coffee or tea?"

"Not made. I can make some."

"I'll do it while you get her into something dry."

Lane disappeared into the kitchen, and I rushed into my bedroom, yanking a pair of sweats from my dresser drawer. On the way back, I grabbed a large bath towel.

Hurrying into the living room, I bent over Josie and threw off the raincoat. Her jeans were sodden, the thin T-shirt plastered to her skin. Getting the clothes off her was a chore. She was dead weight and they clung to her skin like bark to a tree.

Finally, after a battle akin to that waged by Sparta, I managed to peel them from her, then dried her briskly with the towel. Her skin was so pale, it seemed to glow. I tugged the sweats over her body, and Lane came back into the room, carrying a steaming mug. "I made her tea with honey."

"Did she O.D.?" I asked worriedly, spreading an afghan over her.

"No. She's just loaded."

"Should we get her to vomit?"

Lane grimaced. "She already did."

"Oh, in your car?" At his nod, I said, "Sorry about that."

"Not a big deal. I'm a cop. I've had worse things happen."

He squatted next to the couch and put his arm behind her shoulders. "I'll raise her up. You see if you can get her to drink some of the tea."

I did as he asked. Some of it ran down Josie's chin as I tilted the cup to her lips, but some made it inside.

She frowned and tried to pull away from me, but

Lane held her firmly.

"Should we just let her sleep?" I asked.

"She needs liquid so she doesn't dehydrate. She also needs something in her system to dilute the drugs."

I fed her more of the tea. She swallowed noisily. Her eyes flitted open, and she stared up at me. The dark pupils nearly obliterated the green of her eyes. Yep. Loaded.

"What's the…? Roe?" Her words were barely decipherable. "What am I… Oh, God," she groaned and fell back limply against Lane's arm.

"Yes, it's me, Josie. Are you okay?"

"Gotta get offem," she mumbled. "Thas how he keeps me comin' 'round. Keeps me tied to 'im. Knows I need the drugs." Suddenly, she giggled. "Oh shit. Cops 'ere and I'm talkin' 'bout drugs."

I looked at Lane. "Why did you bring her here instead of arresting her? How did you come to be with her?"

"He's a good man," Josie said, her eyes drifting shut once more. "He'll take care…"

"Is there a bed you want her in?" Lane asked. "She needs to sleep this off."

I nodded. He lifted Josie in his arms, and I led him to the guest room. I pulled back the covers so Lane could lay Josie on the bed.

As I tucked the blankets beneath her chin, she said, "Maybe Katie's the lucky one." Her eyes bore into mine, tears swimming, running down her face into the pillow. "At least she's free."

Tears surfaced in my own eyes. "Shhh, sweetie. Just sleep, okay? You'll feel better tomorrow."

She closed her eyes, and I stood next to her until I

heard small snores coming from her and saw the slow rise and fall of her chest.

Lane and I returned to the living room. His hair was plastered to his head, dark with rain. The shirt he wore was probably supposed to be a light shade of blue, but it had also darkened with the water.

"Would you like something to drink?" I asked, itching to know what the hell had happened but trying to be patient.

He shook his head. "I drank some water while I waited for the tea."

"Would you like something dry to put on? I might have a sweatshirt that will fit you. Actually, I think I have a few of my brother's things. He does his laundry here sometimes."

"No. I'm fine. I'll dry."

"Hold on." I went down the hall and got another towel. I returned, handing it to him. "You can at least get part of the moisture absorbed."

"Thanks." He took it and dabbed at his shirt, then rubbed it over his hair.

"What happened? I mean…" I lifted my hands, let them drop. "How did you come to be with Josie?" I repeated my earlier question.

"I got a tip on Lovell's location. By the time I got there, he was gone. Josie was there, though. She was in a bad way, so I couldn't leave her."

"You could have taken her to jail."

He was quiet for a long moment. I waited.

"That's not what she needs right now. She needs to get off the drugs, but not in jail."

A knot of tears formed at the base of my throat. "Thank you," I whispered.

He shrugged. "I know you've been worried about her. Thought you'd worry less if she were here."

I nodded and impulsively stepped toward him. I gave him a quick hug, rain-soaked shirt and all. The brief contact with his hard chest was unexpectedly pleasurable. My breath quickened as I stepped away. "Really. Thanks."

"Maybe you can help her get into rehab," he suggested.

"I will. I've tried, but not that forcefully. I've been accused of enabling."

"Time for tough love."

"You sound like my friend. And my brother."

He smiled and those enticing crinkles appeared at the corners of his eyes. The blue irises sparked like an electrical current moved behind them. A sizzle zipped through the air that I couldn't attribute to the storm. His gaze moved slowly over my face. His voice was husky as he said, "Funny. What I'm feeling right now is far from brotherly."

"Yeah?" I said, but my throat was dry and the word came out a croak.

"Yeah."

Married, married, married.

I let the words beat into my skull and used them as a cloak against the intense sexual attraction building for Lane Brody. His Good Samaritan bullshit didn't help matters at all. Damn him for making me *like* him, too.

"I could actually use something to drink," I said. "You sure you don't want anything?"

"I'm sure. Thanks."

I went to the kitchen, calling over my shoulder, "Have a seat, if you'd like."

I grabbed a bottle of water from the fridge and twisted off the cap, downing most of it in one swallow. I thought about sticking my head in the freezer to cool off, but it was a different part of my body that was affected, so I didn't.

When I returned, Lane was sitting on the sofa. I felt an irrational thrill that he wasn't leaving yet. I sat on the chair he'd occupied the night Matt came to the house.

Searching for a non lust-inducing topic, I said, "So, how long have you been married?"

A cloud seemed to pass over his features. "Ten years."

I tried to quell my disappointment that he didn't add, *But, we're separated, just waiting for the divorce to be final. I still wear the ring because I've been too busy to take it off.*

"Does she worry about you?" I added hastily, "I mean, being a cop and all."

He shook his head slowly. "She's been in the hospital... long term. She's not really... aware... of much these days." His smile had a bitter edge to it. "Even before then, she wasn't particularly concerned about my well-being."

"I'm so sorry," I said, recalling Asia's words about his wife being mental.

He nodded and looked toward the window where a bolt of lightning had just cut a jagged tattoo across my blinds. "Did you know that a bolt of lightning travels up to 100 million feet per second?"

I shook my head and grinned. "I thought it was *50* million feet per second, but what do I know?"

He chuckled. "Sorry. It's kind of reflex." His restless cobalt eyes traveled over my face and hesitated at my lips. He cleared his throat. "Maybe I'll take that water after all."

"Sure." I went into the kitchen and grabbed a bottle of water. When I returned, I handed it to him, holding my breath for just a second when our fingers almost touched. As he took off the cap and tilted the bottle to his lips, I said, "So, why did you become a cop? Let me guess. You grew up watching *Starsky and Hutch* and wanted to be just like them? Or, it's because you come from a long line of cops. Small town southern sheriffs, right?"

I realized I was babbling, but there was something about this night, the rain, the gratitude I felt toward this man, the blue of his eyes, the shirt becoming more their color as the moisture evaporated. Not to mention, I hadn't had sex in a really, really long time.

"Yeah, I watched those shows." Lane laughed. "I didn't come from a long line of cops, though. My dad was a welder, but he left us when I was five."

He looked down for a moment, and I wondered what that must have felt like. A five-year-old boy abandoned by his father. I wanted to ask him more about it. Had his mother remarried? Raised him alone? Had he seen his father since? But I didn't want to pry. He'd tell me what he wanted me to know.

"I didn't set out to be a cop," he said. "I thought I wanted to be an attorney. I was going to law school. One day, I was at the bank, waiting in line in the lobby. Three guys came in with guns. Robbed the bank, terrorized the customers and the poor girls working the teller lines. No one was injured, and the guys were caught that very day. I was back in the bank the following week. The teller who waited on me was young, no more than eighteen or nineteen. I asked her how she was and she said, 'Fine, sir, and how are you today?' I was talking about the robbery, but she still tried to be professional, be brave. There was a quiver in her voice and it infuriated me at the crooks who would dare to do that to a young girl, just trying to do her job. I decided I'd rather be one of the cops who brought assholes like that down than the attorney who got them convicted, or worse, got them off." He looked at me, a smile lifting the corner of his mouth. "Sorry if I bored you. Didn't mean to give you the long version."

"No. You didn't bore me. That's a terrific story."

"So, tell me. Who's Katie?"

"What?" I asked, startled.

"Josie mentioned Katie."

"Oh, yes."

I didn't say more. I hardly ever talked about Katie, at least not to people who hadn't known her. I met his eyes and saw curiosity there. I also saw a glimmer of something else. Maybe he was feeling the same sexual tension I was. The third being in the room. Almost a living, breathing force.

"I saw how you reacted when she said Katie's name," he said. "You don't have to tell me, but…"

"But?"

He stared at me, his gaze intense and compelling, sucking the oxygen from the room. "I don't want to leave just yet." His voice was low, gruff. "Maybe it's safer if we talk."

What would you rather be doing? I wanted to ask, but didn't, because I knew. I could feel the pull, the axis of desire swirling between us.

And, he was married. Happily or not. Ill wife or not.

Married. I didn't need to make any more mistakes. I didn't need any more heartache. From the looks of him, he didn't either.

"Right." I nodded and closed my eyes, swallowing back tears, working up the courage to talk about Katie. Opening my eyes again, but not looking at him, I said, "It happened when we were twelve. Katie, Josie and I were best friends. Inseparable. We were camping out in my back yard. My parents went out for the evening and my brothers were home with us. Actually, I'm sure my parents were home by the time... when Katie..." I sucked in a breath as a jagged pain ripped through me with the memory. "Sometime during the night, Katie disappeared," I whispered. "There was a search party. In the wee hours of the morning, one of our neighbors found her body. She'd been murdered."

I swallowed again... waited for him to speak. When he didn't, I looked at him and went on, "No one was ever arrested for her murder. They had a suspect. He'd done time for a rape. He was also suspected in the murder of another young girl a year earlier. They could never get enough evidence to make an arrest." Standing, I walked to the window and looked out over the darkened neighborhood, not really seeing the falling rain, my mind on that night long ago. I spoke without turning around. "It tore two families apart. A whole neighborhood, really. But my parents were especially devastated. Blamed themselves. Katie's parents blamed them, too. They said if my parents had been home, it never would have happened. Which wasn't true. They would have been inside the house and would have had no idea what we were doing." I gathered the hair on top of my head and squeezed, closing my eyes against the tears. Against the memories. "I think my parents were home by then, anyway. By the time Katie—"

I stopped. Took a breath. Released my hair and swallowed.

I hadn't heard him rise, but Lane was suddenly beside me. He reached out and put a hand on my shoulder. Lightly. Comforting.

"I'm sorry," he said softly.

I nodded. "It wasn't their fault. Katie's parents knew my parents were going out. Knew we were spending the night in the back yard. It was a safe neighborhood. They weren't worried. But after…" I shrugged. "I guess they just needed someone to blame."

"I'm sure they did," Lane said, but I was barely aware of him speaking. I was lost in that time. Now that I had started, it all kept pouring out.

"Although Mom and Dad felt guilty, they were defensive when Katie's parents accused them. It caused a huge rift, and they never spoke again. Funny, but Katie's parents didn't hold it against me or Josie. As a matter of fact, I became even closer to them as the years went by. Katie was an only child, and I guess it helped to have me around. My parents didn't mind. They felt terrible about what happened. Almost guilty about the fact that they had four children left when the Broussards had none. My brothers were devastated. Especially Gabe, since he was left in charge. Coburn, as usual, was a rock, but Mitch and Gabe went to pieces. It had the opposite effect on each of them. Gabe, who'd been wild and out of control, settled down, became quiet. Wound up becoming a priest. Mitch went a little crazy for a few years. Got really heavy into drugs. Josie did, too. Only, Mitch came back."

"Must have been horrible."

"It was."

We started junior high that year. It was miserable. I already had a reputation for being a little morbid since my dad was a mortician. After Katie's death, rumors circulated about my family being cultists. About how we'd put some kind of curse on her. Some even said we'd sacrificed her in a ritual and eaten her flesh. Josie became a stoner and I became an outcast. My brothers, oddly, went unscathed. They were just too good-looking and had too much personality to let a little thing like ritualistic murder affect their popularity.

"I was in Alabama at the time," Lane said. "I guess it didn't make it on the news there. I never heard about it. I would have been, let's see… fourteen. Didn't pay a lot of attention to the news back then."

Fourteen. A shiver ran down my spine. It was silly, though. The pennies meant nothing.

"Even with all the accusations flying around, truth was, if my parents had been home, it wouldn't have changed anything. If Gable had checked on us again, it wouldn't have changed anything. The only thing that would have changed what happened is if Josie and I hadn't teased Katie. Or, if we'd gone with her when she asked."

Lane's hand gently squeezed my shoulder. "The only thing that might have changed is that you might been killed too."

I shrugged again. Maybe he was right. But it didn't feel like it.

I stepped away from his touch and went back to the sofa. He settled beside me.

"I know the guys on the cold case squad," he said.

"They're buried right now. Probably will be 'til the end of time, actually. The stats on unsolved murders are staggering. But, maybe I can check around. See if I can get something going on Katie's case again."

"Yeah?"

"Maybe. There has to be new evidence to start an investigation on a cold case, but maybe something will come up."

I thought of Corrine's penny. I didn't mention it. I doubted that a pennies-from-heaven story from a grieving mother would be considered new evidence.

"What about Maya Pittman?" I asked.

"Who?"

"The girl who was murdered in '06. There were a lot of similarities to Katie's murder."

"I don't know. That was about the time I moved here. Not familiar with that case. I can check into it, though. See what comes up."

"That would be great," I said, feeling close to tears. I wouldn't allow myself to believe that, after all this time, Katie's murder would be solved. But I couldn't control the wiggle of hope that started inside me.

Lane stood. "I'd better be going."

I nodded, standing also, and walked him to the door.

I could hear the rain, still hammering against the doors and windows. It hadn't let up. If anything, it had gotten worse.

We stood silently in my foyer, listening to the rain drum on the roof. I could feel heat emanate from him, although our bodies weren't touching. He reached out a hand and lifted my chin until I stared up at him. His gaze roamed over my face, settling on my lips. A glint of desire flashed in the sea-blue eyes before his lashes lowered over them. His Adam's apple bobbed as he swallowed.

"What are you doing to me?" he asked, almost in a groan.

I didn't answer. I wondered if he could hear my heart galloping in my chest. The sound seemed to drown out even the storm outside.

The heat of his breath fanned my cheek as he sighed. "Goodnight, Monroe," he said, releasing my chin and placing a gentle kiss on my forehead.

I felt the imprint of his lips long after he was gone.

****

Lane sat in his car without starting it, watching sheets of rain cascade over his windshield. Moisture dripped from his raincoat onto the seat, but he barely noticed. The wind howled, buffeting the car, and dark dampness pressed around him. He looked through the deluge to where Monroe's porch light burned like a beacon of warmth.

A hollow void opened up in the pit of his stomach. The feeling reminded him of a time, long ago, when he'd been around nine. He'd bicycled over to his friend, Evan's, house. Lane was going to spend the night with him. Evan had the whole set of Star Wars action figures. Lane didn't have any, but his mom had taken him to see the movie for his birthday.

Lane stepped up on the porch, but before he could knock, he heard bursts of laughter. Looking through the living room window, he saw Evan with his dad. His father had him lifted off the ground, in a headlock, tickling him. Evan roared with breathless laughter.

A funny feeling came over Lane. At the time, he didn't recognize it as loneliness. Didn't know it was an awareness of looking in at something he'd never had and never would have. He just knew it made his heart hurt and made him a little mad at the same time. He stood watching for a few seconds, then realized he had tears running down his face. Embarrassed and miserable, he got back on his bike and went home without letting Evan know he was there.

Lane sighed and started the car, casting one last look at Monroe's house. After she'd opened up to him about Katie, he'd wanted to tell her about Catherine. He didn't, though. It didn't seem to be the right time. After her unburdening herself about the tragic murder of a childhood friend, he didn't want to talk about his cheating wife.

No, he wouldn't expose Monroe to the sordid ugliness of his life.

As Monroe had talked about Katie, he'd watched a barrage of emotions cross her features. Disbelief, grief, guilt, anger, bewilderment. The same expressions he'd seen on the faces of other survivors. He'd always thought that was a good word. Survivors. For many, afterward, survive was all they could do.

The ones where the murder was never solved were the worst. There was no closure. That's what he wanted to give Monroe. He didn't want to give her false hope, but he wanted to do all he could to solve Katie's murder.

Although he wanted to be so much more, being the guy who gave her closure would have to be enough.

Chapter 12

Laurel Lohman threw back her head and let out a scream. Sweat streamed down her forehead, stinging her eyes. Her entire body was drenched in it. Her heart pounded, and her breath came in shallow gasps.

She lifted her head and looked out over the sea of faces. Two-thirds of them wore various forms of clown paint, clown hair, clown noses. Some of them even wore clown costumes, complete with big shoes. And it was all for her. Well, her and her band, Raging Clowns. They had quite a following for a local grunge band.

She gave the audience her signature inverted peace sign and put the mic against her lips. In her throaty, breathless, voice, she said, "Good night, Kansas City. We love you."

Deafening applause followed as she left the stage.

She heaved a sigh once she was backstage and the exhaustion settled in.

"Let me walk you to your car," her drummer, Nate, offered.

"No thanks." She waved a hand behind her and headed to the exit. "I'm in the garage. It's safe." Nate always took forever to change clothes and gather his things. As tired as she was, she didn't want to wait. "See you tomorrow."

No one was around in the parking garage, which wasn't surprising. It was nearly one-thirty in the

188

morning. Only half the spaces were filled, so she easily spotted her red Mustang. Her heels on the pavement sounded overly loud in the eerie stillness. She almost wished she'd taken Nate up on his offer.

When she reached the car, she heard a noise behind her. Turning, she saw a man standing several feet away. One of their fans. He wore an orange wig and a red clown nose, white make-up, and a baggy, brightly striped clown costume. Her heart stuttered and a little shiver of fear ran through her.

Stop, she told herself. *Nothing to be afraid of.* It wasn't the first time a fan had approached her.

"Hello," she called out, forcing friendliness when all she wanted to do was climb in her car and go home. But, where would they be without their fans?

In response, he honked one of those little clown horns. *Puh-lease.* She inwardly rolled her eyes. Some of them got *way* carried away. For the first time, she noticed he held a notepad in the hand that wasn't holding the horn.

"You want an autograph?" she asked.

His own mouth smiled inside the painted red clown mouth. He came toward her, extending the notepad.

"Do you have a pen?" she asked as she took the paper.

His answer was to tap the top sheet of the open notepad. She looked down to see there was already something written on the page. It read, *we're getting in your car. No funny business… no pun intended. I have a gun.*

She frowned in confusion and looked up at him, half smiling, half afraid. "I don't understand. Is this some kind of…?"

One hand went inside his pocket. He gestured downward with the other, showing her something hard and cylindrical protruding from the billows of his costume. It wasn't a boner.

Her bewilderment turned to full-blown terror. She opened her mouth, but nothing came out. Looking around, she saw a couple coming out of the elevator. If she cried out, he'd shoot her.

Her legs trembled with a terror like she'd never known. Through the curtain of moisture filling her eyes, the brightly colored stripes on his costume seemed to come alive, glowing, wavering, sliding into one another. Her breathing quickened, became a pant.

He jerked his head toward her car, the ludicrous bright orange hair swaying with the gesture. She climbed inside, terror keeping her mute… hoping with all her might that he only wanted to rape her.

****

Josie slept through the night on Thursday and all day Friday. I checked on her frequently, occasionally forcing chicken broth and Gatorade down her throat. Other than while I was at work on Friday, I was in her room every few hours. She barely stirred. Her breathing was regular, however, and I tried not to worry.

It was nearly ten on Friday night when she woke. I was in my room, preparing for bed when she came in. Her face was the color of bone, except for the dark, half-moon shadows beneath her eyes. She reached a trembling hand up to swipe a handful of limp hair off her brow.

"What day is it?" she asked, frowning and looking around the room like she'd never been there before.

"Friday."

She nodded as if confirming something she already knew. "I got here last night, right? Or was it the night before?"

"Last night. Lane brought you."

A small smile appeared briefly and she nodded again. "He's a nice guy."

"How are you? I bet you're starving."

"I am, but I feel a little queasy. Not sure if I can eat."

"I'll fix you something. You need to try."

"Okay. In a minute. First…" Her voice cracked. She sucked in a breath and tried again. "I'm sorry."

"I'm sorry, too," I replied. "Sorry that you can't seem to kick the drugs. Sorry that every time you leave, I'm afraid the next time I see you, you'll be dead. Sorry I can't fix you."

She moved quickly across the room and went into my arms. I hugged her tightly as she cried, her tears soaking the shoulder of my pajama shirt.

"I gotta get help," she said when she released me. "I can't keep living like this."

"You need rehab. It's the only way to get the drugs out of your system."

She nodded and wiped tears. Her gaze went to my jaw where the bruise had now turned an ugly yellowish-purple.

"What happened?"

I hesitated, then told her the truth.

"Oh, my God." She sank to my bed, holding a hand to her mouth and shaking her head. "Oh, God. I'm so sorry. That piece of shit motherfucker."

"It's okay."

"No." She squeezed her eyes shut and shook her head. "I told him."

"Told him what?"

She turned tormented eyes to me. "I told him the cops were looking for him. That they were asking you questions. I didn't think..." Her shoulders shook with sobs. "It's my fault he hurt you."

Although surprised to learn that she had, after all, told him, I didn't blame her for what happened. "No, it's not," I said, putting my hand on her shoulder. "You couldn't know what he'd do."

She rose and began pacing in agitated strides. "That motherfucker. I'll kill him. I swear to God."

"Josie." I stood and took hold of her arm, halting her furious movement. "It's okay. The police are looking for him. Just do what you can to get straight. And, if you can, help the cops find him."

She nodded. Tears streamed down her pale cheeks. "I will. Of course, I will. I don't know where he is exactly, but I know some places they can look. I'll talk to Detective Brody."

"Great. That's great, Josie." I felt better about her than I had in a while. I'd never heard her say she even thought she had a problem. Never heard her sounding contrite. Funny how Matt could beat the shit out of her for years, and it didn't seem to faze her. Yet, he hurt me once, and she was ready to nail his balls to the wall.

"He's something else," she said softly.

"Who? Matt? You're telling me."

"No. Detective Brody. I know I was out of it, but I realize what he did in bringing me here. He could have taken me to jail."

"Yes," I said slowly, trying to keep my tone impassive. "It was nice of him to bring you here."

She smiled a knowing smile. "He didn't do it for

me."

"Whatever," I said, crossing my arms, shifting uncomfortably.

"Yeah. Right." Her eyes glinted with mischief. "Whatever."

****

Lane grabbed his jacket and headed to the door. It had been a long, frustratingly fruitless day, and he was ready to go home. He wasn't even going to stop by the hospital as he usually did on Fridays. Didn't want to deal with Catherine... not tonight.

His cell rang as he reached the elevators.

"There's something I need to show you," Lucinda said when he answered. Her voice was low, urgent.

"Okay. What is it?"

"I'll just have to show you. It's about the case. Meet me behind Ziggy's."

Before he could respond, she'd hung up. What the hell? Was there something at the scene they'd overlooked? He hoped it was something good. They needed a break in the case, and they needed it fast.

At Ziggy's, Lane parked next to Lucinda's Toyota and made his way toward the alley.

No sign of Lucinda, but she could still be here, hidden in the darkness.

"Lucinda?" Narrowing his eyes, he moved further into the alley. The faint glow from the street lights cast misleading shadows, and he only found Lucinda because she moved toward him, into the small halo of light.

"Hi," she whispered. Her voice was seductively beckoning; he could hear the innuendo, even with that one small word. She wore a sheer, rose-colored blouse with the buttons undone. Beneath was a black, lacy camisole. Her nipples peeked out through holes in the lace, and Lane caught his breath.

He knew he'd been had, but he said, "You find something we overlooked?"

A smile curved her lips. "Something you've overlooked for a very long time."

Ah, hell. "This isn't about Ramirez, is it?"

She shook her head and came closer. Her scent washed over him, something strong and musky, like forbidden sex.

God or a surgeon had been very kind to Lucinda's chest. The meager light illuminated her full, firm breasts, as if it knew where Lane's attention was drawn.

Reaching up a hand, she trailed her fingers slowly over her breasts, halting at the nipples.

"What are you doing?" Lane asked, feeling his breath catch in his throat.

She stepped even closer, until their bodies were nearly touching. He felt a hand on his crotch, but even before she cupped him, he was hard. A burning heat engulfed him, along with a wave of guilt.

"I can take care of you," she said, still in a whisper, her lips brushing his earlobe. Heat from her breath wafted over his neck. "I want nothing back. Only to please you. Right here. Right now."

Somehow, she maneuvered their bodies to where he was leaning against the back wall of Ziggy's. She leaned forward and pressed her breasts against him while her fingers worked on his erection.

Lane swallowed, his mouth suddenly dry. When she unfastened his pants, he didn't stop her.

"Why?" he managed to choke out.

"Because you need me. I want to give you what you

need."

He closed his eyes and gripped her shoulders. "No. I can't."

"Yes, you can." She took his hand from her shoulder and placed it on one breast. His fingers tingled at the contact with her erect nipple. "You can," she repeated. "Just this once. Feel. Don't think. Take what you need. Let me give you pleasure."

Somehow, in the next moment, she was on her knees. Lane couldn't breathe. His limbs felt weak and he was overcome by desire. He didn't have the strength to stop her, but knew he had to. Her lips rubbed across his groin on the outside of his clothing, and he sucked in a breath.

"I can't," he said again, his protest weak at best. "Oh, God," he moaned when her lips pressed more firmly against him.

He closed his eyes. The face that surfaced in his mind wasn't his wife's, but Monroe's. Not because of guilt, but because he wondered what it would be like to have her hands, her lips, on him. Would he still be able to say no? Even the feeble resistance he was putting up now? Or, would he take her by the arms, pull her up, and crush her body to his? Bury himself deep inside her, get lost in her sweetness, her softness, shut out the rest of the world.

In spite of himself, he let out a groan, wanting release, knowing he couldn't have it. Not like this.

"Oh yeah, baby," Lucinda murmured and slid his zipper down.

He took a deep breath, trying to summon the willpower to end this. It was now or never. If she got her hands directly on him... got her mouth directly on him, he wouldn't have the strength to stop her. Wouldn't want to stop her. Hell, he didn't want to stop her now.

He heard something then, something other than her moans and the sounds of clothes rustling as she worked on getting both of them naked.

Someone was at the back door of the bar, would walk out at any moment…

"Stop," he whispered.

She ignored him.

"Stop," he said, more loudly, so loudly he was afraid whoever was at the door might hear. He gripped her shoulders and pulled her to her feet. "Someone's coming," he said, his voice taut with tension.

Her gaze narrowed. "Could have been you," she bit out.

They stared at one another, both breathing hard. He shook his head, releasing her shoulders.

"Fine," she said, tears of humiliation swimming in her eyes. "Fine," she said again, this time in a hiss. She buttoned her blouse, giving him a hard look as she did so.

She whirled and stalked away, rounding the corner of the alley just as Ziggy's back door flung open. Two men stumbled out, bringing the sound of loud music and mingled voices with them for a brief time before the door swung closed once more.

Lane quickly re-fastened his clothing, but one of the men, a short Asian noticed him and smiled. "Hey, sugar. Wanna party?"

Lane thought about flashing his badge, simply because he was pissed and humiliated, and frustratingly unsatisfied. But they weren't doing anything illegal. Not yet. And he wasn't waiting around to find out.

He slid inside his car, his mind replaying what had happened with Lucinda. He'd like to think he'd have stopped her, even if they hadn't been interrupted, but he couldn't be sure. The ache was still with him. Strong and taunting. Unfulfilled.

****

Laurel didn't know where she was or how long she'd been here. The clown maniac had injected her with something that made her fade in and out of consciousness. She knew they were in a basement. There was a window high on the cement wall, but it was painted black, so she didn't know if it was day or night.

She was tied to a chair, her wrists chafing from the rope. There were times he left the room, and during those absences, she worked on the ropes binding her. They didn't budge. All she accomplished was to cut into the tender flesh at her wrists. She could feel the sting and the blood that had now dried on her skin.

He hadn't touched her. Hadn't raped her or even made her take off her clothes. What the fuck did he want?

The door at the top of the stairs opened and she sucked in a breath. Each time he entered, she would think, *this is it. He'll kill me now. Or rape me. Or something... but what?* It was almost to the point now where she'd welcome it. At least she wouldn't have to wonder. The old cliché was true. Waiting was the hardest part.

She saw his big clown feet coming down the wooden stairs. He still wore the goddamned ridiculous clown costume. Motherfucker. This time, he carried a portable CD player.

He didn't even look at her. He plugged the CD player into a socket and set it on the floor.

"Why are you doing this? What do you want?" she asked again, futilely. Her voice was barely audible. Her throat was raw and tender, painful, as if she'd swallowed broken glass. It was from the hours of screaming, crying, begging, and asking that same, unanswered question. *Why? Why? Why?*

No louder than she could speak, he probably hadn't heard her, wouldn't have answered if he had.

She thought of her boyfriend. What must he be thinking by now? Greg was probably worried sick. He was supposed to come by her apartment after the set. She was to call him. This asshole had taken her before she'd had the chance. Greg was bound to know something was wrong. He'd realize something had happened and save her, wouldn't he?

No. He wouldn't. Even if he knew something was wrong, he'd have no idea where to find her. Unless…

Like she had a dozen times since he'd brought her here, she looked over to where her purse lay a few feet away. In it was her cell phone, tantalizingly close. But she couldn't reach it. And, even if she did, she wouldn't be able to tell Greg where she was. She had no fucking idea.

Just when she thought she had none left, another volley of tears poured from her eyes. She was going to die. She tried to comfort herself with thoughts of what would happen if Greg *did* find her. He was huge. He'd make mincemeat out of this motherfucker.

Clown-bastard punched a button on the CD player and that song about Pina Colada's started. He walked slowly toward her.

"Why?" she asked, choking out the word.

He spoke for the first time. "You know why."

"No. I don't. I swear. Please tell me."

He sighed as if disappointed. "Laurel, Laurel, Laurel. Would knowing why make what's about to happen any easier?"

"Oh, God," she sobbed, dropping her chin to her chest as her entire body shook with terror.

"I didn't think so," he said.

She lifted her head and stared up into his face. "I'll do anything you want. Please don't hurt me. Pleeeaasse…"

His red lips curled into a smile. "You always were easy."

She frowned. "Do I know you—" The words were cut off abruptly when her eyes dropped to his right hand and, for the first time, she saw the knife. Panic gripped her, moving from her heart into her throat.

He gave a soft laugh and reached his free hand up to the orange hair. Slowly, he removed the wig. Her attention was riveted to his actions, the knife momentarily forgotten as she watched in curiosity.

Next, came the nose. Then, he took the collar of his costume and started wiping at the makeup.

As his features were slowly revealed, recognition dawned and she gasped in shock, but no words would come. A small glimmer of hope surfaced. She did know him. And he wouldn't hurt her.

She smiled, found her voice, and made a sound, something close to a nervous laugh. "What the hell? You really had me scared. Is this some kind of joke?"

He didn't answer. She looked into his eyes and felt the smile slip from her face.

Her remaining hope vanquished when the knife plunged toward her breasts. The first cut made her scream.

It was a long while before she stopped.

****

The Blitz was a sports bar owned by Darion Martin, a former Packers wide receiver whose career had ended after an injury. During the fall and winter, one entire wall of the bar was painted like a football field. In the spring and summer, the panels were flipped so that the scene was a baseball diamond.

Lane took a stool at the bar and Darion automatically opened a bottle of Heineken and slid it in front of him.

"How's it going, bro?" Darion wore a Packers sweatshirt with the sleeves pushed up to the elbows, his chest and shoulders testing the durability of the seams. He wasn't overly tall, but still had his playing physique, and was roughly the size of a small automobile. A gold earring glinted in his left ear. On his forearm was a heart tattoo with 'Asia' scrawled in the center. If anyone thought he was a wuss because of it, Lane was pretty sure they kept it to themselves.

"Not too bad, you?"

"Can't complain," his deep voice rumbled. "You look a little tense. Big case?"

Lane took a swig of the beer, shrugging. "Always a big case, my man."

He didn't tell him that, tonight, his mind wasn't on his cases as much as it was his libido. Although Lane had been in a hurry to get home just a few hours ago, now he dreaded the thought. Didn't want to face the emptiness with this urge gnawing at his insides. He was afraid he'd call Lucinda and tell her he'd changed his mind. Or, even worse—yet so much better—that he'd call Monroe.

"Asia tells me you and Monroe are starting to get chummy." Darion wiped down a glass with a bar towel, making the muscles in his forearms jump.

"Not chummy. I've talked to her a couple of times. About a case."

"You could do worse, you know. Monroe's a good person." Darion's broad face broke out in a grin. "Not bad lookin' either."

Lane scowled up at him. "You trying to hook us up? You remember I'm married?"

He breathed out a sound of derision. "That's what you call it, huh?"

"Look, tonight's not the night to give me grief about my marriage or anything else, okay?"

"Sorry, man." Darion shrugged. "Just think you should actually live your life instead of just going through the motions."

"Aren't bartenders only supposed to give advice when customers *ask* for it?"

"Maybe. But friends try to help out when they see a need."

Lane stood and tossed a five on the bar. "How about if I let you know when there's a need."

"You leaving, man? Don't be pissed. Just trying to help out. Have another on me."

Lane sighed and shook his head. "I'm not pissed. It's been a crazy couple of days. I don't need to add drinking to everything else that's going on."

"Okay. Take it easy, then. No hard feelings, right?"

Hard feelings. Lane thought of what Lucinda had done to him in the alley and almost laughed at the choice of words. "Yeah, no hard feelings."

When Lane got home, he took a warm shower,

pulled on boxer briefs and climbed into bed. He tried to fall asleep, but the unrelenting heat in his groin made it impossible. It was a tingling, persistent ache that wouldn't subside. He tried to think of his cases... brutalized corpses and the dregs of society he dealt with every day. Even tried to conjure an image of the ball-busting Lieutenant Michelle Karakas. But it was no use. One image continued to push back the others.

He knew how to attain temporary relief.

Reaching a hand beneath the sheets, he let himself think of Monroe... let himself picture her... conjure her scent... the curve of her cheek... her full lips, smiling... the light dancing in her ebony eyes... her warmth... her softness... her breasts pressing into his chest...

He groaned deep in his throat and shouted her name as he came.

Chapter 13

My mother was in a semi-state of mourning during our family dinner on Saturday. Coburn was still on his business trip, and she missed her little boy severely.

"Look at this," Mom said, beaming as she handed me a postcard she'd pulled from the pocket of her apron. "It's from Coburn."

The card showed a picturesque Miami beach at dusk. Shades of purple and pink from the sunset glinted on the sand. I turned the card over. *'Miss you, Mom. See you soon. Love, Coburn'* was scrawled in Coburn's bold, masculine handwriting. No, *'Having a wonderful time banging the blonde with the fake tits.'* Hmmm… woulda thought he'd give her a complete update.

"Nice," I said, handing it back to her across the table.

"He's so thoughtful," she crooned. "A busy doctor like him, taking the time out to send his mother a card."

Suddenly losing my appetite, I pushed my plate away, the pork chop and mashed potatoes only half eaten.

Naomi was absent from the dinner, probably sitting at home pining for Mr. Wonderful. Gable and Mitchum were unusually subdued. Sighing, I scooted my chair back.

"I need to go right after I clean the kitchen," I announced.

"You can't stay and visit? Why not?"

I took perverse delight in telling her why not. "Josie is at the house. I don't want to be gone too long."

My mother's mouth tightened and her eyes got that look that said I'd disappointed her yet again. "Of course, dear. I know how important your friends are." Slight emphasis on the 'friends.' Translation: Your family is not important. Or, at least, not me, your own mother. "You don't need to clean the kitchen. I'll do it so you can rush off. That way you won't have to waste any more time with your family."

Gable looked from me to my mother, then back to me. Clearing his throat, he said, "How is Josie? I'm glad she showed up."

I knew he was trying to avert a disaster and I smiled gratefully. "She's okay. I think maybe this time, she'll—"

"Your sister's too busy to talk to us, Gable," Mom interrupted. "We need to let her tend to what really matters."

I blew out a breath between my lips and jumped to my feet. Heading into the kitchen without another word, I let the swinging doors hurl back forcefully.

Mom came in right behind me. "I said I'd do these, Monroe. You can leave now."

"I'll do them," I gritted, my back to her as I rinsed food from the dishes into the disposal.

"Then I'll help."

I tensed. The last thing I wanted was to be in close quarters with my mother. The only benefit was that I would finish more quickly and be able to make my escape.

We worked together in a silence thicker than the

gravy I scrubbed from the plates. Nerves tightened my gut. I almost wished we were arguing again. It was better than the anxiety building inside me.

I clenched my teeth and looked up, my gaze falling on the clock. The damned stupid, broken clock.

"Can you tell me something?" I said, trying but failing to keep the ire out of my voice.

"Yes?" she asked, drawing it out in that defensive tone of hers.

"Why the hell do you keep that clock up? It hasn't worked for more than twenty years. Don't you think it's time to take it down?"

Her gaze went to the wall where the clock hung. Her features softened and a wistful smile touched her lips.

"I used that clock to teach you to tell time."

I halted my movements, leaving my hands beneath the running water. "You what?"

"You were six. We'd sit in the kitchen and I'd feed you Rice Krispie treats. You remember?"

I grinned. "Marshmallow creme and cereal. Who'da thought they'd taste so good together? You know, the packaged kind just aren't the same."

Mom shook her head. "They're not made with love, dear, that's why."

Tears pricked the backs of my eyes.

Sighing, Mom said, "You were so willful, even as a child. I know I was rougher on you than I was on the boys, expected more out of you. But, you were just so darned smart, so curious and fearless. Gave me cause to worry, day in, day out. You were always so independent, wanted to take care of yourself. You didn't need me." She took her gaze from the clock and looked at me. "You're still the same way, you know. Stubborn and independent. Almost to a fault."

The words weren't exactly compliments, but she said them as though she admired that about me. Shrugging, I said, "Don't mean to be."

"The older you got, the less you wanted to be around me. I think back over your childhood. All the conflicts we had. The mistakes I made. All the fond memories. I regret that the mistakes outnumber the fond memories. But this," she gestured to the clock, "was one of my fondest. Maybe I just wanted to hold onto it." Her voice grew thick with emotion. "It was the last time you needed me."

The tears that had been taunting me finally fell. I shut off the water and dried my hands. Turning to my mother, I saw that her cheeks were wet, too. She held out her arms.

For the first time in a long time, I went into my mother's hug.

****

Blood was everywhere, the rusty smell of it sharp and pungent in the air. The odor of fresh paint competed with the scent and lost. The basement was in an unfinished home, bare and pristine other than the savaged mess tied to a chair. The girl had been blonde, or so it seemed. Hard to tell. All that blood.

She was slumped over, still tied to a chair. Lane wished the ME would hurry. He wanted her bindings loosened.

He'd been to a lot of crime scenes, but there was something about this one… something heart-wrenching about the lone girl in the abandoned basement. She deserved to be free… deserved to rest.

"Find out who owns the property," Lane told a

patrol cop. "There's a sign out front, Redway Properties. Get me a person to talk to."

The cop nodded, made a note, and fled as if glad to have an excuse not to be in the room.

The walls were freshly painted with a white-ish gray color. Red lettering marred the otherwise clean surface, declaring, 'In You I Trust.'

"What the fuck is that supposed to mean?" Lane snapped.

Tony's eyes flew to him. Probably because he seldom swore. Seldom showed anger. Well, he was angry now.

"I don't know, Huck. Wondered the same thing myself. Different from the other scene, but it's the same guy."

"Yeah. Same lettering, same shade of red. Just decided to wax poetic a little differently this time." Lane felt tension build in his shoulders and he sucked in a deep breath, let it out. The tension remained. "Who found her?"

"One of the construction guys. Came by the house this morning, even though they weren't working today. Some story about leaving his cell phone."

"You don't believe him?"

"Haven't talked to him. Only the first responders have. He's waiting upstairs. Nervous as hell."

A sound at the basement stairs made them turn. The ME came toward them, followed by two crime scene investigators.

"What do you have for me this time?" Keaton asked.

Without waiting for an answer, the ME went to the body. Lane watched as he examined the girl, and the CSIs bagged the items taken from the body.

"Nothing noteworthy on her person," Keaton said. He stood, looked over to where her purse lay. "That belong to the victim?"

"Far as we know," Tony said.

Keaton picked it up with gloved hands, digging among the make-up and mints, the keys and odds and ends, until he found her wallet. "According to the driver's license, her name is Laurel Lohman. Twenty-nine years old." Keaton shook his head. "Someone didn't like her very much." He handed the purse to a CSI to bag. "We'll let you know when we have a positive ID."

After the body was removed, and the ME left, Lane said, "Let's go talk to the guy who found her."

Lane followed Tony up the stairs. The smell of fresh enamel was stronger here, the odor of blood gone, and Lane took a deep breath, cleansing his lungs with the scent of the paint.

"Bronson Edgars," Tony supplied as they walked outside.

They found Edgars, a young, heavy-set guy, leaning against the garage door. He wore a thick, Carhartt coat and had plenty of flesh padding him, yet he shivered like a man with palsy. He smoked a cigarette, furiously drawing on the butt and puffing the smoke out in rapid bursts.

"Mr. Edgars?" Lane asked as they approached.

He turned wild, unfocused eyes on them.

"Yeah?" Another animated drag from the cigarette.

"You found the victim?"

His ruddy face paled. "That was some fucked up shit, man. I just needed my cell phone." He shook his head slowly, regretfully. "Forgot my goddamned cell phone." It was said as if that oversight caused the girl's death.

"Can you take us through it? Step by step?"

"Step by step?" He shrugged. "Not a lot of steps to it. I forgot my cell phone. Went to get it. Saw the basement door open and found…" He shuddered. Tears filled his eyes. He ground the cigarette beneath his boot heel and lit another. "God. She was so… bloody. I called 9-1-1 and got the fuck out of there. No. Wait. Got the fuck out of there first, *then* called 9-1-1."

"Did you see or hear anything? Anything at all, before you went into the house, or while you were there?"

A shake of the head, then the same frenzied attack was launched on the second cigarette.

"Nothing. No one lives around here. The neighborhood is just a bunch of new homes going up. No one around."

Lane figured the killer was long gone by the time Edgars showed up. All signs pointed to some time last night as the time of death.

"Do you know the girl?"

"No." It was almost a shout. "I never saw her. I didn't do nothing, man. Nothing."

Lane was tempted to say, "If you didn't do 'nothing,' then you did 'something,'" but he didn't think now was the time for a grammar lesson.

"Laurel Lohman. Name sound familiar?" Tony asked.

A rapid head shake. "Don't know her, man, I'm telling you."

"We need your name, address, phone number, place of employment. We might have some follow-up questions. Might need you to come to the station."

Edgars nodded and, between puffs of the cigarette, recited the information.

Lane jotted it down, then said, "We'll have to process your footprints and fingerprints."

Tony called one of the techs over to take Edgars' prints and when they were done, told Edgars he was free to go.

"But don't leave town, right?" Edgars barked a nervous laugh, his face stretched in a grimace, then headed unsteadily to a white Ford truck smeared with dirt and bits of cement.

Lane took down the license number. He and Tony headed back toward the house.

They stopped on the porch, the two of them staring out over the neighborhood of partially built homes and no sign of human existence. Lane looked across the empty lots to where a grade school sat half a mile away. It appeared to be within spitting distance, but when the neighborhood was complete, the barrier of homes erected, the more diligent parents wouldn't let their kids make the trip unescorted. Although it seemed close enough, safe enough at the moment, it wouldn't then. Proof positive that safety was only an illusion.

"It is quiet around here," Tony said.

"Quiet as a sinner on Sunday," Lane agreed.

"Good location if you want to kill someone," Tony's voice was low, yet still loud in the quiet of the night. "No one around to hear the screams."

****

I went to work early on Monday morning, before anyone else arrived. I wanted to look up some information from when Katie was murdered. Our computers held software that couldn't be accessed from my home terminal.

I left off all the lights, other than the one directly above my cubicle. Sipping from the mug of hot, strong coffee I'd just brewed, I scrolled through the limited data available about the murder.

The only viable suspect they'd had was Cameron Cooper. He'd been twenty-one at the time. He'd served three years for a rape that occurred when he was a juvenile.

I did a search on his name. He'd be forty-six now. I wondered if he were still alive, if he were still in the area. Had the police looked at him for Maya's killing two years ago? I hadn't found anything to indicate they had in my two years of research. Hadn't found anything to indicate whether or not Cooper was still around. Was he in jail now for some other crime? Maybe another rape? Once a rapist, always a rapist. The question wasn't had he done it again. The question was, had he been caught and convicted.

Nothing came up on the search.

A noise sounded behind me and I turned. A figure lurched toward me from the darkness. I let out a scream.

"Monroe? Is that you?" a male voice said.

My heart pounded furiously, but I recognized him now. Adam.

"Yes, it's me."

"What are you doing here so early?"

He came closer and in the circle from the light above me, I got a better look at him.

His clothing was wrinkled, as if he'd slept in it. His face, however, looked like he hadn't slept at all. Deep lines etched the sides of his mouth and dark circles surrounded his eyes, their vivid green now dulled. His hair was uncombed. He smelled of stale cologne and sweat. He squinted at me, blinking like he was coming out of a daze.

"I came in to do some research," I told him. "What's wrong? Are you okay?"

He peered at the computer screen. "What kind of research?"

Adam knew about Katie, but not everything. In the two years we'd dated, I hadn't told him half of what I'd told Lane.

"It's not important," I said, minimizing the web site I had pulled up. I repeated my question. "Are you okay?"

He shook his head, shoving a hand through his hair. Shaking his head again, he stared at me. For just a moment, I saw a longing in his face. The old feelings I'd buried surfaced briefly, my body responding to the look in his eyes. I shoved them aside.

"Adam, has something happened?"

"Did you read yesterday's paper?"

"No."

"Tabitha's best friend." He sighed and dropped into the chair next to my desk. I waited for him to continue. After a long silence, he did. "Tabitha's best friend was… murdered."

"Oh, Adam. I'm so sorry."

He nodded slowly, staring at his hands where they rested on his knees. "Murdered. Tabitha's a wreck. We were up all night."

"How did it happen? Do they know who did it?"

"Not yet. She was stabbed." He drew in a shuddering breath. "Murdered," he said again.

Not knowing what to say, I sat silently. Reaching out, I placed a hand on his shoulder. I could feel him tremble beneath my fingertips.

"I need a drink," he said.

"It's six-thirty in the morning."

He gave a weak grin. "It's five o'clock somewhere." Leaning back in the chair, he closed his eyes. "I can't believe it. Can't believe Laurel's dead."

A chill weaved its way through me and I shuddered. "Laurel?"

He nodded. "Laurel Lohman."

My blood froze. I couldn't speak.

Laurel Lohman was the girl's name. The one in the obituary with the wrong date.

Chapter 14

Lane woke up thinking about Laurel Lohman. This latest murder had pushed the incident with Lucinda to the bottom of his priority list. He was no longer concerned about how awkward it might be to continue working with her. The mutilation of a beautiful young woman had pretty much rendered that episode irrelevant.

The coroner had made a positive ID yesterday. Laurel Lohman, twenty-nine years old, lead singer for a local band, Raging Clowns.

The newspaper had already decided who the victim was. Yesterday's paper had stated the body found was presumed to be Laurel Lohman, then had launched into a blurb about her being a local celebrity, how the tragic murder had cut a blossoming career short, etc, etc.

As was routine, Lane had looked at the significant other first, but it didn't take long to clear the boyfriend, Greg Rogers. Not only did this have the markings of the killer who'd done Hebringer, and maybe Ramirez, Rogers had an alibi, had filed a missing person's report when Laurel didn't show up after her gig on Thursday night, and was, overall, a devastated mess.

The last time she was seen was by her band when she left the club on Thursday night. Rogers had spent most of two days desperately waiting, desperately searching for her. He wasn't relieved that she'd been found.

Nothing helpful came from the scene. No clues. No DNA. Just like the other murder.

The words on the tree and the wall went round and round in Lane's brain.

"Partners in Crime.

In You I Trust."

There was something familiar about them, something he felt he should remember. It wouldn't come.

After brushing his teeth and taking a quick shower, he headed to his car. He was out of coffee and would have to make the dreaded stop at You Fly, a convenience store a few blocks from his house. He didn't know if the name was derived from the 'I'll buy if you'll fly' saying, or if it was representative of the clerk's perpetual state of chemically induced euphoria.

Although You Fly was on the way to the station and had the best coffee nearby, Lane seldom stopped there. Each time he did, if Russell was working, he had to listen to the burrito story.

He walked in, and as he feared, Russell was behind the counter. "Hey, Detective dude. Long time no see and shit." Russell was tall and lanky. His shoulder-length hair was the color of faded wheat and he wore round, wire-framed, tinted glasses.

"How's it going, Russell?" Lane went to the coffee machines and filled a Styrofoam cup with the house blend. Taking it back to the counter, he had his money ready, hoping Russell would take the hint that he didn't have time for small talk.

"Hey, man, you remember that time we got robbed?"

"Yeah," Lane said, putting two dollars on the counter and starting to turn.

"Dude was a real bone-head," Russell said. "Stopped to heat a burrito in the microwave." He shook his head. "Still munching on it when the cops came."

"Right. Just like the last time I was in here. Same ending to the story."

Russell guffawed. "You're a real hoot, Detective." Then, as if Lane hadn't just reminded him he'd already heard the story, he said, "Dude woulda got away with it if he hadn't had the munchies. What kind of bone-head does something like that? I mean, Taco Bell is right down the street and their burritos beat ours, hands down."

Lane's phone vibrated and he looked at the display, feeling a rush of warm gratitude toward his partner. "What's up?" he said into the cell, giving Russell a wave and heading out the door with his coffee.

"Got the property owner's name," Tony said. "You're gonna love this."

"Yeah?"

"Adam Utley."

"Jesus. The editor at the *Chronicle*."

"Yep. The victim was his fiancée's best friend."

"Damn." Utley had stayed at the inn. His fiancée's best friend was murdered. At a property he owned. Things were not looking good for Mr. Utley.

"I'm following up on the paint found at the scene. Wasn't construction paint. Lab's testing it now."

There'd been traces of some kind of paint on the basement floor. Different color from the paint used in the house.

"Let me know what you find," Lane said. "I'll talk to Utley."

After he ended the call, Lane slid into his car and

took a sip of his coffee. Before he could dial the newspaper, his phone rang again. He felt a jolt in his gut when he saw Monroe's name on the display.

"Brody," he said, trying to keep his tone neutral.

"Lane? There's something I need to talk to you about. Something about the girl who was killed." Her voice sounded frantic.

"Which girl?"

"Laurel Lohman."

"What about her?" Fear replaced the warmth he'd felt at her call. "Is Utley there? Has he hurt you?"

"Adam?" she said. "No. I mean, yes, he's here. He hasn't hurt me. Why would you think that?"

Lane let out a breath. "What about the girl?"

"I received an obituary on Wednesday. The date was wrong. It listed the date of death as Friday, the day after the obit was to be printed. I thought it was just a typo, but…"

"But?" he prompted.

"The name of the deceased was Laurel Lohman."

"What?"

"Yeah. Laurel Lohman. The murder victim. An obituary listing her as the deceased came in. Last *Wednesday*," she repeated impatiently, as if he were too dense to grasp the implication.

"Do you have the obit?"

"Yes. It's here at the office."

"I'm coming by."

"There's something else. Might not be important, but you should know."

"Yes?"

"Last week, it happened, too. An obit with a wrong date, I mean. We didn't think anything of it, but now…

I don't know. Does the name Richard Hebringer mean anything to you?"

"Yeah," he said, his tone low and hoarse. "He was murdered."

"On a Friday, October 24th?" she asked, her voice sounding cold, frightened.

"Yeah. I'll be there in ten minutes."

****

Monroe's cheeks were stained with tears when Lane got to the newspaper. She wore faded jeans and a baggy Kansas City Royals sweatshirt, the color making the blue tinge beneath her eyes even more stark.

"Are you okay?" he asked.

She looked down at the floor, crossing her arms, then said quietly, "If I'd said something, told you about the obituary sooner, maybe she'd be alive."

"No," he said firmly. "You couldn't have known. Don't think like that." It wasn't planned and it wasn't appropriate, but he reached out and pulled her into a hug. Her body felt cold. He stroked his hands up and down her back, feeling the tension in the lines of her spine... enjoying her scent. "It's not your fault."

She nodded and, after taking his comfort for only a few moments, pulled away. The look on her face told him his words hadn't convinced her.

"Is Utley still here?"

"Yeah, in his office." Picking up a newspaper from atop her desk, she handed it to him. "Richard Hebringer's obituary is circled."

The date, October 24th, matched the date of the murder. *Interred at Macon Cemetery.* Macon was the road on which the body was found.

"Laurel's?" he asked.

She handed him another newspaper. The obit was circled on this one, too.

"I left the date out since I knew it was incorrect," she said. "But it came in with this coming Friday listed as the date of death."

The obit stated, *Services to be held at Redway Funeral Home.* The name of the property where Lohman was found. The SOB was playing some kind of sick game.

"Do you have records of who sent the obituary?" Lane asked.

"They were sent by email. I have an email address."

"What about payment? Credit card information?"

She shook her head. "We don't charge for obits up to nine lines. These were both less."

Lane blew out a breath, then looked up from the paper. "When you and Adam stayed at the Highland Lily Bed and Breakfast, do you recall any problems he might have had with the desk clerk? Maybe they had words? A disagreement of some kind?"

Her brows drew together in a frown. "I've never stayed there."

"Are you sure? It shows Utley was registered there in July. You two were together then, right?"

Monroe smiled grimly. "We were together then, but he didn't stay there with me. He was heavily involved in his affair at the time. I just didn't know about it."

"Ah, hell. I'm sorry." Lane felt like an idiot. Not very intuitive, considering he was a cop.

She shrugged. "No big deal. I'm over it."

"Do you know a Garrett Ramirez?"

"Name doesn't ring a bell. Should I?"

"Not sure. He was killed on October twenty-ninth.

No obits with his name?"

"No. None that I recall."

"Okay. Thanks. You've been a big help." He reached out and squeezed her icy hand. "I need to go talk to Utley. Are you sure you're okay?"

"Yeah, fine," she said, but her voice had a hollow, false ring that belied the words.

****

The blinds were drawn on Utley's office window. Lane pulled his Glock from the holster. Holding it down by his side, he entered without knocking.

Utley sat at his desk, looking up when Lane came in. His face was a mask of grief… or pain… or guilt. His hands—free of firearms—lay in plain sight. Utley's golden good looks seemed to have dimmed. Like a sun god who'd suffered an eclipse. Lane might feel sorry for him if he didn't think the man could possibly be a killer. And if he hadn't cheated on Monroe. *And, let's be honest here, if he hadn't slept with Monroe.*

"Detective Brody," Lane said, replacing his gun and pulling out his shield. "I'd like to ask you some questions."

Utley nodded. "About Laurel?" He pointed to a chair. "Have a seat."

Lane remained standing. "How well did you know Miss Lohman?"

Utley's chin quivered. "She was Tabitha's—my fiancée's—best friend." His voice broke. "We spent a lot of time together."

"When was the last time you saw her?"

His eyes closed briefly, as if he was searching his memory. "I think it was a few weeks ago. Tab and I went to hear her band. We went for breakfast after."

"That was the last time you saw her?" Lane let a hint of skepticism enter his voice.

"Yes." No hesitation.

"Did you like Miss Lohman? Did you two get along?"

"Sure. Yeah. She was great." Now a hint of worry entered his eyes. "Why?"

"Just wondered. Trying to get an idea of who might have something against her. Who might have wanted her dead."

His eyes rounded. "You think I killed her? God. That's insane. Why would I want to kill her?"

"Why would anyone?"

Tears filled his eyes and he shook his head. "I don't know. God. I have no idea."

"The obituaries of two murder victims appeared in your newspaper, Mr. Utley. Days before they were actually murdered."

"Yeah. Monroe told me about that. I don't get it."

"Did you know Richard Hebringer?"

Utley shook his head, then, "Wait. The guy whose obituary had the wrong date? Don't know him. Just know the name from the obit."

"What about Garrett Ramirez?"

Another head shake. "Should I?"

"Hebringer was a desk clerk at the Highland Lily Bed and Breakfast. I understand you've stayed there."

Utley's gaze dropped to the top of the desk. "Yeah. But I don't know the clerk. Can't even recall if the person who checked us in was a male or female."

Lane nodded. "I'm sure you had other things on your mind."

Utley's head came back up and his face colored. He

stared at Lane for a moment and opened his mouth as if to say something, maybe to defend his affair, then he thought better of it and didn't speak.

"Do you know where Miss Lohman's body was found?" Lane continued.

Utley scrubbed a hand over his face. "No. Where?"

Lane watched his face as he answered. "Your property, Mr. Utley. In the basement of an unfinished home owned by Redland. Your company."

"Dear Jesus. You're kidding, right?"

Lane just looked at him.

"That makes no sense. Who would…? How…? Jesus," he said again. He sat silently for a few seconds, then his face cleared and he said, "Have you talked to Derek?"

"Derek?"

"Tabitha's ex-husband. He and I owned the properties together. Then, after…" He cleared his throat and looked away. "After Tab left him, he got out."

"He no longer owns the property?"

"No."

"Did he and Miss Lohman get along?"

Utley shrugged. "I guess they did at one time. After the split, I don't think they saw one another. Tabitha has a restraining order against him, so none of us saw him much."

"Why the order?"

"He wouldn't leave her alone. Kept calling. Begging her to come back."

"Did he make any threats? Against your fiancée or her family, friends?"

Utley reluctantly shook his head, as if regretting that he had to be honest. "No threats. Just begging. You know, not ready to let go."

"We'll speak to him. In the meantime, I'd appreciate it if you'd remain in town. Available."

"Do I need a lawyer, Detective Brody?"

"Might be wise."

A disbelieving laugh escaped him. "How crazy would I be to put obits in my own paper if I was the killer?"

"The person who did this isn't exactly rational," Lane said. "I'll be in touch."

Lane was at the door when, out of the blue, the lines from the two crime scenes suddenly popped into his head.

Partners in Crime... In You I Trust.

He realized why they sounded familiar. Song titles. From the Rupert Holmes CD. Catherine had owned a copy.

He turned back to Utley. "You like that song? The one about Pina Coladas?"

"Huh?" Utley's brows drew together. "Pina Coladas?"

"You know, about getting caught in the rain and liking Pina Coladas, that one."

"Oh." Utley shrugged. "Never really thought about it. I guess it's okay. Why?"

"Just wondered." Lane looked at him intently, seeing if his expression, his body language, had changed at all. Couldn't get a read on him. "You know how it is when you can't get a song out of your head. Drives you crazy."

"Yeah," Utley agreed, though he didn't seem to really give a shit.

"Yep," Lane said, shaking his head. "Driving me

crazy."

****

I got home, wanting a drink in the worst way, but with Josie there, I decided I should refrain. Even though drugs were her flavor of choice, any kind of stimulant couldn't be good for her. Not until she was well over the craving. If drug addicts ever got over it.

I'd called a rehab facility and Josie was to go in at the end of the week. It made me worry, made me feel bad, as if I was abandoning her, but I knew it was best.

Josie was watching the first *Die Hard*, like we both hadn't already seen it a dozen times.

The guilt over Laurel Lohman was still with me, and I couldn't seem to shake it. I couldn't stop thinking that if I'd said something, even starting with Hebringer's obit, she might have been saved.

"Something's wrong, isn't it?" Josie asked, hitting the mute button on the remote.

I dropped onto the sofa next to her and told her about my day. She placed a hand over mine. "I'm so sorry. But it's not your fault. You couldn't have known."

I nodded. "That's what Lane said."

"Lane, huh?" she teased. "Not 'Detective Brody?'"

In spite of myself, I smiled. "I'm just not thinking clearly. My defenses are down."

"And that would be a bad thing?"

"You're not implying I should get involved with him? Josie, he's *married*."

She shrugged. "Not happily, right? Isn't his wife in a crazy house or something?"

"Crazy house? She's ill. Some kind of mental problem, I think, but he's still married. Besides, where do you get your information?"

"Asia." At my look, she said, "We might not be best friends, but we talk. She called for you the other day and we chatted a bit."

"Well, bully for you," I said crossly. "Glad I was the subject of your conversation."

"We both just want you to find a guy. To be happy with someone."

I almost said, *Like you were?* but didn't. "I don't think hooking up with a married guy is the answer to my love-life woes."

"Maybe not. But I bet he won't be married forever. Wouldn't hurt to test the waters."

"I don't care if he leaves his wife tomorrow, I'm staying away. I damn sure don't need to jump in a relationship with a married guy *or* one just out of a marriage. Been there, done that. Got the T-shirt."

"Adam's a dick. Lane's not like that."

"You don't know a thing about him. No matter who the guy is, there should be some kind of rule. Some law about a grace period between relationships. Make them simmer a while alone before they start up with someone else." I sighed. "Can we change the subject, please?"

"Sure. I wanted to talk to you about something, anyway."

"Shoot."

"Do you think you could take a few days off work?"

"Maybe. Why?"

"I thought it would be cool to get away for a little while. Before I… you know, go in. Just the two of us. Maybe spend a few days at the lake?"

The idea definitely held appeal. "I'll talk to Adam. I'm sure it won't be a problem. He's dealing with this Laurel Lohman thing, anyway. Probably won't even notice I'm gone." Not to mention, I only had a week or so left on my notice. I hadn't told Josie I was leaving the paper, hadn't told my family, not even Gable. Also hadn't found a job. Was it because I didn't really intend to leave the paper?

No. *Hell* no! I *was* leaving. Wouldn't stay around for more abuse. Couldn't. My old boss would be back in a few days. Maybe he'd have something for me. Then I could tell everyone I was leaving. Of course, I should have been looking for another job in the meantime, but I hadn't been. That didn't mean I was staying at the *Chronicle*. Procrastination, that's all it was. That, and a need to clear my head.

"Yeah," I told Josie. "Let's do it. Let's get the hell out of here for a few days."

"Great." She un-muted the TV. "Now let's watch John McClane kick some ass."

****

Derek Harmon's house was an olive-green two-story on a quiet, tree-lined street in a wealthy neighborhood in North Kansas City.

Harmon answered the door, holding a can of Budweiser and wearing a San Francisco 49ers jersey over black sweats. He was average height and solidly built with short, spiked hair held in place by too much gel.

"Mr. Harmon?" Lane said, showing him the badge. "I'm Detective Lane Brody and this is my partner, Detective Tony Webber. We'd like to ask you a few questions."

He frowned, but his voice was pleasant. "What's this about?"

"We're investigating a homicide. May we come in?"

"Sure." He led them into an untidy living room where a big screen TV showed Monday night football. The 49ers were playing the Saints. "Mind if we watch the game while we talk? I'll mute the sound."

"No problem," Lane said.

"Have a seat, guys. Want a beer?"

Lane and Tony both declined, taking seats on chairs flanking the black leather sofa where Harmon sat.

"Oh, yeah," Harmon said. "On duty. Sorry."

On the wall behind the sofa were two paintings. One a landscape, the other a lighthouse.

Harmon saw Lane looking at them and said, "I did those," with a hint of pride in his voice.

"You're an artist?"

"Art is my passion. Doesn't pay the bills, though."

"What does?"

"Huh?"

"What do you do for a living?"

"I dabble in real estate. I don't have to work. My family has money. I buy properties, investments, just so I don't feel useless, you know?" Harmon looked at the TV. "Come on," he shouted at the screen. "Geez. I thought the 49ers were going to be good this year with their draft picks."

"You're a 49er fan? You from San Francisco?"

Harmon shook his head. "Grew up watching Joe Montana. Sort of kept following the 49ers after."

"Where are you from?"

"Born and raised in Oklahoma. Moved here when I was twenty. Just never became a Chiefs fan."

"Can you tell us where you were, say, from Thursday evening through Saturday morning?"

"Oh, yeah. The homicide." Harmon's gaze once

more strayed to the TV. "I'm afraid I don't know anything about a murder that will help you."

"Your whereabouts, Mr. Harmon?"

He frowned in concentration. "Let's see… Thursday night I was here. Watching football. The Falcons beat the Ravens 26 to 21. Friday I drove to my office in St. Louis. Came back that night. Went to Hooter's and had a few beers. Came home."

"Can anyone verify that?"

"Sure. Part of it, anyway. The people at the office. A few guys I talked to at Hooter's." He grinned. "There was a particularly friendly, particularly well-endowed Hooter's girl who might remember me."

"Are you acquainted with a Laurel Lohman?" Lane asked.

The color drained from his face, and he swung his gaze from the TV. "Laurel? Sure, yeah. I know her well. She's not… It isn't her, is it?"

"I'm afraid so, Mr. Harmon. You didn't know she'd been killed?"

"God." He slid to the edge of the sofa and tipped the beer to his mouth, drinking deeply before he responded. "No. Dear God. What happened?"

"That's what we're trying to find out." Webber now. The two of them taking turns. Like a tennis match.

A hint of tears shone in Harmon's eyes. "Laurel. Who would want to hurt her? She was great. Beautiful." He shook his head. "What a shame."

"Her body was found at a property owned by Redland."

"Huh? How's that possible?" His eyes rounded. "It wasn't… Adam didn't have anything to do with it, did he?"

"Why would you ask that?"

He sighed. Shrugged. "He owns those properties now. He and Laurel didn't exactly..." He wet his lips. "Maybe I shouldn't say anything."

"Did Mr. Utley and Miss Lohman have problems?"

It took him a moment to answer. "Not anything big. She just didn't like it that Adam and Tabitha..." he trailed off. "Laurel and I were pretty close. Got along great. She didn't like it when Tabitha left me for Adam."

"We understand that Miss Carrington has a restraining order against you."

Harmon gave a humorless laugh. "That's just her melodrama. Always likes to keep something stirred up. I never bothered her."

"You didn't harass her? Try to get her back?"

Another shrug. "I called her pretty often at first. I couldn't believe our marriage was over. That she cheated on me with Adam. He and I were partners." He sat back, took another swig of the beer. "It took me a little while to get over it, but I did. I moved on. Tabitha just likes attention. She got a VPO just to screw with me."

They ran Hebringer's and Ramirez's names by him, but Harmon said he'd never heard of either.

"I think that's all we have for now. We'll be in touch if anything else comes up."

They stood and Harmon walked them to the door. "I hope you find the bastard," he said. "Poor, sweet Laurel."

"We'll find him," Lane promised. "Thank you for your time, Mr. Harmon. Please call if you think of anything that might help us." Lane handed him a card.

"Will do," Harmon said as they stepped onto the porch. "And, please, call me D.J."

Chapter 15

At almost perfectly spaced intervals along the roads, plump, green spruce trees were scattered amidst the barren branches of the trees that had lost their leaves.

As I drove to the newspaper office, slate grey winter clouds drifted across the azure sky. Although I hadn't seen a forecast, my internal meteorologist told me snow might be in my immediate future. If Josie and I were going to the cabin, we should get started before long. Didn't want to be out driving on hazardous roads.

Adam wasn't in when I arrived.

"Where is he?" I asked Asia.

"Took off for a few days. Dealing with the little woman."

I frowned. "That was awful. What happened to her friend."

"I know. Still don't like the bitch. How weird is that, though? With the obits?"

"Very weird." I shuddered. Weird was an understatement.

"The killer using the newspaper to let the world know who he's going to kill? Freaky."

I was pretty sure the police wanted to keep those details private, but it was all over the office. Not a chance of keeping it under wraps.

"Hey, listen. I'm going to take off a few days. If Adam comes in, would you let him know?"

"Yeah," Asia said slowly. "What's up?"

"Josie and I are going to the cabin. She's entering rehab soon and needs some time away. A little fun before the hell starts."

"Hasn't that girl had enough fun? *Fun* seems to be her problem."

I rolled my eyes. "This is different. She needs some R and R at the cabin. I told her I'd go with her."

"You need some time away, too. I just think you could pick a better companion."

"Yeah, yeah. Whatever. News flash. You don't like Josie."

"No, but I love you. Take care of yourself, okay?"

"I will. I'm fine."

I left the office, calling Josie from my car. She didn't answer. A niggle of worry started, but I pushed it back. She was probably just in the shower.

I got home and discovered she wasn't in the shower. Wasn't in the house at all. No note on the cowboy desk. Where could she be?

In her room, I found a clue as to where she might be. Or, at least, what she might be doing. A narrow straw and a razor blade lay on the dresser. Small white grains of powder glinted on the blade.

Son of a bitch.

Anger and fear warred inside me. Heroin was her normal choice, but the girl wasn't picky. Coke would do in a pinch. Or, maybe it was heroin. I wasn't sure exactly what the drug looked like, didn't know if it was snorted like cocaine. Whatever it was, it wasn't good. Days before rehab and she was back on the crap. Where had she gotten it? And why would she leave it out like that for me to find?

The answer to the first question was obvious. Matt.

Had she gone off with him? Taken him to the cabin maybe? Surely not. She wouldn't do that. Would she?

I knew the answer to that one, too. There were very few limits to what Josie might do. Especially for the drugs.

I didn't really think she'd be there, but the cabin was a place to start. I had no idea where else to look.

I scooped up the straw and razor blade and dropped them in my jacket pocket. I wasn't really sure why I did. Maybe to brandish when I confronted her. Maybe so the cops wouldn't find it if they happened to come to the house. Not that it was exactly wise to have the items on me. But I didn't expect to get strip-searched by the cops any time soon.

In case I did find her—and, in case Matt was with her—I slipped the .22 in my other pocket.

****

Lane checked out the alibi Harmon had given them—that he was at his St. Louis office the day of the murder—while Tony volunteered to take one for the team by chasing down the Hooter's waitress. Harmon's office confirmed he'd been there on Friday, although that didn't mean he hadn't gone back and forth to where the girl was kept. They knew she'd been taken on Thursday night, killed on Friday night, late. What had been going on in between was still unanswered.

None of the Hooter's waitresses could say for sure if they'd seen Harmon. They admitted he could have been there, that it wasn't unusual for them to flirt with a multitude of customers and not remember their names or faces by the end of the shift.

Lane had told Tony about the song titles, but neither

of them had been able to figure out why the killer was using them, what significance they had. Everything was a dead end.

Lane was at the station, reading obituaries from the past few days. He'd already gone through the *Chronicle* and nothing caught his eye. He was now reading the *Star*. He'd made calls to all the papers within two-hundred miles of Kansas City, asking them if they'd had any obits sent in with the wrong dates. None had. They'd all assured him that, if it happened, they'd call. It was a long shot, but he had to try. This maniac was using obits to forecast his kills. Wasn't feasible that he would suddenly stop. Psychos were nothing if not true to form.

Most likely, if any paper had received an obit with the wrong date, it had been corrected before going to print. Still, he perused the obituary columns, searching for a clue. It was boring work. The less glamorous side of detecting. The old joke about people dying alphabetically came to mind. He knew then that true boredom had set in.

"You busy?" a voice said. Lane looked up to find Lou Vittori, one of the cold case detectives, at his desk.

"Nothing that can't wait. What you got?" He'd asked Vittori to check on Katie Broussard's case after his talk with Monroe.

"I have the Broussard file. Nothing new that I can see, so we can't open the case, but thought you might want to know what we have."

Vittori settled his bulky physique in the chair adjacent to Lane's, placing a Styrofoam cup of coffee on Lane's desk.

He studied the file for a moment from beneath busy grey eyebrows, then read aloud, "The victim was twelve

Alicia Dean

years old. On July tenth, 1983, her and two friends, Josephine Detweiler and Monroe Donovan, were staying in a tent in the Donovan's back yard. Sometime around two a.m., the two friends, Detweiler and Donovan, awoke. Broussard was not in the tent. The girls went to look for her in the woods behind the house. They didn't find her. Woke the Donovan girl's parents, who called the police. The girl's body was found a few hours later, by a neighbor involved in the search."

"What about suspects?" Lane asked, picturing a twelve-year-old Monroe dealing with the horrific tragedy.

"There are three boys in the Donovan family. They were all questioned. Two of them had been hunting that night but were in the house by the time the girl disappeared. Soil was found in the Donovan home that matched the soil near the crime scene, but the same soil was all over those woods. It was determined it was tracked in earlier, when the boys came in from hunting. A neighbor witnessed the boys returning at around eleven p.m., well before Broussard went missing."

Vittori sipped from the cup, then continued. "Another suspect, Cameron Cooper, was questioned and released. He did some time for a rape but had an alibi for that night. Couldn't make anything stick. The girl was strangled and her skull was crushed, her pants and panties down around her knees. No semen was found, no evidence of penetration. Cops figured either the guy was impotent, or something interrupted him. It appears sexual assault was intended, but not completed."

"No other suspects?"

"One more. This one looked like the real deal for a few days. A fourteen-year-old boy who lived in the area.

His girlfriend contacted the police a few days after the murder and claimed he'd bragged about killing the Broussard girl. He also had a solid alibi. He was at a sleep-over with a friend. The friend's parents confirmed the boys never left the house. A few days later, the girlfriend recanted her story. Turns out, she was mad at him, trying to get back for him after kissing another girl. Leads ran out after that."

"Damn," Lane said. "Not much to go on." He put aside the *Star* and picked up another paper. One from Iowa, the *Des Moines Herald.*

"There was another killing a year earlier." Vittori leafed through the papers. "Cassie Carthage. There were some similarities, and some differences. Both girls found in a wooded area. Both strangled. Broussard's skull was crushed, but not Carthage's. Carthage was raped. Broussard wasn't. A few things were kept from the media, though. Carthage's arms were crossed over her chest when her body was found, but not Broussard's. Never could make a definite link. No one arrested in that case, either. DNA wasn't around then. Not sure if they'd have found anything if it was. Hard to gather DNA out in nature. Especially when there were no body fluids."

"The girl who gave the false info in Broussard's case didn't help any."

"That's for damn sure. Tied them up with that for the critical time frame. Ask me," Vittori said, pausing to slurp from the coffee cup, "people like that should be prosecuted along with the fucking criminals."

****

When I rounded the bend and the cabin came in sight, I slammed on my brakes, taking a second look, then a third to be sure I was seeing what I thought I was seeing.

I hadn't expected Josie to be here. I would have been surprised, relieved even, if she had been, especially if Matt hadn't been with her. While the car parked in the drive of the cabin was certainly a surprise, there was no relief to go along with it. I clenched my hair so tight my eyes watered. Fucking Adam.

Maybe I shouldn't have been angry. After all, he was grieving over Laurel Lohman. Tabitha probably needed to get away. But for chrissake, if he wanted to get away and help his fiancée grieve, that was his business. But not in my cabin.

I climbed from the car and slammed the door. As I headed toward the porch, passing Adam's prized Lexus, I just barely resisted the urge to key the flawless black paint.

A thought occurred to me that made me halt at the bottom of the steps. What if they were actually having sex, right now? Did I really want to walk in on that?

No, I didn't *want* to, but I damn sure wasn't letting them finish.

When I stepped up on the porch, I heard loud music coming from inside. Something about the song gave me pause. Chills crept over my skin. What was it about this song? My anger wouldn't let me register anything other than my asshole ex. A distant memory tugged at me, but I couldn't bring it into full focus.

I turned the knob and was pushing the door open before the connection clicked. By then, it was too late. I was already inside.

The music soared...reverberated around me...through me, registering more quickly than the scene in front of my eyes—I recognized the song, but my mind wouldn't quite accept what my eyes were seeing.

****

"This is a favor for a friend?" Vittori asked.

"Yeah," Lane said.

"Tell you what, we can't officially open it, but I'll do some digging whenever I can. See if anything comes up."

"Thanks. Do you see anything about this case that might link it to Maya Pittman's murder?"

Vittori considered this, taking another sip of his coffee. "We looked at the evidence, tried to find a link, but although there were similarities, there weren't enough to tie them together. Pittman's arms were crossed over her chest, which was odd, but with there being twenty-three years between the murders, they decided that was just a coincidence. Best suspect in Pittman's killing was her teacher… also her lover." His lip curled with disgust. "Couldn't get enough to make a case, but we're still keeping an eye on him. His sperm was found on the victim, but there was also sperm from a young boy she dated from school. And, an unknown." He shook his head. "Girl got around for such a tender age. But, then, that's the way things are these days."

"Who worked the old cases?"

Vittori once more consulted the file. "Same guys worked both Carthage and Broussard. McClung and Ramirez."

"You know 'em?"

"McClung. He retired a few years back. Okay cop, but not the most vigilant. Kind that'll cut corners when he can."

"As likely to close a case as to solve it?"

"Pretty much sums him up."

Lane's phone rang and he held up a finger to Vittori. "Hold on a sec." Into the phone, he said, "Brody."

"I'm headin' in, partner. Get anything on the obits yet?"

"Nada."

"Shit. What about the song titles? Lab reports on the paint?"

"Nothing yet," Lane said, sighing in frustration.

Tony echoed his sigh. "All right, then. I'll be there soon."

Lane hung up and looked at Vittori. "Sorry. Current case is starting to make us a little crazy."

"No problem. Mine have all been around for a while. Not a lot cooking. Not like the fresh ones. Still, this Broussard thing. Kind of tugs at you, you know?"

Lane nodded, his attention going back to the Des Moines paper. His eyes locked on an obit near the end of the list.

"I'll be damned," he whispered.

"I know. Shame. Little girl like that. Never getting the guy. Dirty, rotten shame."

Lane didn't acknowledge him. His eyes once more scanned the obit and his blood chilled. It wasn't a date that caught his eye, but a name. Two names, actually.

The obituary read, *Adam Utley and Tabitha Carrington passed away unexpectedly and violently on November 11th. As they loved together, they died together. Services to be held at Sausalito Funeral Home.*

Utley most likely wasn't the killer. Or, if he was, it would be a murder/suicide. Either way, they needed to find him and Tabitha Carrington. And they needed to do it quickly. According to the obit, the two of them would die today.

"Sorry," he told Vittori, "Got something breaking on a case."

"No problem. I'll get out of your way. I'll let you know if anything comes up on Broussard."

"Kramer," Lane called out, "I need you to check out a residence." He gave him Utley's name and a brief rundown of what had developed. "Don't know the address. Look it up. I'm heading over to the newspaper."

Lane called Tony's cell. "You here yet?"

"Almost. What's up?"

Lane explained seeing the obit. "Kramer is on his way to Utley's. I'll head down and meet you in the parking lot. We'll go to the *Chronicle*."

Lane took the stairs instead of waiting for the elevator. Tony was in the parking lot when he got outside.

"What about the funeral?" Tony asked when Lane slid into the passenger seat. "Does it list where?"

"Sausalito funeral home. Mean anything?"

Tony shook his head. "Nothing."

They pulled out onto the street while Lane dialed the newspaper's number. A recorded voice answered, "You have reached the offices of The Northland Chronicle. Please say the department you want when you hear it."

"You've got to be kidding me," Lane muttered.

"Did you say classifieds?" the voice asked.

Lane let out a breath. "No," he said clearly, loudly.

Tony looked over at him and raised his brows. Lane shook his head. If he explained, the voice might send him to Antarctica.

"I'm sorry," the voice continued. "Please say the department when you hear it." It then began listing the departments. Lane didn't know which one would get him to Utley, so he said, "Operator," into the phone.

"Please hold for an operator," the voice, eager to please, said.

Lane held for an operator, but before a human came on the line, they'd reached the *Chronicle*.

Chapter 16

Adam and Tabitha sat side by side in two dining room chairs that had been placed in the center of my living room. Their hands were behind their backs, and when I saw their bound feet, I realized their hands must also be bound.

At first, I thought Adam was naked. Then I noticed the black bikini briefs. Tabitha wore a white, lacy Teddy. Even under these bizarre circumstances, I felt a brief flash of envy at how tanned and toned her bare legs were. Her face was pale and splotched with tears. Her blue eyes were wide and bewildered, like someone receiving bad news they hadn't quite accepted.

A man stood with his back to the door, but he swung around when I came in. We stared at one another, the silence almost palpable, as mutual recognition bloomed between us.

It took a few seconds to really register who he was. Without the tattered watch cap, the grimy, shredded coat, and the wires connecting him to the ever-present CD player, I almost didn't know him.

Finally, I found my voice. "I don't understand. What…?"

But I did understand. Headphone was the killer.

"Monroe? What are you doing here?" He sounded angry and confused. It occurred to me it was the first time I'd ever heard him speak. His voice was deep, melodious, not at all what I'd have imagined.

He held a pistol pointed straight at my chest. I thought of the .22 but knew he'd shoot me before I could possibly fumble it out of my pocket. I was dimly aware that the song, "Escape," had ended… and started again. The professor was right. Headphone really *did* like this song.

"I'm sorry." Headphone said, sounding truly sorrowful. "I really liked you. I don't want to do this."

Oh, God. He was going to kill me. Tears welled in my throat, but I was so frozen with fear, they didn't fall.

"Drag a chair in here," he said.

"Huh?"

He motioned impatiently with the gun. "Get a chair. I'll have to tie you up, too."

I was never so relieved at the thought of being bound to a chair and held captive. Damn sure beat the other option that had flitted through my brain.

I headed into the kitchen, aware of the gun pointed at my back, and grabbed one of the two chairs left. Headphone took it from me and placed it a few feet away from Adam's.

"Sit," he commanded.

I sat. He took a length of rope from a duffle bag and bound my hands and feet.

"That's not too tight, is it?"

I shook my head, bewildered by his conciliatory manner, combined with his decidedly non-conciliatory actions. Now wasn't the time, however, to puzzle out a conundrum such as this. Now was the time to figure out how to get out of this alive. And maybe get Adam and Tabitha out alive, too. The jury was still out on that one.

The bulge in my pocket caught Headphone's

attention and he reached in and took the .22.

"Sorry. Can't let you keep this."

"Who are you, really?" I asked once he had me secured to the chair.

He turned to Tabitha. "Tell her."

She slowly lifted her head, frowning. "What?"

"Tell her who I am."

Her lips tightened and a fresh wave of tears poured from her eyes. "My ex. He's my ex-husband."

Headphone nodded like she'd passed some kind of test. "Yes. I'm Tabitha's ex-husband. Derek. D.J."

"But you…" I shook my head. "Why were you outside… homeless?"

"It was the only way to be close to her." His gaze swung to Tabitha. "I watched you, you know. Every day. You thought you were so smart with your restraining order, thought you could keep me away. But I was closer to you these past few weeks than you would have possibly thought I could be. Of course, had you not been so self-absorbed, I wouldn't have gotten away with it. But, you never really saw me. Never saw them. As if they're not worth your notice. Less than human."

Tabitha frowned again. "You're doing this because I treated homeless people badly?"

A burst of laughter left him. "Oh, my dear. You are beautiful, but not exactly God's most intelligent creature. I'm doing this because you betrayed me. Because, you're mine. Only mine. You know, I kept thinking that you'd come back to me. That you'd see you really loved me. Then, when I found out about your engagement, I knew. You were never coming back." His eyes narrowed and he shook his head. "But you're still mine. Always will be. You'll die mine."

Tabitha let out a little whimper and a fresh rush of tears fell from her eyes. Headphone—no, *Derek*—laughed. "You're scared? Hurt? Now you know how I felt. How I *feel*."

The song started again. Tabitha squeezed her eyes shut. "Can you please turn that off?"

"Why, honey," Derek said, "it's your favorite song, right?" He started singing along with the song, loudly and out of tune.

Tabitha's whimpering turned to a high-pitched wail. "Please," she begged. "Please stop this, let us go. I'm sorry, please, please…"

"Remember?" Derek said, ignoring her pleas. "We listened to it constantly during our honeymoon. The beach, the moon, the umbrella drinks. And, this song. When you left me, I found this CD on the floor of our bedroom. Discarded, cast away just like our marriage."

"Look, man—" Adam began. Derek pounced on him and cracked him across the jaw with the gun.

I yelped. "No! What are you—"

"Shut up!" Derek screamed at Adam. "You don't speak, got it?"

Adam stared up at him, a line of blood oozing from his jaw. His eyes were wet and glittered with pain… or rage. Maybe both.

Derek's gaze swung to me. "They have to pay, Monroe. You know that, right? I won't kill you… can't. You're a victim just like I am. Plus, you have a good heart, unlike this self-centered whore I married. You *saw* the homeless. Really saw us. You cared. Not them, though. They only cared about themselves. What they wanted, no matter who it hurt. You do see why, right? See why they have to die?"

"No one has to die," I said. "You can stop this." I glanced to where Tabitha and Adam sat, their expressions frozen in terror. "Don't you think they've been punished enough?"

His gaze followed mine. He shook his head. "No. I don't think they've been punished enough. Not nearly enough."

****

"Is Adam Utley here?" Lane asked the receptionist as soon as he and Tony stepped off the elevator. He flipped open his badge, even though they were here a few weeks ago and she probably knew they were cops.

"I'm not sure," she said, smiling pleasantly and reaching for the phone. "One moment and I'll check."

As he waited, the phone on his belt vibrated. He picked it up. "Brody."

"I'm at Utley's. No one's answering the door." It was Kramer.

"Is his car there?"

"Not in the driveway. Could be in the garage, can't see through the window. Want us to go in or wait for a warrant?"

"Can't wait. They're in danger. Try again. If no one comes to the door, go inside. Call me when you're in."

"Lane?" a female voice.

He slipped his phone back in its case and turned to find Asia coming through the glass door. His gaze searched the room behind her, trying to catch a glimpse of Utley. Hoping he might also catch a glimpse of Monroe.

"Asia, hi. Is Utley around?"

She shook her head. "He took off for a few days."

"Shit," Lane murmured.

"Is everything okay?" Then she shook her head and laughed, a short, humorless sound. "Well, I know everything's not okay. I mean, come on. The murders, the obituaries... weird. But, I mean, is everything okay with Adam?"

Lane ignored her question. "What about Tabitha? Do you know where she might be?"

Asia's brows drew together in a frown. "No. I don't. What's going on? Is Monroe okay?"

"Monroe? Why wouldn't she be? She's not here?"

Asia shook her head. "She took off for a few days, too."

Lane tried to ignore the tight feeling in his chest. "With Utley?"

"No. No way. With Josie. They went to the cabin."

"Cabin?"

Asia nodded. "She and Josie have a cabin at Lake Viking."

"Do you know where Utley went? Was he planning a trip?"

"Have no idea. You might try the cabin."

"I thought you said Monroe went there and they didn't go away together."

"I did. But that asshole has used her cabin before, without permission. He might be doing it again."

Lane's phone rang again.

"We're inside," Kramer said. "No one's around. No sign of a struggle, but the bedding is rumpled."

"I'm heading that way. What about a car?"

"There's a pink Ferrari in the garage. It's a four-car garage and there's just the one. I'm betting the Ferrari belongs to the girlfriend. You know what Utley drives?"

"No, but I'll find out."

"Let's go," Lane told Tony when he ended the call. "No one's at Utley's place."

"What's happening?" Asia asked.

"Not sure," Lane said, heading for the exit.

"You'd tell me if something was wrong with Monroe, right?"

"This has nothing to do with her. She's fine," Lane said, but worry had started to slither in his gut. The killer was using her obituaries, after all. She'd dated Utley. She still worked for him. Could this have something to do with her? Could she be in danger?

"What about Harmon?" Tony's question interrupted his thoughts. "Should we talk to him?"

Lane nodded as they stepped back onto the elevator. "We'll call him. Also, we need to call Utley and Carrington's family members. See if anyone knows where they might be."

He reached for his phone. First, he was calling Monroe.

****

"Don't you want him… want them, to pay for what they've done to you?" Derek asked.

"No. I've moved on. I realized that if we were meant to be together, we would be. I'm better off without someone who would cheat on me," I said, trying not to think about how bizarre it was to be discussing my emotional journey with a killer.

Between the slats of the plantation blinds on the living room window, I could see the encroaching darkness. Evening had started to fall and I hadn't been aware of its arrival. How long had I been here? Would someone be looking for me? Would Lane?

Derek paced between the chairs, first behind Adam

and Tabitha, then between us, then behind me. All the time, he kept a running litany of all the wrong that had been done to him.

"What about Richard Hebringer?" I asked. "Laurel? What did they do to you?"

He stopped in front of my chair, but his eyes were on Adam and Tabitha. "They were conspirators. They aided in the deception."

I wasn't sure exactly what he meant, but figured if I waited, he'd elaborate. Not to have ever heard him speak before, I was certainly getting a large dose of his voice now.

I wasn't disappointed.

"Hebringer was the desk clerk at the bed and breakfast where the lovebirds liked to sneak off. He knew they weren't married. He catered to the sleazy clientele who wanted to sneak away and betray the ones who trusted them. Then, Laurel—"

At that moment, my cell phone rang. I jumped. Derek turned and looked at me. "Was that yours?"

I nodded.

"Ignore it."

I nodded again. I hadn't really thought he would allow me to answer and chat with whoever was calling. I wondered if it were Josie.

"Laurel," he continued, "knew the whole time. She pretended to be my friend. She even acted indignant that you would betray me, pretended to feel bad for me after you left me. But, in reality, she helped you. Helped you hide it from me. Helped you sneak away, made excuses for you so I wouldn't know what you were doing."

Tabitha didn't respond. She sat in the chair, trembling, still crying. How many tears could one woman shed? I would have thought she'd dry up by now. Adam had been silent since Derek struck him. His jaw was starting to swell. He looked miserable and terrified. I couldn't help but feel sorry for him. I even felt sorry for Tabitha.

Were we all going to die? Derek said he couldn't kill me, but the man didn't seem very trustworthy. Besides, I didn't want to watch him kill Adam and Tabitha either. I mean, admittedly, it had been a fantasy I'd entertained from time to time, but I didn't really mean it. I wanted them to be unhappy, sure. Fat, poor, disease-ridden, yeah. But not *murdered*.

Because I'd seen a lot of movies, and because stalling seemed to be a popular tactic used by kidnap victims, I kept Derek talking.

"What about the obituaries? Why did you put them in the paper?"

Derek shrugged. "Thought it would be a good way to fuck with our boy here. His paper, after all. Kind of an extra little dig, you know. To announce the murders in his paper."

"Clever," I said, and was surprised that I really meant it.

Derek looked at Adam and shook his head. "Do you have any idea what kind of woman she is? You had so much better before. And you threw it all away for her?" He shot Tabitha a disgusted look and shook his head. I didn't bring up the irony of the great lengths *he'd* gone because of his love for Tabitha.

"Did she tell you about the baby?"

"What baby?" Adam mumbled, obviously having difficulty speaking through the pain.

"When I met Tabitha, I had a child. A little boy. He

was two. I wasn't married to his mother, but had visiting rights. We were close. I would have made a good dad. Tabitha didn't want me to see him. Didn't like that he took part of my time, not to mention money that could have been spent on her. We had several fights about it, but I finally gave in. I signed away my rights to my son. For her." His eyes misted over. "I loved my son. I really did. But I was so madly in love with Tabitha. And, she promised me we'd have a child of our own. Promised me she'd spend the rest of her life making me happy." He went silent for a moment, then slowly walked closer to Adam and Tabitha. "Did you tell him, Tabitha?"

She didn't answer.

He looked down at Adam. "Did she? Did she tell you she was pregnant?"

Adam flinched and I knew she hadn't.

"Yes," Derek went on. "She was pregnant with my child. Only, she never told me. Instead, she killed our baby. She had an abortion without telling me."

I gasped, and Adam's face paled. He looked at Tabitha with something close to disgust. I thought it a little incongruous that we could be held by a murdering psychopath and still be shocked by Tabitha's callous act. I knew how much Adam wanted children. His first wife hadn't given him any. Although he and I never discussed marriage, he said many times he hoped someday to be a father. I guess Tabitha's betrayal hit close to home. If she could do it to her first husband, she could do it to him, too.

"Adam, he's lying. I would never—"

"Shut up!" Derek screamed, and I thought he was going to hit Tabitha, too. He didn't. Instead, he smiled.

"I want to hear the story," he said, his voice as

pleasant as if he were inviting her to afternoon tea.

"Story?" Tabitha said in a trembling rasp.

"The story of how the affair started. Tell us all about it. I never really got the chance to find out. How did it start? We want details, don't we, Monroe?"

I said nothing.

Tabitha didn't respond right away, and Derek leaned down, so close to her face it looked like he might kiss her. "Tell us!" he screamed. "Tell us how the fuck it started."

She shrank back from him, her eyes as big around as softballs. "I don't... I'm not..."

My phone rang again, and Derek whirled toward me. "Where is it? Where's your phone?"

"In my jacket pocket," I said, then, remembering the razor blade and afraid he'd search me and find it, even though I wasn't sure if or how I'd be able to use it, I said, "The same one where the gun was."

He came over to me and reached into that pocket, pulling out my phone.

Holding it up, he peered at the display. "Detective Brody?" he said. "Why would a cop be calling you? What have you done? Did you get a message to them somehow?"

I shook my head, feeling my heart soar that it was Lane calling. "No. How would I have? He doesn't know anything. We're seeing each other," I blurted.

Derek's eyes narrowed suspiciously. "Then why do you have him stored as *Detective* Brody?"

I rolled my eyes, as if it were obvious. "I programmed him in before we started dating. I just haven't bothered to change it." I wasn't sure if he was buying it or not. Before he had too much time to think, I rushed on, "He doesn't know anything's happening, but if I don't answer, don't call him back, he'll start to wonder. He'll be worried. Might even come out here to check things out. Cops have a way of finding people, you know. He could track my phone."

He hesitated, then said, "Okay, call. But I'm listening in. Don't try anything."

"Will you untie me?"

He shook his head. "I'll dial."

He punched the callback button on my phone and stuck it to my ear. He put his head close to mine, so he could hear what was said. Although I would have expected foul odors to emanate from him, instead, I smelled mint and some kind of musky aftershave. Even while posing as a homeless person, he obviously paid attention to hygiene.

In seconds, Lane came on the line. "Monroe?" His voice was so full of relief, so very precious, I almost cried.

"Hey, sweetie," I said brightly.

There was a pause. "Hi. Is everything okay?"

"Yeah. Fine. I just miss you. We haven't been apart for this long since we started seeing each other."

Another pause. "Right. Yeah. I miss you, too."

"Just thought I'd let you know, I'm on my way to meet Katie." I hoped he'd get the message that something was wrong, although I wasn't sure what he'd do about it... what he could do about it. I couldn't say I was at the cabin. Derek wouldn't be very happy about that.

"Katie?"

"Yeah. I'll be there soon."

"I thought you and Josie were heading to the cabin."

"No. Josie had to work."

Between the pretend dating, going to see Katie, and the idea that Josie had a job, surely he'd know all was not well. Even if he did, though, I didn't think he could find me. Yes, as I told Derek, the police could trace cell phones, but I was pretty sure they had to have a warrant. And, I wasn't sure how exact the trace would be, even if he could do it immediately, which I doubted.

"You're going to see Katie," he said incredulously.

"Yes." A loud static sounded in my ear and I held my breath, afraid I'd lose the signal and Lane would be gone.

I almost cried with relief when I heard his voice through the distortion. "Where? Where are you going to see Katie?"

I looked up at Derek. I couldn't think of a way to give Lane a hint without tipping Derek off. My mind wasn't working properly, although in my defense, it was no wonder under the circumstances. "Her place," I said, then wished I hadn't. I might send him on a wild goose chase to Katie's grave, but I couldn't think of anything else to say. I'd meant 'her place' as in, death, but Lane wouldn't know that.

"I see," he said slowly. I sensed his uncertainty, his worry, through the phone. Derek motioned for me to cut it off.

"I have to go. I'll talk to you later," I said, feeling tears clog my throat. I didn't want to break the connection. Didn't want to lose the sound of his voice.

"Take care of yourself. I'll see you soon, okay?" he said, as if making me a promise.

"Yeah, okay." I tried but failed to keep the tremor out of my words.

"Monroe?" Lane said, his voice low, soothing.

"Yeah?"

"I love you."

I drew in a sharp breath that turned into a sob and briefly closed my eyes, savoring his words. I hadn't expected that. I knew we were playacting, but the way his declaration affected me was so very real. Too real.

"Yeah, you too," I said, barely able to squeeze the words past the knot in my throat. "I'll see you soon."

Chapter 17

They had just pulled up to Utley's house and climbed from the car when Monroe called. Until that moment—until their conversation—Lane hadn't known she was in danger. Had worried, yeah, had known it was a vague possibility, but now it was confirmed and he felt like his heart was going to explode inside his chest.

On the way over, Lane had made calls to every friend and relative he could get hold of. None of them had any idea about Utley's or Carrington's whereabouts. Lane had also called Utley's cell. Kramer answered the call. Both cell phones were at the house, along with Carrington's purse. It was starting to sound more and more like they were snatched. Or, there was still the possibility that Utley was the killer and had taken off with Carrington.

"Wow, dude." Tony whistled after Lane clicked his cell closed. "You sly dog. You *love* her?"

Lane scrubbed a hand over his face. "She was trying to get me a message. I said that for the benefit of whoever was listening."

"Well, if what you *said* will benefit them, imagine how happy they'll be if you bone her."

Lane turned on him, grabbing him by the shirt collar. "Shut the hell up. You hear me?" His rage was totally out of proportion to the comment, and he tried to shove aside the dark curtain falling over his vision.

"Hey, hey," Tony said, his hands rising defensively. "Take it easy, man. It's me. Just trying to lighten the mood a bit. Didn't mean anything by it."

Lane let out a breath and released his hold. "Sorry. I'm just wound a little tight, you know?"

"Yeah. I can see. Hey, for what it's worth, you're a really good actor."

Lane narrowed his eyes. "What's that supposed to mean?"

Tony shrugged. "I'm just sayin'. You know. The love thing? You had me convinced."

Lane glared at him, but chose to ignore his remark. "Someone definitely has her. Utley and Carrington are probably with her, too. Hell, Utley may be the one holding her. But where? No time to get a warrant to trace the cell signal." He slapped a palm on the hood of the car. "Damn."

"What makes you so sure something's wrong?"

"She said they were going to see Katie."

"Yeah, so? Couldn't she really be going to see Katie?"

"Hope not," Lane said tightly as they headed to Utley's door. "Katie's been dead for twenty-five years."

****

"I meant what I said," Derek told me. "I don't want to kill you, but if he shows up, I will. You better not have tipped him off."

"I didn't," I said, hoping I had, but that Lane could do something about it that wouldn't get anyone killed.

"Was is worth it?" Derek asked, his attention now on Adam and Tabitha, seeming to have forgotten about my call to Lane. "The sex? Was it worth what happened? The murders?"

"It wasn't our fault." Tabitha's voice was thick with tears. "You didn't have to—"

"Oh, but I did. You drove me to it. You betrayed me with someone I thought was my friend. You made a fool of me, took away everything I had, then left me. Like I was nothing." He ran the gun along Tabitha's cheek and she flinched. Slowly, he let the gun trail downward, over her neck, then to her breasts where he let it linger. "Must have been really good. The sex. So, tell us. How good was it?"

"Stop, please," she whimpered.

"No. I want to hear about it. Right after we married, you became a prude. Wouldn't let me touch you. All you cared about was yourself. Your looks. The spas, the exercise, the facials. Sex would just cut in to your beauty sleep. Your beauty regimen. Is she that way with you, Adam? Or does she give it to you like a prostitute? Any time you ask, but it's going to cost you?"

"Knock it off," Adam said.

Derek laughed. "I want to know about the sex." The gun traveled down to between Tabitha's legs. She gasped. He laughed again, then moved the gun over to Adam, aiming toward his crotch. "If the sex isn't worth talking about, I might as well shoot off your dick, right? Is that what you want, or you want to tell me about it?"

"I'll tell you," I said.

Derek turned. "You? What do you know about it?"

"More than I want to, trust me. I've seen the signs." I met Adam's eyes and put as much hatred as I could into mine. "I found the sex toys they used. When he screwed her. Here. In my cabin. My bed."

"What are you doing?" Adam's eyes rounded. "You'll just piss him off."

It was true, but I had a plan. Maybe not the greatest, but it was all I could come up with at the moment. Had to try. I didn't think Derek would be any angrier at evidence of what he already had in his head about the two of them. Maybe I could have thought of a better way to get him out of the room, but I was under duress. I didn't do my best thinking when I was tied to a chair, in a room with my almost naked ex-lover and his equally naked fiancé, being held captive by a harmless, slow-witted homeless man turned ranting, murderous, psychotic, kidnapper.

"Let her talk," Derek told Adam, then to me, "Tell me."

I nodded. "First, though, I want the ring."

"What ring?"

I pointed. "Her ring. It should have been mine."

Tabitha glared at me. "You're out of your mind. It's mine. He didn't love you."

"Take it," Derek said, giving her a smug smile. "Want me to cut her finger off for you?"

"No," I said quickly. "Untie me and I'll get it." At his hesitation, I said. "Come on. You have my gun. You're standing there with yours. What am I going to do?"

He thought about it. "Go ahead. But make it quick."

"I want his, too."

Derek laughed. "Miss goody-two-shoes has a mean streak. I like that."

He loosened my bindings and I stood, rubbing my wrists to get the circulation going again. I walked over to Tabitha.

"Please," she whispered tearfully. "Please don't take my ring. If I'm going to die, I want to die with it on."

A surprising surge of sympathy rose. Moving behind Tabitha, I squeezed her hand, hoping to convey reassurance, although not sure what I was reassuring her about. I tugged the ring from her finger and slipped it in my pocket, at the same time, gripping the razor blade. Behind Adam, blocked from Derek's view, I pulled his ring off also, putting the blade in his hand.

Moving around to the front of him, I leaned in and said, "Goodbye Adam." Moving closer, as if to kiss him, I put my lips against his ear, whispering so quietly, I wasn't sure if Adam heard me, but I didn't want Derek to. "If you get a chance, use this. Escape."

I rose and turned to Derek, opening my hand where the rings lay in my palm, triumphantly displaying my success.

"Good for you. Where they're going, they won't need them anyway."

Tabitha sobbed out, "Please, Derek. God, think about this. You can't really mean to—"

"Where are they?" he asked me, cutting her off. "Where are the toys? Maybe we'll make them give us a demonstration."

I shuddered. He was lumping us together, as if we were a team.

"Upstairs. In the bedroom. Maybe in the nightstand drawer, but they could be in the closet." I was pretty sure Gable had gotten rid of all the paraphernalia, but looking for it would keep Derek busy long enough for us to get away, even if he tied me up again before going upstairs, which I was certain he would.

My hopes were dashed with his next words. "Okay, but you're going with me."

Correction. Maybe just long enough for Adam and

Tabitha to get away.

I cast Adam a look I hoped he understood. *Now's your chance.*

Then, I led Derek up the stairs.

****

There was nothing at Utley's to indicate where they'd gone, or to indicate whether he was the perp or a victim. They'd tried to reach Harmon, to no avail. He could possibly be involved, too. Or at least know where Utley might have taken Tabitha.

Now, Lane had the added concern over Monroe. The added urgency. She was in danger. And, he had no idea how much, or by whom, or where she might be.

His phone rang and he snatched it off his belt. "Brody," he barked.

"This is Chris at the lab. Got results back on the paint at the Lohman scene."

"Yeah?"

"There were two different kinds, actually. One was a water-based paint, like face paint."

"Face paint?"

"Yeah. Like clowns might use."

Lohman's band was the Raging Clowns. Lane and Tony had gone to the club where they performed and learned that their fans dressed like clowns. A crazed fan had killed her?

"And the other?"

"A water soluble oil paint. Artist's paint."

"Artist's?"

"Yep."

Artist's.... Why did that seem to trigger something? Artist's paint...

Then it hit him. Son of a bitch. Harmon.

"Thanks, Chris." Lane slammed the phone shut. He looked at Tony. "It's Harmon. Let's go."

"Harmon?"

"Remember his paintings?" Lane said as he and Tony climbed in the car. "Artist's paint was found at Lohman's scene. It's him."

"Shit. And he seemed like such a nice guy."

"Right. Don't they all." Lane's gut tensed as they sped to Harmon's. Would Monroe be there or did he have her somewhere else?

Please let her be there, he prayed. *But mostly, please let her be okay.*

****

Harmon's house was dark when they pulled up. Nothing to indicate anyone was inside.

"Police, open up," Lane shouted, banging on the front door.

No response.

Tony went around to the back while Lane waited on the front porch, continuing to knock. When Tony reappeared, he shook his head. "Nothing back there. I tried the doors, locked."

Lane considered for a moment, then said, "Stand back. We're going in."

Tony nodded and backed up.

Lane hoped 'probable cause' would fly. If not, he was willing to deal with the consequences. He aimed his Glock at the knob, firing until the lock, and parts of the wood, shattered. They pushed the door open and stepped into the darkened house.

"Harmon?" Lane called out. He and Tony made their way through the house, into the kitchen, bathroom, pantry. Up the stairs, into each bedroom, each bathroom, each closet. Back downstairs. Not a sign of anyone.

"Where the hell is he?" Lane said, fighting down panic.

Tony shook his head as they both re-holstered their weapons. "Have no idea." He walked over to the entertainment center where the CD rack was filled with CD's and began to thumb through them. "I'll be damned," he said after a few seconds.

"Any of them Rupert Holmes?" Lane asked.

Tony turned to look at him and sighed heavily. "All of them."

Lane could feel the blood drain from his face. "We had him," he bit out. "We were right here in his goddamned living room."

"Yeah. We had him. What now?"

Lane's shoulders dropped and he swiped his hands over his face. He replayed his and Monroe's phone conversation in his head, trying to figure out if she'd given him a clue as to their whereabouts. She'd said they were going to 'Katie's place.' Did that mean they were at her grave? At Katie's parents' house? He had no idea where either of those was, but he could find out. He didn't feel convinced Harmon had taken Monroe there, but he had nowhere else to look.

He picked up his phone to call headquarters and nearly dropped it when it rang in his hand. He looked at the display, praying it was Monroe. It wasn't.

"This is Schwinn." Lane had the computer guy at the station running a check on Sausalito, the place mentioned in Utley and Carrington's obit. Lane had told him to find out if it were a street, a business, a town, anything. "Got a hit on Sausalito."

"Yeah?" Lane's heart sped up. Wherever this

Sausalito was, most likely that was where Harmon had taken them.

"It's a road. Not sure if that's what you're looking for, though. It's not here."

"Where is it?"

"Lake Viking."

****

I slowly led Derek to my bedroom, one part of me hoping Adam and Tabitha would escape, the other part not sure, not wanting to be left alone with a killer... wondering what would happen to me then. Did Derek really mean it when he said he wouldn't kill me?

"Where are they?" Derek asked when we were inside my room.

It took me a moment to answer. My gaze was on the bed where an unfamiliar comforter had replaced my grandma's quilt. *Gabe.* I'd forgotten about his promise to replace the bedding, but he'd been true to his word. A rush of emotion swept through me. Would I ever see my brother again?

"Monroe?" Derek barked. "Where are the toys?"

I started at his voice. "Maybe over here." I went to the nightstand and slid the drawer open, rummaging through the few items—hand lotion, a Dennis Lehane book, reading glasses. No sex toys.

"Well?"

I shook my head. "They might be in the closet."

We went to the closet, but there wasn't much to rummage through. Since I didn't stay at the cabin often, I kept only a few items there. It didn't take long to figure out there were no sex toys.

"They must have taken them with them the last time they stayed. But, they were here. You can't imagine how hurt, how humiliated I was when I found them." At least that part was true.

"Yeah, as a matter of fact, I can." Derek sighed. "Doesn't matter. I'm tired of the games anyway. Time to put an end to all this. Let's go."

He motioned me in front of him and I slowly walked to the top of the stairs. Peering down, I saw a flash at the front door as Tabitha slipped out, Adam close behind. Derek saw it, too.

"Shit!" he yelled and raised the gun.

Automatically, my arm went up and shoved at his.

The gun went off and a stinging, burning sensation pierced my hand. I jerked, flailing backward, grasping with both hands, including the injured one, but making contact with nothing but air. I lost my balance, stumbling, then falling, toppling down the stairs. I cried out as a sharp pain stabbed through my chest, much more painful than the hand that had taken a bullet.

"Son of a bitch." Derek raced down the stairs, past me, running to the door.

In moments, he was back, cursing, storming over to where I lay on the ground. "You let them go," he raged. "You helped them escape. I know you did."

Wooziness swam through me, and I thought I might throw up, but the pain had cut off my breath, and I couldn't do anything but gasp, fighting the blackness closing like a curtain over my eyes.

"Couldn't let you kill us," I managed to whisper, not sure if the words really came out. "Not all of us."

He aimed the gun at me. I closed my eyes, tears of pain and fear squeezing between my lashes. I didn't want to die. I was terrified and would have been begging for my life if the pain wasn't so bad that I could barely breathe, let alone speak. I couldn't decide what hurt the most, my chest and side where I thought I might have broken a few ribs, my ankle I'd injured in the fall, or the hand with the bullet hole that was now starting to burn and throb like a mother.

Didn't matter. All of the pain would soon go away, because in seconds, I'd be dead.

****

"You should have let me drive, dude," Tony said, the words a tense warble as he stared at the speedometer's climbing needle.

Lane didn't respond. His hands tightened on the wheel, but he decreased his speed, just a little. Asia had given them the address to the cabin. They'd passed the graveyard and the church she mentioned. From what he could gather, they were only a few miles out. He was having trouble breathing. Fear had taken hold of his throat and was spreading through his chest. Monroe with this maniac. An image of Laurel Lohman's bloody body strapped to the chair flashed in his mind, and he almost gasped out loud.

Shit, shit, shit.

He felt Tony's eyes on him, but he kept his on the road. They pulled into the lake entrance and passed a brick sign with a replica of a ship mounted on top, displaying the words "Valkyrie Valley" in red, another landmark Asia had mentioned. They were close. He peered through the gloom for the Sausalito street sign.

In moments, he found it, and then the cabin. Lane slowed , lights off. A dark colored Lexus was parked in front of the porch. Next to it was Monroe's car.

Lane parked at the end of the drive so the killer wouldn't spot them if he happened to look out the window. It might make him freak out and do something to the hostages. If he hadn't already.

He and Tony exited the car, both sinking into a low crouch, guns drawn. Lights glowed in the windows of the cabin, but he couldn't see figures, couldn't make out anything from this distance. He'd have to get closer.

"Cover me," he whispered to Tony and started to head toward the cabin. Before he had gone two steps, he heard the boom of a gunshot. He froze. His intestines twisted and fingers of ice climbed his spine.

Two figures ran out the front door, illuminated by the cabin's porch light. Lane raised his gun, then slowly lowered it when he saw the man wasn't Harmon. Both people were half-naked, the woman wearing some kind of lingerie, the man nothing but bikini briefs. Neither of them were Monroe. It was Utley and Carrington, their hands in the air, their faces clenched in terror.

"Please," Utley screamed. "He's got a gun... Monroe's in there."

Behind them, a man appeared in the doorway. He spotted Lane and ducked back, but not before Lane recognized him. Harmon. Shit. They'd had him. Right there, right at the tips of their fingers, but had discounted him as a suspect. And now Monroe's life was on the line. She might already be dead.

"Is she okay? Who was shot?" Lane asked, panic nearly cutting off the words. He wanted to rush into the cabin, but knew it could possibly endanger her even more. He had to figure out the best way to do this, the way that would save her life.

Utley shook his head. His eyes were moist with tears. "I don't know. It happened as we were... running." The last word came out quietly, as if from shame.

"Monroe gave me a razor blade, then distracted Derek, got him to go upstairs so we could escape." He sucked in a deep breath. "He saw us trying to run and was going to shoot us. I think Monroe might have blocked it. She saved our lives."

God. Foolish, brave woman.

Next to Utley, Tabitha Carrington trembled violently, her face pale except for the streaks of red on her cheeks. Utley didn't touch her. He stood, arms crossed over his chest, his expression that of a crash victim.

"Get them in the car to warm up and call an ambulance," Lane told Tony. "Tell them to keep sirens off."

"Don't need an ambulance," Utley said. "We're not hurt." His gaze went to the cabin. "But I don't know what's happening inside. Monroe might be."

****

I lay at the bottom of the stairs, gasping for air, willing myself to unconsciousness so the pain would go away. The blackness kept threatening, teasing, but it didn't follow through on its promise.

Derek came back in seconds. I wondered if he'd shot Tabitha and Adam. Had I heard shots? No. Then why did he come back without them? Was he more focused on me now? Was I his number one nemesis?

"Son of a bitch," he said through clenched teeth. "You helped them escape. Now the cops are out there."

Cops? Was it Lane? A wave of relief swept through me, but it didn't last long. Cops might be outside, but I was inside. With a killer.

Derek peered down at me, his face a mask of uncertainty. "You're injured. Now what?"

I shook my head. Why was he asking me? He was the one in charge.

"You need medical care."

I almost laughed, but knew it would hurt too badly. He'd slaughtered people, took delight in torturing his captives, would most likely kill me, but was worried that I needed medical care. Nice.

"I can't let you die. You're a good person."

I opened my eyes long enough to peer at him in surprise. "Turn yourself in," I managed to choke.

He shook his head and looked away, rubbing a hand over his face. "Can't. Too much has happened."

I wanted to talk him into it, to make him see reason—if a psycho such as him could see reason—but I couldn't speak. The pain was increasing, cutting off my breath. I stared up at him, silently begging him to put a stop to this, to let the cops in.

He looked at the door, then down at me. "Okay," he said, nodding, coming to a decision. "It's time. You can't wait much longer. You're in bad shape."

Then, I saw something in his eyes. I wasn't sure what it was... resignation, doom, fatalistic acceptance.

"Goodbye, Monroe," he whispered. He whirled and disappeared out the front door.

A volley of gunshots erupted before the blessed blackness finally took me.

Chapter 18

My eyes slowly opened. I was in a hospital. That much was clear. Beyond the window, the sky was black with a light smattering of stars. I remembered the cabin. Derek. The gun shots. Everything in my body hurt, but mostly, my chest, my side, felt like someone had plunged a knife in me.

Painfully, I turned my head to find Josie sitting by my bedside. I frowned in confusion, trying to remember the last thing that had taken place regarding her. Oh, yeah. She'd disappeared, left drug paraphernalia in my house. Was she here to steal my pain pills?

"Roe?" Tears choked her voice. She scooted to the edge of her chair and looked at me, her eyes wet. I immediately felt guilty about my suspicions.

"Hi," I croaked.

"How are you, sweetie?"

"Hurts."

"I'll get the doctor."

She rose and it was then I noticed Adam. He stood just inside the door.

"Hey," he said, coming over to my bedside. "You gave us all quite a scare."

Before I could respond, the doctor appeared behind him. "You'll need to leave, please," he told Adam. "You can come back in a little while."

Adam nodded and reached out to squeeze my hand

before leaving.

"I'm Dr. Mesnick," he said, patting my arm. He was middle-aged with graying hair and kind, hazel eyes behind dark-rimmed glasses. "How are you feeling, Miss Donovan?"

"Sore, thirsty, strange, woozy."

He smiled, nodding. "Not surprising after what you've been through. If it weren't for the pain meds we're pumping through you, you'd be feeling a lot more than sore."

"What happened? What's wrong with me?"

"You were shot in the hand. Not a serious injury, but painful. The bullet passed through. You broke your ankle falling down the stairs, but the worst of your injuries are three broken ribs, one of which punctured a lung. Much longer without medical care, and you might not have made it."

I remembered Derek's look of concern, his decision, his running out the door. Had the man who'd caused all the trouble also been the one to save my life?

And, what had happened to him? The gunshots… had he shot someone or been shot himself? Or both? Cops were outside, was…

"Lane? Is he okay?"

The doctor frowned. "Lane?"

"Detective Brody. Cops were outside the cabin. What happened?"

"I'm afraid I don't know. But, there is a detective who's been anxiously waiting to speak with you. He's right outside. Let me check you over and I'll send him in."

I closed my eyes, happiness sweeping through me. *Hurry, Doc, hurry.* When he was finished, I could see

Lane.

The doctor took what seemed like hours, but was really just a few minutes, to check me over. He nodded. "Everything looks good. I'll send the detective in, but just for a little while. You need your rest. Tomorrow you'll feel more like having visitors. Your family is outside, too, but I'd rather them wait until tomorrow to come in."

I nodded. Who cared? Lane was here.

"I'll be back in to check on you tomorrow," Doctor Mesnick said, then he left.

I stared anxiously at the door, but felt like my lung had been punctured again when Detective Webber walked in.

"Miss Donovan, how are you?"

Tears surfaced and I shook my head.

His brows furrowed with concern. "Should I get the doc back in?"

"No," I said. "I'm okay. Just a little…" Confused? Worried? Broken-hearted? "Lane? Detective Brody? Is he okay?"

A knowing look came into his eyes. He nodded. "He's fine. Taking care of some paperwork."

Ah, yes. Paperwork. Great. Paperwork had to get done.

"What happened? With Derek?"

A heavy sigh. "He ran out the front door, shooting at us. Didn't hit anyone, but we…" A shrug. "We had to take him out."

"Dead?"

Webber nodded. "We'll need to ask you some questions, if you feel up to it."

I wondered why cops always said 'we,' even when

there was only one of them. Maybe silly, inane thoughts like that would keep my mind off Lane, and the fact that he wasn't the one here. That he wasn't concerned enough about me to come check on me himself. Instead, he was doing *paperwork*.

I pushed back the disappointment, pushed back the tears. "Okay," I said. Starting to feel my eyes droop, figuring the pain meds were taking hold, I said, "Ask away. But you might want to make it quick. Not sure how long I can stay awake."

****

The next morning, Josie was once more at my bedside. "I only have a minute," she said. "Your mother is chomping at the bit to come in. We've been taking turns in and out of your room, but I was lucky enough to be in here when you woke up."

"How are you?" I asked. I was feeling better. The pain was still there, but dull and not as severe.

"I'm fine. How about you?"

I nodded. "Getting better."

"I was so afraid." Her eyes filled with tears. "I thought you might die."

"I was afraid when I got home and found the…" I looked around. We were alone. I lowered my voice. "The drug paraphernalia."

"Matt came by. He did the coke, not me. He insisted I go with him and I was afraid if you came home while he was there, he might hurt you. So, I went with him. I didn't do drugs. I promise. I'm still clean."

"Where's Matt?"

She shrugged. "I'm not sure. I managed to get away from him."

"He's still not in custody?"

"No. But, the cops are looking for him. I told them where I'd last seen him, all his hangouts. Hopefully, they'll find him soon."

There was a noise behind her and I looked up to see Adam come in the room. Josie turned, too, then looked back at me, rolling her eyes. "I guess it's his turn. If you want to see him."

"It's okay," I said. "We'll talk again later."

Josie stood and gave Adam a quelling look before she left. He took her place in the chair.

"How are you?" he asked, his handsome face clenched in worry. I was quickly growing tired of the question.

"I'm okay. You? Tabitha?"

"We're both fine, thanks to you. You saved our lives."

I shrugged. "It all just happened so quickly."

"Did you see this?"

Adam held a newspaper out. I took it.

The headline read, 'Serial Killer Shot to Death in Showdown with Police.' Underneath, there was a smaller caption: 'Jilted Lover takes a Bullet for Ex.'

"What?" Fury swept through me. "I'd say that's twisting facts just a bit."

"Well, you did risk your life to save us."

"I didn't mean to take a bullet for you. I was just trying to deflect his aim. I don't particularly want you dead," I ground the words through clenched teeth, "but I wouldn't risk my own life to prevent it. At least, not on purpose."

"Hey, calm down. You did a brave thing, whether it was instinctive or not."

I closed my eyes. "I'm really tired. I appreciate you

coming by, but I think I need to rest."

"Okay. But, I wanted to say a few things first."

I sighed and gave a weary nod.

"Tabitha and I are through."

My eyes flew open. "What?"

He shrugged. "I've always sort of known she wasn't the best person in the world, but I had this uncontrollable fascination with her. She was like a fantasy woman, you know?"

I didn't know. I wasn't sure what kind of fantasy would conjure up a cartoon-voiced, egotistical, narcissist, but, to each his own.

"But after what Derek said about her. After what you did. I couldn't help compare you two, and I was an idiot to let you go."

"What are you trying to say, Adam?"

He sighed. "I want another chance. I realize how shallow Tabitha is, how shallow I've been to choose her over you. Do you think there's a possibility we can try again?"

I lay there, waiting for the surge of elation, or at least the surge of satisfaction, but neither came. I didn't want Adam. Didn't want to have this conversation.

"I'm sorry, Adam. It's too late for us."

He looked down to where his clenched hands rested between his knees. "I was afraid of that. It's someone else, isn't it? Lane Brody?"

I shook my head. "There's no one else. There doesn't have to be someone else for me to know I don't want to be with you."

His head rose and he stared at me for a moment, then slowly nodded. "I see. Well, even so. Would you stay at the paper?" Before I could respond, he rushed on. "Not writing obituaries. I want you to have the crime desk."

"A pity promotion?" I asked, knowing I'd take it even if it was. I hadn't found another job and this was what I wanted.

"No. You deserve the position. Deserved it all along."

"What about Phillip?"

"I can't take it away from him. You can both do it. How does that sound?"

"I'll let you know for sure when I'm out of here."

I was sure my decision had been made, though. Already, my adrenaline was pumping at the thought of sinking my teeth back into crime stories.

"You know, I don't blame you for not wanting to be with me. Truth is, you're too good for me."

I peered at him. I wasn't used to humility from him. Wasn't sure what his angle was. "You're in hero worship mode right now. You'll come to your senses."

"Nah," He shook his head and stood. "I might be blind, but I'm not a total idiot. I know what I lost. I just hope the next guy realizes what a catch you are. If not, I'll be waiting to take my shot."

I didn't remind him there was no next guy. Didn't mention that the only guy I wanted to be next was married. Unattainable. And, nowhere around when I so desperately needed him to be.

****

Over the next few days, I had a steady stream of visitors. Asia, my mom, my dad, my brothers, Naomi, my co-workers, Josie again, Detective Webber. Almost everyone I could think of. Except for the one person I wanted to see most.

Finally, on the third day of my hospital stay, the day

before I was to be released, Lane showed up.

I was breathless and a little shaky from showering and brushing my teeth, more activity than I'd had in days. My body ached, but the majority of the pain was masked by the pain meds pumping through my system from the IV.

Mom and Dad were there, as were Gable and Mitchum. Coburn and Naomi had just left.

When Lane walked in, Mom turned to him. "Who are you?"

"Detective Brody, ma'am."

"Well," she said in her ready-to-do-battle voice, "I'm glad you're here. I've wanted to give you people a piece of my mind. How dare you let my daughter get hurt, almost killed? It's your duty to protect the citizens and you—"

"Mother," I interrupted. "Detective Brody isn't here in an official capacity." He was, but I wanted to stop her tirade. "He's here to see me, personally. Lane, this is my mother, Rosalyn." I introduced the rest of my family members and Mom's expression softened.

"Oh, my. I see." A hand fluttered to her heart. "Lane, so nice to meet you."

Lane shoved his hands in the pockets of his jacket, then smiled, and my pulse sped up. "Nice to meet you, too, Mrs. Donovan. Trust me, I'm devastated that Monroe was injured." His eyes went to me. "If I could have done anything to prevent it, I would have. I haven't been able to sleep knowing she almost died."

Oh, brother. He was pouring it on thick. If he meant even half of that, he probably wouldn't have waited three days to come see me.

Mom turned to me. "Monroe," she said, her

276

conciliatory tone morphing into admonishment. "Couldn't you have at least combed your hair?" She brushed my hair down with her fingertips and straightened my covers, adjusting the hospital gown around my shoulders.

"Thanks, Mom," I said.

She placed a kiss on my forehead, whispering, "Don't slouch, dear, it makes you look heavier than you are."

I gritted my teeth until my family made their exit.

Lane stood beside my bed, staring down at me. Beard stubble shadowed his jaw and, even though it had only been a few days since I'd seen him, his hair seemed longer—hanging just below the top of the collar on his black button-down shirt.

He looked good, very good, but tired. Dark shadows rimmed his eyes and his features were tight, drawn with lines of tension. I looked into the stormy blue of his gaze and my heart nearly burst with joy. Just because he was here.

"So," he said after a few moments of silence. "How're we coming along, comb-wise?"

I laughed, feeling the tension ease from my spine. "Hard to look at, huh?"

He shook his head and took his hands from his pockets. Dropping into the chair next to my bed, he said, "Not hard to look at. Hard to keep my hands off you."

I drew in a breath. "Yeah? But not so hard to stay away from, right? This is the first time you've been by."

"I've come by quite a few times, actually. Each time, though, you were out like a puppy in a pickup."

I smiled, kneading the blankets with my fingers as I spoke. "Must be the drugs."

"Did Tony tell you about Harmon's will?"

I shook my head.

"He left all his money to the homeless shelter."

I remembered the look in Derek's eyes just before he ran out the door. He had to know he wouldn't survive. "Suicide by cop?"

"Looks that way." He didn't say which of them shot him. I didn't ask.

"Kind of sucks that Carrington and Utley were the targets," Lane said. "Yet you got the worst of it."

Yeah, I thought, *I got the worst of it all right. Because I'll never have you.*

We sat in awkward silence for a bit, then Lane said, "I'm not sure what to do here."

"About?"

He sighed and reached out to take my uninjured hand in his. "About the fact that I think I might be crazy about you."

I lifted my brows. "*Think* you might? That's not the most ardent declaration I've ever heard. Where did you learn your wooing technique, from Attila the Hun?"

He laughed and his eyes locked onto mine. "Okay. How's this? I *know* I'm crazy about you, and it scares the hell out of me."

I pulled my hand away, liking the warmth that coursed through me from his touch a little too much. "Since you're married, this probably isn't a discussion we should even be having."

"I know." He looked down, then back up at me, his eyes filled with agony. "How much do you know about my marriage? My wife?"

I shrugged, not wanting to tell him Asia told me she was a mental patient. "Really not anything. Other than that she's ill. You know, what little you told me."

"My wife cheated on me during our marriage. She had an affair with a friend of mine. A fellow cop."

"I'm sorry," I said.

He nodded. "Yeah. That's not the worst of it. Although I left Catherine when it happened, I took her back. I thought the affair was over."

"But it wasn't?"

"No. I was called out one night to a shooting at a motel. It was Catherine. She'd murdered her lover because he was going to leave her."

I drew in a sharp breath and let it out slowly. "That must have been..." I couldn't find the words.

Lane gave a humorless laugh. "It was pretty rough. She showed more passion in killing her lover than she had toward me during our entire marriage."

"She was found unfit to stand trial?"

"Yeah. She'd already been under a psychiatrist's care. Had some episodes throughout her life, even as early as her teens. I knew she was unstable when I married her. I just had no idea how unstable. Besides, I thought I could help." He gave a self-deprecating laugh and shook his head. "She's in a mental institution now. Not really aware of what's going on. Or what happened back then."

"Yet you haven't divorced her?"

"It's been a difficult decision. I've always felt I should wait until she wasn't so... I don't know... defenseless." He raised his gaze to the ceiling, then back down, shaking his head. "My mother was horrified at the thought of me abandoning my wife. No matter what she'd done. Mom is still bitter over my dad's desertion and thinks only the lowest form of humanity would do that to another person. I know how passive, how wimpy this must sound, but it was easier to give in to the pressure, since I didn't have to actually live with Catherine. I wrestle every day with whether to cut her loose and reclaim my life, or see it through to its bitter conclusion."

I nodded, but I didn't understand, not really.

"Now, though. After meeting you. After falling—" He stopped and I held my breath, wanting him to say it, yet not wanting him to. He didn't. "After all that's happened, I've realized. I want to be free. I can't live like this any longer. I spoke with an attorney today."

"You're not... you didn't do it for me, did you? I can't have that burden on me. You need to do it because it's the right thing for you. For your life."

"No. It needed doing. It was way past due." He came to his feet and stared down at me. "I'm not sure what will happen now. What I'm facing as far as the divorce, but I don't want to lose whatever you and I might have."

"Lane, I can't be romantically involved with you. Even with the divorce. It's just too soon after. I've been down that road."

"I understand," he said, but I heard the disappointment in his voice. "No pressure. I just want to be in your life. Be around you. I want to take it slowly with you, but I do want to take it."

I closed my eyes, feeling a lump of tears in my throat. "I'm not sure that's a good idea. Feeling the way we do... I don't know. Maybe it would be best to put some distance between us. I'm afraid if I'm around you, I won't be able to..." I opened my eyes and looked at him. "I'll want you too much," I finally confessed.

His eyes roamed over my face, as if taking in every

detail. They stilled when they reached my lips.

"A human heart beats an average of 100,000 times every twenty-four hours," he said softly. "Mine just did that in sixty seconds."

My throat and lips suddenly felt so dry I wouldn't have been surprised if tumbleweeds formed inside my mouth. I slowly ran my tongue over my parched lips, wishing for ice chips, but I couldn't speak, not even to ask for them.

His gaze followed my movements and he gave a long, ragged sigh. "Monroe…" he whispered hoarsely, bending toward me.

My breath caught as his head drifted down. I knew what was going to happen, but I didn't stop it. Just waited for that first touch of his lips on mine. And then, it was there. First, I felt the rasp of his whiskers against my face—slightly painful, yet in a good way, a delicious, thrilling way—then, the burning touch of his mouth. Shock waves coursed through me and I whimpered as his lips—first tender, then more insistent—pressed against mine.

It was inevitable, had been from the moment we'd first met. This kiss… this explosion of pent-up yearning. His hand wound into my hair as he pulled me from the pillows, melding me even closer to him. My ribs twinged from my injury but I barely noticed, and I most definitely didn't want to end the kiss.

His tongue was warm and insistent, probing against mine. I opened to him, feeling the need to cry… to laugh… to shout from the rooftops as my heart thumped its painful, rapturous rhythm.

Then, just as abruptly as it started, it was over.

He released me and I almost groaned in frustration.

Or, maybe I did. My ears were ringing and I wasn't sure which sounds escaped and which ones were trapped inside my body.

Lane dragged in a swift breath and ran shaking fingers through his hair. He looked down at me, guilt and longing showing on his face.

"I'm sorry," he said softly. And then he was gone.

Chapter 19

Two Weeks Later

A cherub flanked either side of the tombstone. Engraved in the granite were the words, 'Our precious Katie, taken from us much too soon. Rest in peace, our little angel.'

Dusk was approaching, nearly swallowing the other headstones in its darkness. Cool wind whipped around my legs and I drew the leather coat more tightly around my body, thinking I should have worn something warmer. Kneeling, I placed a bouquet of tulips and baby's breath on Katie's grave. Today was her birthday. I hadn't been to visit her in a while. The least I could do was be with her on her birthday.

Since I'd been back on the crime desk, I'd started a series of articles about unsolved murders. Particularly those of young girls. Particularly, Katie's, Cassie Carthage's and Maya Pittman's. I was hoping that by bringing attention to them, something new would surface. Even though the police didn't believe the murders were related—and they might not have been— they were at least related in that none were solved.

"I'm sorry, Katie," I said aloud. "I promise I'll never stop trying to find out who did this. Never stop trying to help you finally rest."

My eyes grew wet and my visions blurred. Tears spilled in warm rivulets that quickly chilled on my cheeks.

I heard a cracking sound behind me, like someone stepping on a twig. Whirling, I spotted a man materializing from the fog and I gasped. "Lane? What are you doing here?"

He moved toward me, not speaking. I hadn't seen him since that day in the hospital. Since the kiss. I didn't realize until now how hungry I was for the sight of him. I stood, silently drinking him in while I waited for him to reach me. He wore jeans and a brown bomber jacket. His hair was ruffled by the wind, his eyes an intense glitter in the murky gloom.

"I was looking for you. Asia said you were here." He studied me with an unfathomable expression. "How are you?"

"Still a little sore, but healing. You?"

He shrugged. "Not bad. How was your Thanksgiving?"

"Fine. You know, the whole crazy family thing." I rolled my eyes. "Oodles of fun. Yours?" I regretted the question as soon as it was out of my mouth. Lane didn't really have family, at least, not any close by.

"Quiet," he said, smiling briefly. "Tried to keep busy during the holiday." He crossed his arms over his chest. "I've read the articles you've written on the unsolved murders. You're a good writer. I had no idea."

I shrugged. "Kind of hard to flex your writing muscles on an obituary paragraph."

He grinned. "I suppose so. Your articles certainly bring out your talent. Pretty detailed. You've done your homework."

"I keep hoping something will trigger a memory, a clue. A way to find the killer."

He tucked his hands in the pockets of his jeans and said, "I convinced the cold case squad to open the case and I've been helping."

"Have you?" I asked hopefully.

"Yeah. And I've found nothing. Not likely that we will. The best suspect from back then, Cameron Cooper, is dead. He died five years ago in prison where he was serving time for assault. We have no DNA. There are similarities between Katie's killing and the other girls', but distinct differences, too." He shrugged. "It's likely you'll just have to accept the fact that her killer might not ever be found. A lot of murder cases are never solved." He let out a long, weary sigh. "Too damn many."

I shook my head, clenching my jaw. "I'm not sure I can accept that."

His voice was gentle, sympathetic. "I'm not sure you have a choice."

I stayed silent, not wanting to believe him, but knowing he was probably right.

Lane took his hands from his pockets and hooked his finger under my chin, lifting until I was looking up at him. He cupped a hand to the side of my face and brushed a tear away with his thumb. I let my eyes drift shut and for a moment, savored his touch, fighting against the urge to nestle into his warmth.

"Katie is resting, you know."

"What?" I said, my eyes slowly opening to meet the electric blue of his.

"The dead are at peace. She doesn't know her killer might still be out there. She doesn't know how the people left behind are suffering. How they mourn her. It's the ones left behind who can't rest."

"You think so?"

"I know so," he said. His gaze roamed over my face with a yearning intensity. "I've missed you." The admission was an agonized whisper, almost an entreaty and I steeled myself against the jolt it sent through my body. "You've been living in the past for twenty-five years," he said. "Don't you think it's time to look toward the future?"

The future.

I had the job I'd always wanted, the job I deserved. Adam had been properly repentant, almost groveling, since my return. Josie was clean, for now. The man I cared deeply about—maybe loved—was here and would soon be free.

The future.

I met his eyes again and shivered. He must have thought it was from the cold because he pulled me into a hug, warming me everywhere his body touched mine. A deep wave of contentment moved through me as we stood silently, together, in the shadow of Katie's headstone.

The future was starting to look pretty good.

A word about the author...

Alicia Dean began writing stories as a child. At age 10, she wrote her first ever romance (featuring a hero who looked just like Elvis Presley, and who shared the name of Elvis' character in the movie, Tickle Me), and she still has the tattered, pencil-written copy. Alicia is from Moore, Oklahoma and now lives in Edmond. She has three grown children and a huge network of supportive friends and family. She writes mostly contemporary suspense and paranormal, but has also written in other genres, including a few vintage historicals.

Other than reading and writing, her passions are Elvis Presley (she almost always works in a mention of him into her stories) and watching (and rewatching) her favorite televisions shows like Ozark, Dexter, Justified, Breaking Bad, Sons of Anarchy, and Vampire Diaries. Some of her favorite authors are Michael Connelly, Dennis Lehane, Stephen King, Lee Child, Lisa Gardner, Ridley Pearson, Joseph Finder, and Jonathan Kellerman...to name a few.

Email: Alicia@AliciaDean.com
Website: http://aliciadean.com/
Blog: http://aliciadean.com/alicias-blog/
Facebook:
https://www.facebook.com/AuthorAliciaDean/
Twitter: @Alicia_Dean_
Instagram: AliciaDeanAuthor

BookBub: https://www.bookbub.com/profile/alicia-dean
Pinterest: https://pinterest.com/aliciamdean/
Goodreads:
http://www.goodreads.com/author/show/468339.Alicia_Dean

Thank you for purchasing
this publication of The Wild Rose Press, Inc.

For questions or more information
contact us at
info@thewildrosepress.com.

The Wild Rose Press, Inc.
www.thewildrosepress.com